superheroes
ANONYMOUS

heroes
ANONYMOUS

E DUNNE

HARPER
VOYAGER
IMPULSE

An Imprint of HarperCollinsPublishers

This is a work of fiction. Names, characters, places, and inc[...]
are products of the author's imagination or are used fictiti[...]
and are not to be construed as real. Any resemblance to a[...]
events, locales, organizations, or persons, living or dead, is [...]
tirely coincidental.

EPub Edition NOVEMBER 2014 ISBN: 9780062369116
Print Edition ISBN: 9780062369123

10 9 8 7 6 5

To Dad and Mom:
For proving you don't need a cape to be a superhero.

"I'll play swapsies anytime, Doc. Just say the word."

"I'll let them know. It seems Razor dosed some guards on his way out of Detmer. Looks like he got you with the same stuff, according to the bloodwork."

I looked down at the crease of my elbow. Bright pink medical tape held down a bit of gauze. It made my skin, washed-out thanks to the hospital lights, look even more diseased and sickly. "Any side effects?"

"The main side effect just seemed to be pain—some psychosis, so we had you strapped down until that passed. Memory loss is consistent with the stories we got from the guards. Now." He looked down at me, putting his scholarly doctor face back on. "Any headaches? Double vision?"

I answered in the negative as he ran down the medical checklist I'd memorized a long time ago. "Has Jeremy been by?"

"You'll have to check with the nurses. They'll know if Mr. Collins has been in." He moved over to the computer to make one final notation and gave me a nod before he left.

I sat up slowly (every muscle in my body shouted) and nudged aside the covers. Starting at my ankles, I began to probe up my legs, across my stomach, chest, and shoulders, and finally down to each individual fingertip. When the only pain turned out to be a minor bump on the back of my head and a bruise on my jaw that made the world go temporarily blurry, I breathed a sigh of relief. No new scars.

Finally, I turned to my empty bedside table and frowned. No new flowers, or old ones either. While this sometimes fit Jeremy, it was definitely out of character for Blaze. No matter which supervillain I faced, or how bad things had gotten, there was always a single white rose on my nightstand whenever I woke. Today, there was nothing.

The clock on the wall told me that it was four thirty. Afternoon, I deduced, eyeing the gray drizzle of light coming in through the window. I shifted and turned on the TV, clicking over to the news. "Let's see what the villains are up to today, shall we?"

There'd been one threat of Armageddon in the Big Apple, two threatened nuclear attacks in Houston, and one hostage kidnapping (not mine) in Arkansas. Every threat, the newscaster assured me with plastic compassion, had been neutralized by the local superhero. Even the Raptor had emerged for the threat in New York, which added a hell of a lot of legitimacy to the whole situation. Very little drew the Raptor out of retirement these days.

At least Armageddon had a way of keeping the news cycle from covering me provided I wasn't directly involved. I flicked over to *The Bird Also Sings* to see which of my favorite characters had discovered a heretofore-unknown half sibling in the time I'd been unconscious. Nobody had, but Chance was now seriously debating sleeping with Lucille. Luckily, some of the characters in the show had already reminded him she might be his half sister, so I wouldn't have to shout it at the TV later.

"Ah, she lives."

I tore my gaze away from Chance's soulful eyes (blue, unlike Jeremy's and Blaze's green stare). Jeremy stood in the doorway, hands shoved into his pockets so that his thumbs stuck out. They drummed against his hipbones. He was smiling, so I must not have looked too horrible.

"Hey, you," I said, reaching out a hand.

He took it and kissed my hair, careful to avoid the bump. "How do you feel?"

"Like I went a few rounds with a sledgehammer and lost."

Jeremy wrinkled his nose. He had such an attractive face, sometimes I wondered what he was doing with somebody who looked like me. I'm not a hag, but I'm not a stunning beauty, either. Jeremy, on the other hand, was a paragon of male perfection. His eyes were direct and wide-spaced, his features aristocratic. A sprinkling of dark freckles under his eyes somehow made him even cuter. "And which villain did the sledgehammer belong to?"

"Razor X. The mask with the yellow bug eyes, terrible breath. Not so good with the people skills."

"Oh. Right." Jeremy searched his memory for a minute, now playing with my fingers. "Red cape?"

"I don't know if I'd call it a proper cape. It's a little half cape." I reached over for the remote and muted Damien and Lucille's argument—one that would probably lead to the bed. "Apparently, he got me with some sort of pain juice. You called Angus and let him know I'm shored up in the hospital again, right?"

"Right. I said you'd probably be released tomorrow."

I groaned. "Why would you do that? Now he'll expect me back tomorrow."

Jeremy shrugged. "Wasn't thinking. Sorry."

Something felt off, I realized. He'd always been good

about visiting me after one of the supervillain attacks, but now he had yet to fully meet my gaze. He kept playing with my fingers, his hands never still. "What's up?" I asked him, sensing there was an elephant that I couldn't see somewhere in the room.

"Nothing." He attempted a smile. "How d'you feel?"

I narrowed my eyes. "You asked me that already."

"Well, I was worried. You know." One of his shoulders moved in his patented half shrug. "My girlfriend's in the hospital. I'm not allowed to be worried?"

"Something's definitely up," I said, squinting at him. Jeremy was usually direct and honest—at least when it came to me. Though I'd been told before that I could be unnecessarily blunt, the kidnappings had turned me into a rather squirrelly person whenever emotions were involved. I didn't like sharing feelings, while Jeremy regularly announced whatever was on his mind to the world. Sometimes he even filtered it first. "What's going on?"

"It's nothing." Jeremy dropped my hand, but he still didn't look at me.

For a second, I was tempted to let it go. The last couple of weeks had been rough. We were close to print on two of the magazines at work, there had been a train holdup on the way home from work last Tuesday, and Razor X had seriously put a crimp in our plans for a nice anniversary dinner out. By all means, I should have dropped it.

Instead, I gave him what he calls the Girl Look.

"Gail . . ." Jeremy ran an exasperated hand over his shoulder, pushing down on an unfelt ache.

I stared harder.

He got up to pace. Given how long his legs were, it didn't take many strides to reach the other side of the room and return. Once. Twice. Finally: "I got a job offer."

"Really? That's great!" Jeremy hated his job. In truth, he would have hated any job that took him away from his video games, but Jeremy hated his boss. And unlike me, he could afford to do something about it. After all, *he* didn't have to worry about the healthcare plan. "Where is it? Doing what?"

"It's . . . it's the same stuff I'm doing now. Same company."

"Oh."

"The thing is, it's in Miami."

"Wait, what?"

"Girl." Jeremy paused and took a deep breath even as he shot me an annoyed look. "I didn't want to get into this until you were better. I still don't."

A new job in Miami? Miami was half a country away, and I certainly couldn't afford to fly. Nor could I really afford to move. Any other employer would have found some reason to let me go, what with the constant danger I caused everybody around me. I was lucky to have what I did. But I'd been with Jeremy for years. I knew what that look on his face meant.

"You're going to take it," I said.

A mutinous scowl crossed Jeremy's face. "We don't have to talk about this now."

"Just tell me."

Now Jeremy looked deeply unhappy. His hands had started moving once more, thumbs tapping a new rhythm against his hips as he resumed pacing, albeit more slowly. "The pay's better," he said at length. "And it's a promotion. I'd be an idiot to turn it down."

"And what about us?"

"We could do the long-distance thing," Jeremy said, but it sounded halfhearted. I didn't blame him. A long-distance relationship was hard enough without having to wonder if your girlfriend wasn't picking up the phone because she was in the shower—or in the claws of a supervillain.

So I shook my head, and Jeremy sighed.

"Look," he said, dropping back down into the chair by my bedside. "Let's just not think about this right now. We'll get you feeling better, get you out of here, and then we'll talk, okay?"

I opened my mouth to tell him that with my luck, there was always going to be sometime when I was in the hospital or recuperating from some supervillain's attempt to get Blaze's attention, but Jeremy knew that. He'd lived the past few years with me, even when all signs indicated that he should bail, should run fast and run hard. He knew just as well as I did that it was only a stalling tactic, and I didn't have the heart to point that out.

So instead I sat there dumbly, with my soon-to-be-ex-boyfriend holding my hand in the hospital, and tried not to think about how much breaking up was going to suck.

Chapter Two

"WHAT KIND OF douchebag dumps somebody in the hospital?" Portia McPeak licked foam off of her thumb, ignoring the napkin right next to her. "More importantly, what kind of girl just lets him?"

"It wasn't like that," I said, though I couldn't exactly work up much enthusiasm to defend either one of us, not when I had the latest text from my landlord on my phone screen. Jeremy had dropped off a box of stuff with him since I was at work.

It was really over.

"Then what was it like?" Portia asked.

"The job in Miami pays better, and he hates his job here."

"Hey, I'm on your side—he dumped you in the hospital, and that makes him a douchebag."

"Thank you," I said.

"I mean, so what if he's a tool, and we all think you should have dumped him years ago?"

"I take that back." I lifted my head to glare at Portia.

Five days had passed since Jeremy had walked out on me. I'd gone back to work, sore, limping, but otherwise alive, to find that my coworkers had oh-so-thoughtfully saved all my work for me. So it wasn't like I had time to miss Jeremy at all. It just stung that I'd been dumped so callously.

Since Angus was out of the office on a business trip, I'd tried to sneak away for coffee at the Daily Grind to gain back a moment of sanity. Unfortunately, Portia had decided to tag along.

"I mean, I get why you didn't kick him to the curb." Portia, with her too-expensive bag and her designer shoes, didn't fit in with the hipster crowd at the Daily Grind. But she didn't seem to care. "He's hot. And what girl doesn't want a hot boyfriend? But, hey, now that he's out of the picture, I think I might be able to set you up with someone."

"No way." I picked up a sugar packet and flicked it at her, and she sniffed. "No blind dates. Ever. I'm just going to sulk and be single for a while."

"Then who'll bring you clothes at the hospital?" Portia asked. "And before you can say me, I'm not going into a hospital unless I'm *dying*. So forget about it, Girl."

"I'll figure out a way," I said. "Besides, maybe I'll stop ending up in the hospital if Jeremy lets enough people know he's in Miami. You know all the villains think he's Blaze."

"Because he *is*," Portia said, rolling her eyes as though it was obviously my gamer ex-boyfriend pulling on a superhero suit to save the city on a daily basis. "Duh."

"So with him in Miami, I'll get a break from the kidnappings. Stranger things have happened, right?"

"To you?" Portia considered. "Not really. Remember that time Venus von Trapp turned you green?"

"Thank you for that depressing reminder of the worst two weeks of my life. I got a paper cut this morning. Would you do the honors?" I handed her the saltshaker.

Portia blinked at the saltshaker. "Huh?"

"Never mind." I rested my head on my arms. Portia was probably the friendliest worker out of everyone in the office, and some days I wished I'd never drawn her attention, so I could drink my coffee in peace. She'd been standing next to me during one of Blaze's epic fights with Dr. Death and had subsequently ended up on the front page of the Domino. She'd been lucky: people who spent time around me had an equal chance of winding up on the front page or in the hospital. But Portia was too fame-hungry to care about that.

"I'm going back," Portia said, and I looked up. "Walk with me?"

Yes, because who knew what could happen to a long-legged blonde in three blocks? In broad daylight? I refrained from pointing out she was safer without me, cleared my coffee cup off the table and into the trash, and followed her out though I had absolutely no desire to go back to work.

I'd been working at Mirror Reality for a couple of years, and while I knew I was lucky to even have a job, it wasn't a picnic. The work itself wasn't bad, but the office was stuffed with idiots. Portia could probably be considered the smartest of all of them. My boss regularly hired men and women hoping to break into print modeling by constantly putting themselves in Angus's line of sight. He found them amusing, but he knew better than to actually expect quality work out of these people, which meant I had to pick up the slack.

I hated my job. Every morning, I turned off the alarm clock and rolled over to stare at the window of my fourth-story apartment. And for ten minutes, I contemplated rolling out of bed and out of that window, and not having to go to work. I even set my alarm clock back ten minutes just so that I would have time for my daily existential crisis.

Once I decided that I had too much to live for, I dragged myself out of bed and headed into the office, two hours before anybody else came in. I used the quiet to prep meeting materials, research stories, and even occasionally ghostwrite a few articles if the regular writer didn't live up to Angus's standards. My coworkers trickled in between nine and ten. They left right on the nose at five. You could set your watch by that, at least. If I was having an efficient day, I'd be out of there at seven. The earliest I'd managed in a couple of years was nine.

Why did I stay there? That's easy. The healthcare plan.

Angus paid for the gold plan for his employees, probably to keep the idea men and the overworked happy. Even if I tried to find another job at this point, the insurance company would have taken one look at my record and burst out laughing.

I don't ask to get kidnapped. In fact, in the grand scheme of things, I'd prefer if the villains focused on something else. One of them—I think it might have been a mind reader—got it into his head that Jeremy is Blaze, savior of Chicago. And even though I'd been insisting for over eighteen months that there was no way my boyfriend was Blaze, everybody insisted right back. So, people asked, why were Jeremy and Blaze never been seen in the same place? Because Jeremy was usually at his computer, playing games. How come Blaze came to save me every time? He must be a nice guy, but I assure you, he's not Jeremy.

So I stayed for the health care. And I think Angus knew it. He was the first to start calling me Girl instead of Gail after the media named me Hostage Girl. Others followed suit, no matter how many times I insisted that it was Gail. Gail from Nowhere, Indiana.

When Portia and I strolled back into the seventh-floor offices of Mirror Reality, the receptionist was already mid-fit. "There you are!" she said.

"It was just a coffee run. Don't worry so much, Adrianna." Portia barely glanced up from her phone as we walked through. Angus insisted that the front office be kept spartan and minimal, so there was only the coatrack, two chairs, and Adrianna's desk. Which was mostly empty anyway, usually of Adrianna herself. "What can I do for you?"

"Not you." Adrianna waved her away. With an affronted look, Portia stalked off, and Adrianna turned toward me. "Angus has been calling for the past half hour. *Why* did you pick today of all days to leave?"

I refrained from pointing out that I was legally allowed to take breaks. "What does he want?"

"He's got a meeting with Edward," Adrianna said, grabbing my arm.

I raised my eyebrows. "Gonna need more than that. Who's Edward?"

"*Davenport*. Edward Davenport!" Adrianna practically melted back into herself before she remembered that I didn't care. "He wants the entire office prepped, and with Guy leaving today, you're it."

"I'm taking a meeting with Edward Davenport?" I blinked. Edward Davenport, CEO of Davenport Industries, was practically a celebrity in Chicago. And why not? He had the smashing good looks of a movie lead, the brains to tackle the country's top law school at nineteen, a tragic past, and the world's formidable most company behind him.

"Not you." Adrianna rolled her eyes. "Guy and Asiv are, but the meeting room, it's a wreck and—"

"Get the cleaning crew up here, then," I said. "That's not my job. If Angus wants to meet with Edward Davenport, he'll want all the materials prepped. I need to start that."

"He's going to be here at three!" Adrianna looked frantic at the thought. "The maintenance staff takes *hours,* and I'll never get the office cleaned in time. You know how hopeless I am with cleaning products—we always kept a maid."

"Get somebody to help," I said.

"But what about the phones?"

"Have one of the McClavens do it."

"You know they hate that."

"What's this? It appears my well of compassion has dried right up. He pays them, they can answer the phones for an hour. I have to prep the materials."

On cue, the phone rang. "Oh, that'll be Angus," Adrianna said, fluttering her hands worriedly. Yes, she actually fluttered her hands. Like an old-time movie actress.

I waved a hand at her. "Send it back to me. He wants to talk to me, anyway." And with that, I trudged the familiar path to my cubicle.

"Girl!" Angus's European accent (I'd never been able to quite place its source) thundered through the handset. "Where have you been?"

"On the phone with a potential client," I lied as I sat down behind my cluttered desk.

"I'm sure. Have Adrianna get fresh coffee—use the corporate account, don't put it on the company card until we teach that idiot in accounting how to actually pay the bill—and have it waiting, and hot, precisely at three. We'll need the sales packet for the millennium clients, not that piddly one you put together for the golds and the silvers."

I bit my tongue over the retort that those "piddly" packets had taken me the better part of a month of arguing with Angus to perfect, and continued to jot down his demands. Once he'd finished, he sighed. "And for heaven's sakes, Girl, put on proper shoes before Edward and I get into the office, will you?"

I glanced around, but Angus was nowhere to be seen. "How did you know that—?"

"I didn't, but you just confirmed it."

Damn.

Thankfully, Angus just chuckled. "Proper shoes," he said, and hung up.

I dug into the bottom drawer of my desk for the pair of

plain black flats I kept on hand. As long as nobody came too near my feet, which had been sweating a little in the heat that morning, everything would be fine. Feet shod, I headed across the office to where Asiv and Guy shared a glassed-in office. Asiv, as usual, was tilted back in his office chair, asleep. Guy sat behind his mahogany monster of a desk, his hands steepled as he regarded something on his computer screen. I tapped on the door; he straightened.

"Hey," he said once I'd entered. "Something up?"

"You haven't heard?" I rolled my eyes for emphasis. "Angus scored a meet with Edward Davenport. And since you're not blowing this joint for a few more hours, you get to sit in on it."

"Fantastic." Guy's lips quirked up in a smile. "Does that mean you have paperwork for me?"

"Millennium packet." I handed over a thick manila demo folder. Edward Davenport would naturally get the one in the slick black binding, presentation-perfect. "You'll want to look over that before the meeting. Review the numbers. The usual."

Guy rose to his full height to take the packet from me. Standing, he towered over me—and everybody in the office. Actually, sitting in his office chair, he was almost of a height with me. Nobody would ever consider me tall. Diminutive, maybe. Elfin was how one ex-boyfriend had described me.

I preferred "short."

"Are you coming to my going-away party tonight?" Guy asked, not looking at me as he paged through the packet. His hair came down his forehead and over his stylish glasses. The sleeves of his seersucker dress shirt were rolled up to his elbows. He looked like exactly what he was: a trust-fund boy idling the days away in publishing.

On the side of the room, Asiv let out a snort in his sleep.

I bit my lip. Hang out with my coworkers outside of the office? You couldn't have paid me enough, even if Guy was the only nice one in the office.

"I'm sorry," I said, twisting my fingers together behind my back. "I'm behind on work."

"Really?" And this time Guy did look up from the paperwork to chuckle at me. "Can't get away for one night?"

If I could, I definitely wasn't going to spend an evening with my coworkers. So I smiled at Guy and prepared for my retreat. "Come say bye before you leave, will you?" I asked him, and before he could answer, I turned and left.

BY THE TIME Edward Davenport descended on the offices of Mirror Reality, every spare inch had been scrubbed and polished until the shine on the chrome wall panels threatened to give me a headache. Angus paced like a general surveying his troops. In truth, he was the furthest thing from a general, being stoop-shouldered and a little bit pigeon-toed. He made up for the former with expensive Italian suits and the latter with expensive Italian shoes.

Angus P. Vanderfeld was nothing if not classy.

The phones rang once: the signal that Edward Davenport had arrived. Since my desk wasn't anywhere near the route they would take to the meeting room, I hunkered down to look over some client requests.

I jumped about three feet into the air when a shadow fell over the desk.

"Hello."

The media hadn't done Edward Davenport justice, I saw when I looked up. Dashing, I thought right away. He was in his mid-forties—though you wouldn't know it apart from laugh lines alongside crystalline blue eyes— and he wore an Italian suit every bit as expensive as Angus's, only he filled his much more nicely. His teeth were slightly crooked, but on such a handsome, rugged face, it was only endearing.

And he was smiling right at me.

"I'm Eddie," he said, holding out a hand.

I rose somewhat unsteadily to shake his hand. "Gail," I said. "It's nice to meet you."

"What do you do for Mirror Reality, Gail?"

"What doesn't she do for Mirror Reality is the proper question." Guy came forward, smiling. He'd rolled his sleeves down. "She keeps this place running, Eddie."

Guy Bookman was on a nickname-basis with one of the most powerful men in the world? I'd apparently missed that memo. I probably should have paid more attention to him while we'd been in the same office. It was too late for that now.

"Hold on." Eddie paused, still studying my face. "You look familiar. Are you—you're her, aren't you?"

I sighed. Should have seen that coming.

"What is it the media calls you?" Eddie went on. "Hostage Girl? Hostage Girl Gail Godwin."

Now I barely swallowed my surprised look. Not only had he recognized me, but he'd remembered my real name when most of the world had forgotten it.

And he wasn't done. "Can I be honest with you? That has to be the most uncreative nickname the press has published in ages. No offense."

"None taken," I said.

"How are you doing today?" Eddie said. "No bank holdups? Hostage situations? Time bombs ticking down?"

"Not yet, thank god." When the answer seemed to dim Eddie's smile a little bit, I hastened to add, apologetically, "But it's early."

"I like that attitude." Eddie smiled again and patted my shoulder. If he weren't a hot lawyer, the move would have seemed grandfatherly. "I see the big man's getting impatient, so Guy here had better shuffle me along to this all-important meeting. Very nice to have met you, Girl."

"Same to you, Mr. Davenport."

"Eddie, please." One last roguish smile (well, roguish for a man who sat behind a desk all day), and he was off, Guy and Asiv in tow, to meet Angus. Even as I sat back down, I noticed that he didn't stop again. He nodded at some, smiled at others, but the only one he'd stopped to talk to was me. And minor celebrity that I was or not . . . well, that was a bit odd.

ONCE FIVE O'CLOCK hit, and Eddie Davenport was still in the meeting, the office did not become a desert. Instead, my coworkers all sat at their desks, adjusting their faux-reading glasses as they squinted at their screens and tried to look as if they actually knew what work was. I, on the other hand, actually got stuff done.

Eddie left a little before six. The instant the elevator dinged closed behind him, there was an immediate rustling as people went for their coats and purses and tromped out together, no doubt headed to The Nine to drink and send Guy off to his greener pastures. I waved. Finally: the office to myself. I cranked up the music, pulled my hair out of its French twist, and hunkered down for some serious editing.

Outside the floor-to-ceiling windows—seen through Guy and Asiv's office—the sun dripped out of the sky in a glory of color. I switched on my desk light. The stars came out. I nuked a cup of microwaveable noodles and slurped them up while I double-checked numbers in a report. Angus had a meeting with the board coming up, and he wanted everything looked over at least twice before he made any presentations. Being anal hadn't always won him fans, but it had never lost him business.

I was still checking those figures when the tapping began.

After the third or fourth time I was kidnapped from the office—and the first time my kidnapper had actually done some damage—Angus installed a set of high-powered alarms. "Great," I'd said at the time. "Now I'll *know* I'm a sitting duck. Thanks, Angus."

He'd merely smiled and pointed out that forewarned is forearmed.

When the tapping started now, I froze and glanced

at the alarm console Angus had purposely put above my desk. Steady green—no threat. Yet.

The tapping persisted. Slowly, I opened my desk drawer and withdrew the letter opener I'd borrowed from Adrianna. Thankful that I'd never bothered to return it, I held it in a death grip and turned.

Somebody was outside the windows.

Angus's offices are on the seventh floor of the Shrewfield Building in the Loop. The only people who hover outside the windows are the heroes who can fly and the window-washers who come by every other month. A memo always went out so that we'd know they were coming and wouldn't startle us, so I knew it wasn't the latter. Besides, they never cleaned at ten o'clock at night.

So the only possibilities of somebody outside the windows were superheroes or supervillains. Given my luck, it was usually the latter.

This time, it wasn't. My hand, fisted around the letter opener, dropped to my side. I held up one finger to hold off my visitor, and disengaged the alarm. It could have been an impostor, mind-controlling me to believe it was Blaze hovering outside the window, but I doubted it. For one, mind-control villains have always had a difficult time with me. One of the more notable, Sykik, had offhandedly claimed that there just wasn't much there to control.

Seeing as I'd never met a test I couldn't ace, I think he was probably just trying to cover up the fact that I was one of the 20 percent with a mental shield that was naturally hard to break. Didn't mean it couldn't be done, the supervillain expert I'd talked to had claimed. But it would take a lot of energy and forethought to make me believe in things that weren't there.

And besides, it was obviously Blaze hovering outside of the window. Most flying superheroes and -villains pointed their toes when they hovered, as if they were going to be more aerodynamic while standing still. Blaze never did. He stood on the air like he stood on solid ground. Every part of him was still, from the hands crossed over his chest to his black (rather scuffed) boots.

He was outside Asiv's office, about three feet away from the building itself. I pushed the window open as much as the safety bar would allow me. "What are you doing here?"

His green eyes, seen through the slits of his black mask, cut from my face, down to the letter opener left forgotten in my hand, and back. Even through the mask, I could see the raised eyebrow of amusement.

"Well, you know," I said, dropping the weapon on Asiv's desk. "Every little bit helps."

A tiny tilt of the head in acknowledgment, an isolated movement.

"So I guess you don't know what you're doing here?"

Now I could tell he was smiling behind the mask. I'd always been able to tell.

Apparently, he wasn't going to talk. And he wasn't going to reveal why he was hovering outside though I figured I knew that much. I'd come to suspect that Blaze was usually nearby wherever I was. That never bothered me. It was something akin to having a security blanket, albeit dressed in green and with the ability to take a bullet to the face.

But he had never made his presence known before now.

I decided to try again. "Am I in danger?"

An emphatic shake of the head, no.

Something occurred to me. "Oh, right," I said mostly to myself. "Thank you for getting me away from Razor X. Again. You have no idea how much it means to me, you taking time out of your day all the time just to save my scrawny ass."

Now, an incline of the head, and an amused look in those green eyes. Spring green, I should say. Not hazel, but a true, bright, outstanding green, just like Jeremy's.

"And thank War Hammer for me, too? If you see him?"

The amusement vanished. War Hammer and Blaze weren't friends? I'd always assumed they were, being the headlining superheroes of Chicago. Had I unknowingly been the central figure in a temporary truce between enemies? Given how much I hated my coworkers, I'd never foist the need to work with a distasteful partner on somebody else.

Seeing my mortification, Blaze quickly shook his head and tried to look as contrite as is possible behind a face mask.

As absurd as it was, holding an entire conversation with Blaze wasn't silly, like trying to converse with a mime would be. Blaze's eyes were by far the most expressive eyes I'd ever seen. And even more than that, he seemed to be able to interpret my reactions far better than anybody in my life ever had, even my boyfriend of two years (well, ex-boyfriend now).

Which was why I found myself saying, "Do you want . . ." What, Gail? I asked myself. To come in and have some tea? Nope—couldn't drink through the mask, and there was obviously no way he was unmasking in front of me. Who knew if he even liked tea? Or if I had any left in my cubicle? So I said, "To go for a walk with me?"

Surprise flared in those green eyes. Well, more like shock. And then one tight nod.

So I went on a walk with Blaze, my savior. The man sure to deliver the antidote if I'd been poisoned, who'd personally pulled me out of more fiery buildings than I cared to count and, on one notable occasion, a live volcano. He waited for me to take the elevator down after closing the window. And we walked, silently. Mercifully, the streets were bare, save for us, so nobody gawked at Hostage Girl and her own appointed superhero.

Neither of us said a word. Blaze because he wasn't going to talk and reveal his identity to me. Me because I had no idea what you say to the man who had done all of the aforementioned. We strolled along with the polite distance of acquaintances between us as though he hadn't carried me in his arms like a classic damsel in distress every time he rescued me. Etiquette is such an odd thing.

Around us, the night was misty and foggy in the way only true autumnal nights can be. The bridge glowed green in the mist, evenly spaced light poles creating brief pools of yellow. I kept my hands in the pockets of my jacket to avoid the chill. Blaze didn't seem to feel the cold at all even though his green shirt was thin, defining his muscles nicely. It made me wonder if superheroes had gyms, or if he'd woken up on the day he'd become a superhero to find a set of washboard abs and pecs to die for.

Finally, when we reached the top of the bridge and had paused by mutual agreement to stare into the murky river below, I broke the silence. "You're not Jeremy."

Again, surprise. And a bare shrug.

"So you are Jeremy?"

Another shrug.

"What you are," I said to myself, "is no help whatsoever."

This time there was no shrug. But there was a definite smile behind that mask.

I didn't say anything else—and neither did he—while we were on that bridge. After a while had passed, I turned and began to head back to the office. I had more work to do before I could go home that night. Blaze kept pace with me even though his legs seemed to be twice as long as mine. Jeremy never bothered to slow his loping stride down, so I was sometimes forced to jog to keep up. Blaze matched my stride perfectly.

When we reached my building, Blaze nodded at me, and then the door behind me. Our odd little walk was over. He would wait for me to get safely inside. I mustered a smile for him and headed inside, peeking over my shoulder. It was so rare that I got to see him when the world wasn't in peril. He stood, arms crossed, a shadow thrown over his face from the streetlamp behind him. I turned away to go inside.

In the elevator, my phone buzzed. The display screen showed Jeremy's name and picture. It was only a text: *Leaving on a jet plane. See ya when I see ya.*

I texted back: *Have fun in Miami*, and magnanimously did not call him any names.

The office was just as I'd left it, save for the rose on my desk. A single white rose with a green ribbon tied around its stem. I stared. That was Blaze's trademark, but when on earth had he had time . . . ? Confused, I whirled, but the windows were all locked. The alarm beeped a steady green. I carefully picked up the rose and fingered the ribbon. Only then did I see the note, written in black ink on plain (if heavy) cardstock.

I'm sorry. Good-bye.

Blaze's signature drawing—just a little cartoon flame—was doodled beneath the words.

"The hell?" I asked, turning the rose over. It took me a full minute of staring to realize what it meant: the walk hadn't been because he'd wanted to see me outside of the confines of danger. He'd been saying good-bye.

So where was Blaze going?

And though every feminist in history would throw her hands up in disgust, my next thought was, who would save me now?

Chapter Three

A LOT CHANGED after Blaze left.

I guess when he left town—publicly showing up to save supermodel Victoria Burroughs from the evil clutches of Lieutenant Lunatic in Miami two days later—the villains just lost interest. Supervillains ignored me to chase the more classically pretty damsels in distress. Months passed without a single kidnapping. For the first time since Sykik had seen me on the train tracks, I could walk into a bank without expecting a holdup.

It was like there was some sort of secret code. But since my landlord was so relieved that he could stop replacing random walls in my apartment after supervillain attacks, I decided not to think about it.

That is, until the pictures started showing up on the Domino.

"You know, she's really pretty," Portia said. She was perched on the edge of my desk with her tablet, clicking through a slide show on the Domino's front page. "Doesn't that bother you?"

I grabbed a stack of annual reports and stapled them together. "Why would it?"

Portia leaned forward and tapped one lacquered nail against her mouth. "Just saying. It would bother me. Of course, all of *my* ex-boyfriends are photographers, so it makes sense that they'd date models. But Jeremy's just in sales—"

"Accounting."

"—and it's not like you meet a lot of models working in sales." She paused to think about it. "Unless you work here."

I closed my eyes and wished for some sort of excuse, any excuse, something shiny—anything to get her to wander off. "You need a new hobby."

"Nah." Portia popped her gum. "Check this one."

I made the mistake of looking when she swiveled the tablet around. The picture wasn't anything special: it was outside some kind of juice bar in Miami, and there was no mistaking my ex-boyfriend. He wore a stupid little trilby hat and a white button up shirt over his khakis, his arm around the tiny waist of Victoria Burroughs.

And if things weren't bad enough, he was grinning like a kid in a candy store.

"Huh," was all I could say.

"You're telling me that *really* doesn't bother you?"

"Do you want me to swear on the Bible or something?" I reached around her for my little bin of paper clips. "I'm trying to work here."

"You know it's weird that you don't care, right?" Portia

hopped off the desk. The move nudged her top up another inch.

June had attacked Chicago, bringing with it an unrelenting, wet heat. My coworkers had answered by dropping layers. I'd conceded to the heat with a skirt, something that I could finally wear since I probably wouldn't have to run for my life. My shirt, which had looked cute on the rack, had already wilted, and my hair had fallen out of its classy updo into a mass of frizzled curls. Curls that, with my lack of height and petite form, would always keep me away from adjectives like "sexy" and "sultry," and steer me towards "cute" and "doll-like."

Though that usually wasn't a problem, as I was so busy working for Angus that I didn't really have time to date anyway. Which was precisely why Portia had come over to my desk, unfortunately.

"If you say it doesn't bother you," she said, "then it doesn't bother you. Either way, it's time you had a date. It's been what, a year since Jeremy?"

"Eight months," I said, glancing over my shoulder in time to see Portia's puzzled look. "What?"

"Oh, nothing," she said, too quickly.

"What?" I said again.

"It's just, the reporter I talked to this morning mentioned it had been a year since your last kidnapping."

"Were you hitting on a reporter this morning?" I squinted at her.

"No. Well, sort of. She called, and she sounded cute. So I talked to her—it's not a crime, don't give me that look. She said it had been a year since you'd been kidnapped."

"Somebody's not keeping track, then," I said. "Razor X kidnapped me twice last October."

"Uh-huh."

"But, really, we need to talk about you talking to reporters about me."

"What about it?"

"Don't."

Portia's lower lip jutted out. "Girl, that's so mean. You know I need all the exposure I can get! I'm not even a proper tag on the Domino yet. Maybe we could go out for drinks and get threatened by some villains or something. I'll let you borrow a cute outfit."

"As delightful as that sounds, I think I'm good." I swiveled around to face my desk. I heard her heels click on the tiles as she sulked off, and I smiled. Finally. Got rid of her.

Unfortunately, my peace didn't last long. Asiv came up, papers overflowing from the folders in his hands. "Girl! Girl—I need help—quick—" He thrust the whole mess at me; papers spilled onto my desk, nearly knocking over my tea and destroying my careful system. "I've got a meeting in twenty minutes, and I can't figure out how to organize these. Please."

A quick glance through the scattered paperwork had me giving him an unimpressed look. "These just need to be collated, Asiv. That's Adrianna's job."

"She's out to lunch."

"Still?" She'd left two hours before.

"Please, Girl? Can't you do this for me?"

I gave him a frown that I wished was intimidating. "You're really making me miss Guy, you know." Say what you like about the Bookmans, but Guy had always been organized. And he'd never made me do his busywork.

"You think I don't miss Guy, too?" Asiv crossed his arms over his chest. "He was the one who knew how to do all of this."

"I suggest you learn," I said, and began to sort the paper into stacks. "When's the meeting?"

"Twenty minutes—no, make that eighteen now. Thanks, Girl!"

I tracked him down in his office fifteen minutes later. "Your paperwork," I said, and thrust the stack of files at him. A single glimpse of the monitor was all it took to get my blood pressure rising. "Please tell me you didn't pawn your work off on me so you could play video poker."

He flicked his fingers. "Oh, come off it. Like you had anything better to do."

"Asshole." I turned on my heel and very carefully did not stomp out. Outside the office, though, I had to breathe through my nose a few times. I swallowed and grabbed my purse.

"For anybody who cares, I hate this place, so I'm getting coffee. And no," I said as four heads popped up like deranged prairie dogs from the cubicles, "I'm not bringing any back. I am not your pack mule."

With that said, I stomped off. And found myself ambushed the instant I set foot on the pavement outside.

"Girl—Girl Godwin!" A young woman with unremarkable features and a slouchy beanie pulled over her hair hurried up to me. I took an involuntary step back in surprise, hand already wrapped around my mace. "I'm

Naomi Gunn. I run Crap About Capes, the blog? I wondered if I could ask you a few questions."

"Were you waiting around for me to come out?" I asked.

She raised both eyebrows. Because she was so much taller than me, it felt a little bit like she was looking down her nose at me. "Serendipity, actually. I happened to be walking by and spotted you."

She had to be a writer to use the word "serendipity" though I wasn't sure I believed the rest of her story. I didn't have to ask how she'd recognized me. "Questions about what?" I asked instead. "About Blaze? I can't tell you who he is. Because I *don't know*."

Naomi Gunn scoffed. "You really should drop the act. Everybody knows Jeremy Collins is Blaze. I mean, even the Domino is in on it, and you know those morons, they take forever to get the real news."

I glared at her.

"Anyway, never mind that. I'm here to ask about your year of not getting taken hostage. Getting in on the ground floor." Naomi pushed her cap back to scratch at her forehead, which the June sun had dampened. Her fingers twitched as she straightened her dark-rimmed glasses. "What's that feel like? And how do you feel now that Blaze has decided to protect Miami instead?"

"The citizens of Miami should feel very fortunate." I was willing at least to give him that much. "And for your information, it hasn't been a year since my last kidnapping. Razor X kidnapped me *twice* last October. So check your facts. And off the record, quit calling my coworkers for stories about me. Now, excuse me. You're between me and caffeine."

"A scary place?" Naomi said.

"Move," I said in a quiet voice that had once made Captain Cracked do a double take. Before he, of course, had knocked me out. But it had still made him pause. Naomi Gunn of Crap About Capes was clearly no match for Captain Cracked. She stumbled as she dodged out of my way. I sailed by, sending her one last glare.

"Try not to get kidnapped for four more months, okay?" she said. "Because I still want to write this story."

I closed my eyes. "You just had to say that, didn't you?"

Her entire face folded with confusion. "What are you talking about?"

"Never mind." I strode off.

In the Daily Grind, I ordered my usual and forced myself to relax. Naomi couldn't have jinxed me. I wasn't Hostage Girl anymore. I was safe. I was just a normal worker on a much-needed caffeine break.

I paid for my coffee and waited by the little counter for the barista to deliver it. At least Naomi Gunn had temporarily shifted my annoyance away from my coworkers. Did I really need my job? The economy wasn't great at the moment, but with my experience, I could find a new job pretty easily. And it *had* been a year since the last major kidnapping. Maybe I didn't need to stick around and be treated as a stevedore in the name of great healthcare. Maybe I could be one of those people who saw the doctor for things like annual checkups and not Venus-von-Trapp-turned-me-green-again.

I swear, in that moment the universe laughed at me.

The front wall of the coffee shop creaked so loudly that everybody in line turned as one. I recognized the sound—it was impossible to forget—but it had been so long that my shouted, "Get down!" was too late.

Something hit the front window with enough force to send glass and wood splintering across the shop. The ground shook, throwing me into the counter, as a second blast hit the wall. Brick dust exploded. Debris hurtled through the air, joining the screams of the patrons. I turned to duck behind the counter and tripped over a guy in a suit. Both of us cursed as we crashed to the tiles.

Hot coffee rained down like an angry waterfall from the counter above me, dripping on the back of my neck. The villain couldn't have waited until I was out in the open, away from scalding liquids?

"What's going on?" the man in the suit asked. "Is it Captain Cracked?"

"Not unless he's escaped Detmer in the past two hours," I said. I tried to pull myself out of the way of the dripping coffee, only to discover that my foot was wedged between the counter and a fallen chunk of concrete. "Crap! My foot's stuck. Can you help?"

But the man gaped at me. Around us, the tenor of the screams changed; I had to assume the maniacal laugh cutting through the air meant the villain had stepped inside. The man continued to gawp. "Y-you're her, aren't you?"

I didn't bother to ask who he meant. "Please help me."

Instead of helping free my foot, though, the man stood up. "She's right here!" he said to somebody I couldn't see.

"There's no need to hurt anybody else. I've got Hostage Girl right here—"

He broke off with a gurgle as he was briefly engulfed in a bright purple corona. His eyes went wide, and then he slumped to the floor, out cold.

"Huh," I said. Karma usually took a lot longer than that.

A spindly man in plaid and a gruesome Halloween mask stepped around the counter. He sniffed down at the unconscious man. He cleared his throat. "Hostage Girl, I presume?"

"No, sorry, I think she went thataway," I said, jerking a thumb behind me as my heart hammered twice as fast against the side of my sternum. I jerked at my ankle, hoping some miracle would free my foot and allow me to run.

He only smiled. How he could do that with the mask, I had no idea. "Cute."

He raised his wrist and pressed a button on his cuff. For a split second, everything turned purple. I only had time for two thoughts as my reality shrank to nothingness: the first, there was no way the Daily Grind was going to let me keep my frequent customer discount card after this. And the second? The minute Blaze came to rescue me, I was going to send Naomi Gunn a *very* strongly worded e-mail for jinxing me like this.

IT TOOK THE purple a long time to recede, and when it finally did, I was no longer on the floor of my favorite roasthouse but at an 'L' stop several miles away.

June had become November, my ankle was free, and I'd somehow jumped back in time. Though it was a dull day, the sun well hidden and the wind cutting, I recognized it. Under my new coat, which wouldn't be new much longer, the hair on my arms stood on end. How had I come back? I hadn't thought about that day in months, so why was I revisiting it now?

Apparently, my questions weren't to be answered, for my legs kept moving up the steps. Chicago was brand-new brand new to me, fascinating and dirty and still a little marvelous without the dull layer of drudgery it would soon gain. My breath puffed around my face as I reached the top step, and just like I remembered, the screaming began.

Across the wide network of tracks, a woman was screaming, long, horror-movie screams. My friends in Indiana had warned me about moving to the city, but I'd laughed them off. Villain attacks weren't *that* common, I'd argued. The news just didn't like reporting positive things, bad news sold better.

I was about to discover exactly how wrong I was.

Around me, people scrambled for the exits, shouting and shoving other people aside. They'd all recognized the villain, but all I saw was a skinny guy with a mohawk, laughing a bit hysterically. Two things stood out about him: despite the fact that it was lose-your-fingers cold, he wore a tank top, and he was hovering eight feet over the 'L' tracks, cackling like a lunatic. He hovered about twenty yards away, but it wasn't difficult to make out the two kids huddled on the tracks, gazing up at him with slack looks on their faces.

The oncoming train was a little bit more of a pressing concern.

I started running, my shoes sliding against the icy platform. "What are you doing?" I shouted. A crowd gathered close to the screaming woman, who was beating on the air like it was a solid wall, her screams hoarse and desperate. The crowd, on the other hand, watched all of this with something akin to disinterest. None of them looked at the fleeing pedestrians or at me.

I snatched up an empty beer bottle from an overflowing trash can and flung it as hard as I could, pitching forward and losing my balance. There was a world of difference between breaking up a bar fight in Nowhere, Indiana, and hurling beer bottles on a frozen train platform.

Apparently, my aim had improved, though.

The bottle hit the floating dude square between his shoulder blades. He whipped about, looking around until his gaze speared right through me.

He tilted his head. "What are you?" he asked, and lifted his index and middle finger to rest against his temple. "Don't smell like a tourist, don't look like a local. Let's take a peek, hmm?"

The headache that had hit me then had been akin to slamming full force into that train still racing down the tracks. Or it had been like that then. Now, I didn't feel anything, so I stayed crouched on the platform, gasping with the phantom memory of pain as what felt like tiny fingers picked my thoughts apart like bits of cotton batting. I hissed out a breath between my teeth and scooted backward, hoping only to get away from the instant migraine.

Unfortunately, I hadn't realized how close I was to the edge of the platform, the bumpy concrete of the safety lines digging into my knees. Teeth still clenched, I tipped right over the edge.

For a second, it was like flying.

I didn't hit the ground. I saw a blur of vivid green, and the breath whooshed out of me as something snatched me from behind. One second of disorientation later, I was back on my feet, well away from the edge of the platform.

The green blurred away again. It was a man—no, not just a man, this was a superhero. Where had he come from? I looked around, bewildered, as the man took three running steps away from me and launched himself off of the platform. He swooped across the tracks, flying in a zigzag pattern because the ugly guy with the mohawk kept trying to glare that daggery mental gaze at him. The man in green scooped up the children; an instant later, we all felt the blowback of the train race by. He set the kids on the platform next to their sobbing mother.

The man with the mohawk, who'd nimbly dodged out of the train's path, glared at my mystery savior. In a blink, a lightning-quick change, he whipped around to smile at me. "Don't worry. I'll see you again."

And he sped off, right as the man in the green suit and mask leapt at him. The man's fist punched through empty air.

When he turned to look at me, purple light crept around the edges of my vision the way it had in the coffee shop, and I had only a second to meet Blaze's eyes, even greener than his uniform, across the platform before he flew away.

It had been the first time he'd saved my life.

MY EYES OPENED, though the rest of me didn't follow. I floated in a haze. There wasn't pain; there wasn't anything. Though I was in my body, it no longer existed. Did that mean I no longer existed? I wasn't missing much, if that was the case. An unenviable job, no boyfriend, a tiny apartment. Shallow coworkers. Late nights with Ramen and early mornings with instant oatmeal.

I was probably better off without all of that.

Slowly, details trickled into my world. I could feel my hands and my fingers, and finally my shoulders, which ached a little. Sensation returned next to the littlest toe on my left foot, followed by my right leg. It crept up my shins and calves, into my thighs and butt. And it was *cold*. Less cold on my upper thighs and butt, but frigid nonetheless.

When the feeling entered my back, I gasped and felt my lungs expand with it. For one startling eternity of a second, I was aware of every single atom, every molecule, and every fiber of my body. I was Gail. I was. And then it faded away.

But one thought slipped in before everything became nonsensical again: "Why am I strapped to a table?"

Chapter Four

WHEN I SURFACED again, I wasn't alone.

"Would you wake up already? If I didn't know better, I'd say you were a narcoleptic, and the solution only exacerbated matters."

Slowly, I blinked my eyes open, my vision focusing surprisingly quickly. It only took a glance to see that I was in some kind of basement, and not a well-kept one. A single halogen light swung on an exposed wire over my table, casting awkward shadows across floor-to-ceiling metal shelves all around me. They contained metal instruments with suction cups and pointed ends, chemical phials and vials, some with liquid inside, binders that leaned against each other like a bunch of drunks. All of it was covered in an unbelievable amount of dust. I was grateful once again for the fact that I'd never suffered from allergies. When I moved my head, black sparks skittered across my vision, and I felt my reality begin to slide away . . .

"No, no, none of that now. Quit that."

A sharp twinge in my left arm dragged me right back, and I found myself staring up at the horror movie mask from the coffee shop. No, I realized. That was no mask. It was a face, one attached to an actual person. Even worse, he was using it to sneer at me. He blocked the lightbulb for a second as it swung in that direction, throwing a ghoulish halo over features that were far from pretty to begin with. His nose was bulbous, his eyebrow thick and slashing over the expanse of his entire forehead. Skin sagged at his jowls; he had yellow, crooked teeth and the breath to match.

This time, I didn't bother to recoil. "Who . . ." My voice cracked and rasped as if I'd been chain-smoking for twenty years. "Where . . ."

"Who am I?" Satisfied that his victim was awake, Ugly leaned back so that I could see more of him, giving me a reprieve from the halitosis. He wore a lab coat over a flannel shirt, which I took to be a very bad sign—the lab coat, not the flannel. Mad scientists had been the bane of my existence for a long time, but I could honestly say I'd never had the honor of being kidnapped by a lumberjack before. He rubbed spindly, liver-spotted hands together. "I, dear girl, am Dr. Mobius. Tell me what's wrong with you."

My throat hurt, my head was pounding, and I couldn't feel my fingers or toes. "You mean, besides the fact that I'm strapped to a table?"

"Yes, yes." He waved impatiently. "Besides that. How do you feel?"

"Cold."

"Interesting." Dr. Mobius rubbed his chin, looking away so that the light got lost in the crags of his face. Mostly to himself, he said, "Why is that?"

"Probably because I'm strapped to a metal table," I said. "But I'm just spitballing. I could be wrong. Hey, here's an idea—untie me so I can get off the table, and I can tell you for sure. Think of it as removing a variable."

Dr. Mobius's eyes flashed. "Nice try. How do you feel? Any effects? By my calculations, you should be feeling a bit . . . a bit *off*."

Giving kidnappers information never ended well, so I swallowed down steadily rising nausea and dizziness. There was a persistent throbbing nexus of agony behind my right eye, but I gave him my sunniest, most sarcastic grin. "Feeling great," I said. "Except for the part where I'm strapped to a metal table."

"I'm not going to be moving you for a while, so I'm afraid you'll just have to get over that."

"Look, Dr. Nutball. You have officially broken the eight-month record I had going for not getting kidnapped. I was *fond* of that record." Despite the fact that it made my head spin, I sat up as far as the chains on my wrist would let me to glare at him. It ended up being more like doing crunches, which wasn't the worst thing for my abs. "Going along with your plans like a good little hostage is not on the agenda, okay, so save us both time and let me go. It'll end better that way, trust me."

"Eight-month record of not getting kidnapped?" Dr. Mobius stared at me as though I'd grown an extra head. Since the idea wasn't entirely outlandish in this situation,

I had to check. I still had the same number of craniums. "What do you mean? Have the villains not been doing their job?"

"Villains have other things to do," I said. "Thankfully."

"But you're still Blaze's Girl, aren't you?"

"Not anymore." Since my abs were screaming, I lay back down on the table. "Not since . . ."

I never got to finish my sentence. The black sparks, having been threatening at the edge of my vision all along, came back to finish the job. And even though I felt that pinch on my left arm again, I ignored it for the cool bliss of the unknown.

"OH, COME OFF IT." Jeremy risked a glance away from the TV eating his entire wall to look over at me. His brilliant eyes were incredulous. "You really don't think I'm Blaze?"

"No." I flicked my index finger, scrolling to the next page of the Domino on my tablet. I hoped they would have a good picture of Blaze this week. He usually flew so fast that it was hard to get a clear shot. So far, the only great pictures had been while Blaze was flying slow enough to carry me. And I never looked good unconscious, I'd discovered.

"Really?" Jeremy returned his gaze to the screen. "I mean, it didn't strike you suspicious at all that Bla—*I* started rescuing you right before we met?"

"Mm." There was an excellent profile shot of War Hammer, looking as serious and sober as he always did. I paused to study it. War Hammer had just that touch of sadness in the eyes behind the mask. I wondered what his story was. "Sorry, Jer. I know it hurts your ego, but I don't think you're Blaze."

"Why not?"

"Well, if you are, why don't you go grab that uniform that you fill up so nicely and show me?"

Jeremy rolled his eyes. On-screen, he obliterated the three Nazis that were guarding the base, while his partner threw a grenade to destroy the rest of the compound. "That ruins the principle of the thing, Girl." Though we'd been dating six months, he'd picked up the habit of calling me by my nickname. "You have to have faith in these things."

"Inspire my faith, then. Show me the uniform."

"That's the exact opposite meaning of faith."

I smirked and went back to reading the article on War Hammer. It was a Saturday blissfully free of work, so Jeremy and I were taking the opportunity for a little alone time—just us and *Call of War*. Tired of fighting with a video game to spend time with my boyfriend, I'd resorted to browsing social media.

"Why don't you think I'm Blaze?" Jeremy asked.

I shrugged. "Faith?"

"You know, you're a bad girlfriend."

Purposely, I looked over at the screen, then back to Jeremy. "Says the man who's ignoring his girlfriend on her first full day off in two months . . . to play video games."

"Oh, did you want attention?" Jeremy's grin turned wolfish. In a flash, he'd clicked pause and was on top of me on his ratty couch, his weight comfortably pressing into me. He grinned and nipped at my neck. "Guess I'm a bad boyfriend then, eh?"

"Eh?" I repeated, and all talking ceased for a bit while our lips were otherwise engaged. I felt Jeremy's fingers moving down the buttons on my shirt and moved to return the favor, but he eased back. "What is it?"

"Nothing." Jeremy clambered off of me, leaving my shirt open. "Stay like that a minute, will you? I've just got to kill some Nazi scum and level up, and then we can pick up right where we left off." He looked over his shoulder to waggle his eyebrows at me. "Only maybe we should take it into the bedroom?"

"And you wonder why I don't think you're Blaze," I said, and buttoned up my shirt.

WHEN I WOKE again, it was because something very insistent was prodding my left elbow. Mostly I awoke to tell whoever it was to knock it the hell off so that I could back to sleep.

Only to find myself staring into the face of my captor, yet again. Oh, joy.

"Is Blaze dead?" Dr. Mobius shoved his face into my line of sight. The halitosis alone was enough to knock away the last vestiges of sleep.

"What?"

"Blaze—is he dead? I knew he was going to bite it in some stupidly heroic way before I could pull this off.

How'd he go? Saving a bus full of orphans? Kittens?" Mobius stroked his chin while he gave the matter some thought. "Puppies?"

"Blaze isn't dead. He's in Miami. You're barking up the wrong tree if you did this to get his attention." In an attempt to get away from his foul breath—had he just been *feasting on roadkill?*—I leaned as far away as I could. Why did I feel so dizzy? What was going on?

"What!" The walls seemed to shake from the rage in Dr. Mobius's voice. "Why didn't you tell me this sooner?"

"I don't communicate well when unconscious. Never was great at multitasking." I closed my eyes. "Tell you what, you let me go, and I won't even tell the police. I'll just go back to my life and let you live yours. We can forget the past few hours ever happened."

"Few hours? I've had you here twelve days."

My eyes shot open. "Tw-twelve days? You've kept me here *twelve* days? What are you, nuts? I've got work!"

Mobius paused and gave me a peculiar look. Belatedly, I realized my priorities might be a little out of line, but I hunched my shoulders and tried not to throw up. "What?"

Dr. Mobius moved away to pace back and forth across the lab. With every footfall he made, things on the shelf beside him tottered. "So Blaze has decamped for sunnier climes. That does put a wrinkle in my plans."

"A wrinkle? You? That must be a new one," I said, glaring at his lined face.

He snorted, unimpressed with my rather lame insult. "You had better hope Blaze discovers that you're missing soon. Or else I might be tempted not to . . . give you your upgrades."

Upgrades? He had my full attention now. "You turned me into a robot?"

"Don't be foolish, Girl. Do you feel like a robot?"

"How would I know?" I said. "I've never been a robot before."

"And you're not one now."

Whew.

"You're just radioactive."

There went that "whew."

"*What?*"

"You heard me." Dr. Mobius moved away to putter at a desk in the corner. "Relax. I've already swallowed a supplement—of my own design, naturally—that will prevent me from getting radiation poisoning. You won't contaminate anybody here. I am perfectly safe, my dear Girl."

He wouldn't be if I could snap out of these damn shackles. "Yeah, because I was *so worried about that*. Why am I radioactive?"

"Well, why wouldn't you be? I injected you with a solution containing a synthesized isotope of—well, let's call it Mobium after yours truly—among other nasty little things. You don't recall? You were awake for it."

My memories produced nothing but a blank. I remembered the coffee shop and some fever dreams, but that was it. "What are you talking about?"

"I distinctly remember that you were lucid," Mobius said, turning away from the desk. He did not, thankfully, have a syringe in his hand (I've been suspicious of people who keep their backs to me in secret laboratories ever since the incident with Nurse Wretched). The clipboard he held didn't much reassure me. He peered at it. "I'll have to check my records to be sure, but—hmm. Oh, yes. Yes, you were most definitely conscious and cognizant. I noted several colorful adjectives you chose to employ in the use of describing a certain part of my anatomy."

That sounded like me, but I still didn't remember any sort of injection. And I tended to remember those things. A lifelong fear of needles had taken care of that long before I had ever been kidnapped.

"Why?" I said. "Why would you inject me with this— this whatever the hell it was you gave me? What kind of sick game are you playing here?"

"Sick game?" Mobius looked affronted. Or as much as somebody with a face appropriate for the Halloween aisle of a department store could. "My dear Girl—"

"Don't call me that."

"—this is no game." Mobius sighed to himself. "The plan was simple: I inject you with the solution until your blood would become accustomed to it—yes, even crave it—and Blaze shows up and saves. In two months, you'll fall ill without another dose, and Blaze will be forced to come to me to get more. For his precious Girl."

"Making me the perfect bargaining chip," I said, dull horror gnawing at my middle.

"A coup de grace, if you will." Mobius's face twisted back into its scowl. "Only your Blaze does not seem to be following the program."

I'd been up excrement creek without a paddle before (as the polite saying goes), but this blew every near save to pieces. My only hope of getting out of here alive had no idea I was here. Because he was in Miami. The only way I was going to walk out of here was if I broke through the shackles myself, or if I convinced Dr. Mobius just to let me go. And the likelihood of either of those happening—I'd better just start gnawing on a limb if I wanted to escape.

I decided to focus on the other reason for panic. "So you injected me with something that's made me dependent upon it?" I demanded. After years of avoiding needles, white powder, and cigarettes, I had nonetheless become a junkie. For a mad scientist's formula. Which I had a feeling I wasn't going to be able to pick up from a shady guy on a street corner.

As if already preparing for the life of an addict, my hands began to shake. They jerked left and right so that the shackles bit into my wrists. I yelped, but the convulsing extended, pushing up my arms and into my shoulders, bouncing my head hard against the metal table. I shouted. With my last waking coherent second before the seizing overtook me, I saw Dr. Mobius reach for what looked suspiciously like a clipboard. He might have said, "Again?"

But I couldn't be sure. I was too busy blacking out to double-check.

I OPENED MY eyes to find myself in Dr. Mobius's basement lair once again.

He leaned over me, his long nose pushed disturbingly

close to my face. He smelled rank. "Gah, what are you doing? Get away from me!" I said.

He didn't move. "Who's Naomi Gunn?"

"You'll find her in the file named 'Business Comma None of Yours.'"

"You were muttering her name." Mobius eased back to check his clipboard. "She must be somebody important. From what I can gather from your little outbursts, you've been reliving important moments in your life."

"I was hallucinating." I began to search the room for the source of the smell. Surely something that stank that badly would make itself obvious.

Dr. Mobius tapped one finger against a wart on his chin while he studied the clipboard in the flickering light. "You mentioned a Jeremy Collins—Blaze, understandably. Angus Vanderfeld is a noted entry, and never with happy emotions attached. And Blaze himself, as his superhero identity. Of course." He looked up from the clipboard and down at me, and I quite suddenly wished he'd go back to the clipboard. His eyes, too large and too bulbous for his sockets, bugged out at me. "I find it curious that you deny even in your subconscious that Jeremy Collins is Blaze."

"Blaze isn't Jeremy Collins."

Mobius twitched a shoulder.

And I realized where the smell was coming from: me. I stank. I reeked badly enough that I was causing myself to gag. No wonder I'd been shaking so badly. I'd probably been trying to break the restraints and run away from myself.

"Evidently, I could use a shower." I breathed shallowly through my mouth. "How long was I out?"

"Eight hours. I felt it best to sedate you during your seizure so that you didn't try to swallow your own tongue and suffocate. Death is such a messy, pointless thing. You're of much more use to me alive." Mobius put the clipboard away.

Since I'd been kidnapped by villains who hadn't shared that philosophy and hadn't cared whether I lived or died, the sentiment was actually a bit touching. The seizures were worrying, though.

Mobius, of course, ruined the effect. "Granted, if Blaze doesn't show soon, I may have to revise my policy. Every minute you're here is one where we might be discovered. As spry as I am—I'm quite spry; that's how I was able to escape the guards at Detmer—I'd rather not have to live with the messiness of a civilian rescue."

Detmer, where they kept the most dangerous, deranged supervillains. I swallowed hard.

"They had me in solitary, you know." Mobius's voice took on that distant quality that only supervillains could get while they lectured about their evil plans: smug and with a hint of wistfulness. "It took me nearly two years to come up with the perfect escape plan. I shan't tell you what it was—it's the most forgotten rule in the Villain Handbook that to give away the intricate details of one's plan or escape is to concede defeat on the spot. And, Girl, I will not be defeated."

Why did it not surprise me that the villains had a handbook? I probably had my own chapter and designation, and they likely included the words "handy to kidnap in a pinch."

"Where was I?" Dr. Mobius pushed his scaly index finger up the side of his face, thinking. "Oh, right. You're troublesome. I've had you here thirteen days, and frankly, I'm tiring of cleaning up your messes, of feeding you, and of your lack of gratitude. I mean, even if you weren't forgetting every day left and right, you really are a most ungrateful creature."

"Sorry I'm not grateful that you strapped me to a table."

"That's precisely what I mean." Dr. Mobius stalked to the other side of the laboratory and back, a short trip. His scowl turned into a mutinous frown, and he let out a gusty sigh. "Every day that passes increases the likelihood of you escaping that table, and there are several caustic chemicals around that could hurt me."

"You think?" I asked, eyeing the bubbling green beaker.

He flicked his fingers at me. "I think it's time for a new location."

"Where? Will I be able to move around again?"

"Unfortunately."

"And will I be able to shower?"

"The entire world would be grateful, so I'm tempted to say no. But as I'm the one that has to have to live with your ungodly stink, I will grant you a shower."

"Hey!" I lifted my head to glare at him better. "You brought this on yourself."

"There's a chemical shower through there." Mobius's long fingers undid the shackle around my ankle. Though my skin crawled that he was touching any part of me, I had to sigh when the foot was released. Mobius's eyes narrowed. "No funny business. The solution has the side effect of making you rather weak. So I recommend you don't even bother."

I didn't roll my eyes though I considered it. After two weeks on a table, I was going to be as useless as a newborn puppy. But I had to try *something*, so when Mobius released my wrist, I swung at him.

Both of us watched my hand as my arm made it halfway into the air and flopped uselessly at my side. He raised his eyebrows at me. "Is that it?"

"Apparently," I said, sighing. It took everything I had to gingerly ease over the edge of the table and lower my legs. My feet were so frozen that touching the cold concrete did absolutely nothing. I gritted my teeth and slowly transferred my weight to my unused legs. It took everything I had to keep upright.

Mobius seemed to be one of those scientists who had never developed the necessary wells of patience. He grabbed my arm above the elbow and hauled, shoving me over to a door. Inside was a room no larger than a closet with a drain on the floor and a showerhead suspended from the ceiling. A pull chain appeared to be the only type of faucet the chemical shower had.

I stumbled into the shower and braced my hands on the walls as I tried to get my breath back. I wasn't precisely winded, but everything just felt *weird*, like my body had been disassembled and reassembled with different parts. Was that an effect of the radiation?

"Don't come out until you smell better."

"Kind of not that possible without soap, Doc."

"Fine, fine." I heard his muttered grumbling as he puttered around the basement-lair. A few seconds later, a bar of soap was tossed at my feet.

I plucked at the shoulder of the soiled, rotten gown. "Am I just supposed to wear this?"

He scowled again. "I'll find you something and leave it outside the door. Hostages are a lot of work."

Even if I weren't Hostage Girl, I could have told him that.

Chapter Five

CHEMICAL SHOWERS APPARENTLY aren't very warm. Or at least this one wasn't.

The instant I pulled the cord, cold water sluiced over my head, making me gasp out loud. It was like an icy rain of death, but at least it seemed to shake most of the feebleness out of my limbs. Swearing viciously, I fumbled around in the dark until I found the soap. My hands shook as I yanked off the gown and scrubbed as fast as I could. Thanks to a complete lack of coordination and the danger of frostbite, I stumbled more than I cleaned. I grunted when I banged my shoulder into the wall.

Honestly, would it have killed him to put in a light?

I had to use the soap on my hair since there wasn't any shampoo, but after two weeks, anything was better than nothing. I ducked my head fully under the spray, closed my eyes, and held my breath for ten seconds.

When I eased open the door to find clothes waiting for

me outside, I was shivering so hard that it was hard to pull on the ratty corduroy trousers. The white T-shirt had seen better days, and the flannel shirt made me grimace. Now Mobius and I would both look like lumberjacks. The pants needed a belt and were far too long, so I rolled the waistline over and over until the extra cloth held the pants up on its own. Underwear seemed like too much to hope for, so I went without. The clothing didn't smell exactly fresh or anything, but it had the advantage of being clean. I finger-combed my hair, pulled it back into a wet knot, and for a moment, just enjoyed the rare feeling of being human.

For all of two seconds.

Mobius had been waiting for me to emerge; he grabbed me by the arm, yanked me out of the lair, up a staircase, and down a brief hallway with bare walls and no defining features. Summarily, he shoved me in a closet and locked the door.

Habit from dozens of other kidnappings made me explore the walls and corners with my hands, searching for any trapdoors (it's amazing how many villains forget to hostage-proof their lairs), but the storage room was all it appeared to be: a dark, empty hole. Thanks to the corduroy and flannel, I started to warm up almost immediately, but other than that, it didn't have much to offer me.

Leaning against the wall, I dozed off—maybe I did have narcolepsy—and when I woke up, my hair was drier. Thumping repeatedly on the door raised no response from Dr. Mobius, so I leaned back and finally took some time to do a mental inventory. By my calculations, I'd spent the past two weeks asleep, or close enough to it. Dr. Mobius had said I'd been awake for part of it, so why was everything during that time blank?

Focusing as hard as I could produce nothing but a vague, blurry memory of watching a giant needle being shoved into my arm, and an accompanying dizzy spell. The entire room seemed to shake, so I fell forward, hugging the ground until the vertigo had passed. It took me nearly a minute of lying on the floor to convince myself that it was all in my head.

I pushed myself back up. Belatedly, I froze. That push-up had been really easy.

Shouldn't I be as weak as a baby kitten? I didn't know how long it took muscular atrophy to set in, but I was pretty sure two weeks on a table wasn't exactly healthy. Testing, I propped myself up on my hands and my feet and did a push-up. And then I did another.

I began to count in my head. One. Two. Five. Ten. Thirteen, fourteen. Fifteen.

I wasn't even tired yet.

Eighteen. Nineteen. Twenty.

My arms felt fine. In fact, they felt better than they had in a long time. I kept going.

Twenty-nine, thirty.

Forty. Fifty.

Sixty.

Nothing burned. I was doing full, military-style push-ups, my palms biting into the ground right below my shoulders.

Seventy.

I hadn't even broken a sweat.

By the time I reached ninety without any signs of

fatigue, I began to panic. When I passed a hundred, my hands began to shake. It wasn't exhaustion. I'd just done a hundred push-ups when twenty usually did me in. Breath scraping against the insides of my lungs in terror, I dropped to the ground and looked around, like the empty walls surrounding me would have an answer.

There was nothing but silence in reply.

What the hell was happened to me? What had Dr. Mobius done to me?

Slowly, hand shaking, I felt my upper arm, where the flab normally had a lot of give. It was like pushing against steel. I yanked off the flannel shirt—the white shirt beneath was old to the point of see-through. In the flickering light, every muscle was defined in perfect, video game lines.

"Uh," was all I could say to that.

Dr. Mobius might have turned me into an addict who would die without her fix, but he'd also apparently given me *muscles*.

A part of me had to marvel. Not at the fact that my arms had become streamlined ropes of wiry muscle and sinew, not that I had washboard abs better than my exboyfriend's (and he'd worked several hours a week on those abs). No, I marveled that I'd somehow missed out on all of this during my shower.

You'd think it would have been obvious.

ABOUT TWENTY MINUTES after my bout with the pushups, hunger began to gnaw away at my stomach. By the time Dr. Mobius opened the door twenty minutes later, I was curled up on the floor, almost delirious. He sniffed. "There's no need to resort to histrionics," he said.

I managed to find the energy to lift my head and give him what I hoped was a glare.

He set a plate inside the door. "So you'll stop mewling," he said, and closed the door again. Two sandwiches using Wonder Bread, a handful of chips covered in orange cheese dust, and a juice box. I hadn't had a lunch like this since I was twelve. But that hardly seemed to matter since I gulped most of the food down without tasting it and licked my finger to pick up any crumbs left on the plate. It seemed to appease the hunger, so I lay back down and waited for my strength to return.

Since I had only the bulb above my head, and no signs of night or day, time became a meaningless entity. It flew, it crawled, it moved in any number of animal ways, while I lay on my back and stared at nothing.

You know what the problem with confinement is? Besides the lack of freedom, I mean? It gives you time to think about everything you've been avoiding. After only a couple of hours in my cell, I couldn't help but ruminate on the fact that I hated my job. The problem with being a workaholic is that there's very little to your life but your job. And I'd been too passive to find a new one. In fact, my forced confinement made me realize how passive I was in every area of my life. My boyfriend had dumped me while I was in a hospital bed. Instead of hunting him down and exacting some form of revenge, I'd stood silently by while he'd moved to Miami to date supermodels.

I'd let Blaze rescue me over and over without prying to find out why it was always him, and why it was always me. I'd allowed Angus to walk all over me until I was little more than an emotionally stunted pancake on the floor of Mirror Reality.

I defined the word "loser" all too well.

Depression began to sink in, deep and dark and oppressive. Once more, I was a hostage, but now I was an addict as well, hooked on a substance that only one man in the world knew how to create. A man who wasn't exactly sane. Was I going to lie down and accept this as my lot in life, as I had with all of the other villains?

What a depressing thought.

For lack of anything better to do, I lay down on my belly. "Okay, Gail. Let's see what you can do."

I pushed up so that my back was straight once more. And I lowered myself. Raised myself again. One. Two. Ten. Fifteen. Twenty. I hit fifty and kept going steadily, breathing perfectly fine. Soared by seventy-five. Passed a hundred without a hitch. Even as my mind marveled and balked, my body never stopped. My arms and shoulders just continued to move, lowering my rib cage to the floor—stopping before it touched—and lifting again. Every time, my elbows broke the ninety-degree mark. Perfect, military-style push-ups.

A hundred.

Two hundred.

Three hundred.

Lactic acid began to break through the barrier that my body had formed against pain, leaking in so that I began to really feel my shoulders. At 350, the ache crawled down my arms.

Four hundred.

Near five hundred, I gave in to the pain and the shaking, and collapsed.

For a long time, I lay there, shocked and stunned. I'd completed nearly five hundred push-ups—not counting the hundred I'd done earlier. Sure, I had muscles now, but that seemed well beyond ridiculous. I didn't know how many push-ups the old trainers at the gym could do without stopping. One thing for sure—it probably wasn't five hundred.

I was still lying on my stomach when the door opened again. A sliver of yellow light cracked the wall, and Dr. Mobius's face loomed over me. With the light behind him giving him a demonic halo, he peered at me. "Why are you sweating?"

"Confinement gives me terror sweats," I said. The first rule about being a hostage is that if you have an advantage, don't let your captor know. "What do you want? Gonna get me addicted to crack cocaine? Or are we skipping straight to meth? I'll have to clear my schedule."

He cocked his head. "What use would I have for a meth addict?"

"You don't seem to have any use for a Mobium addict," I said, pushing myself up to my knees.

"If your Blaze were more diligent in his efforts to protect you, you'd be on your way, and you would only have to see me when the cravings threatened to kill you."

I didn't figure logic was going to take my side on this one.

"In any case," he said, "I figure Blaze will catch on eventually, and it might be easier to convince him not to kill me if I present you well fed and well kept. I have a remarkably low pain tolerance, and I'd prefer not to end up dangling from a building or some such nonsense. It's happened before."

I wasn't surprised. It was one of Blaze's—and War Hammer's—trademarks to leave their villains dangling from a building until the police could collect them and send them to Detmer. I imagine that it amused them though it was probably a lot of hassle for the police.

"So it's time I fed you properly. I advise you not to attempt any funny business. The solution should be keeping you pretty weak, and everybody knows you don't fight back, but I'd rather not have to deal with any unpleasantness."

My stomach sank. It figured that even my passivity was well known among the villains.

Thankfully, I didn't have to play the aching weakling as I rose to my feet. The push-ups had done that for me. So, meek and docile as a lamb, I followed Dr. Mobius. There was nothing on the walls to give me a clue as to where we were or if we were even in Chicago anymore.

Dr. Mobius led me into a different room. Unlike the dirty storage closet and the dim laboratory, this one was relatively normal. A scarred wooden table with mismatched chairs sat in a room with two doorways, one of which we'd just come through. The doorway opposite led to a small, relatively tidy kitchen area.

We weren't just in Dr. Mobius's evil lair, I realized. He lived here.

"Eat." Dr. Mobius pushed a plate in front of me. Steam curled off a grilled piece of chicken and the vegetables around it. "I've decided you're no longer a hostage."

"I'm not?" I perked up. "I'm free to go?"

"That would be rude. You're a guest here now."

"So . . . a fancy hostage," I said.

He ignored me. "I'm moving you to the guest bedroom for the duration of your stay. Which, hopefully, won't be long. You'll put in a good word for me with Blaze."

"I don't know if that's in my best interests," I said, and took a bite of chicken. A little dry, but not bad. And I'd had much, much worse in previous kidnappings.

He chuckled and took a sip of wine, none of which he offered to me. I had a glass of water that I had to trust wasn't doped with something. "But of course it is."

"What's your beef with Blaze, anyway?" I cut a large piece of chicken free and managed to chew a couple of times before swallowing. The gnawing, pervasive hunger was back, possibly because I'd just pushed myself beyond regular human limits. "Did he run over your dog?"

"Ha!" Mobius sipped his wine again. "Ha, ha."

"You're not going to answer me, are you?" I asked.

"I like a bit of mystery. It gives me a certain *je ne sais quoi*, don't you think?" He rubbed his rubbery mask of a face. "Makes me debonair."

I gagged on a bite of vegetables.

Once I cleaned my plate—and I mean that almost literally, for I nearly began to lick the dish when my belly realized the dry chicken and vegetables had reached its end, and I was still hungry—Dr. Mobius led me from the dining room to a new room just down the hall. I cringed, expecting another storage closet, but when he pushed the door open, it was obvious that the room belonged to a seven-year-old.

A seven-year-old in love with the color pink. Light pink wallpaper, dark pink carpet, lacy white curtains, unicorns and rainbows on the bed pillows. "You'll be staying here," Mobius said, shoving me inside.

I blinked at the light pink wallpaper, dotted with tiny cartoon stars, and the purple carpet. Lacy white curtains hung over a window that had been blacked out. There were rainbows on the pillows on the bed. "What the . . . is this your daughter's bedroom? Where are we?"

Mobius glared. "You ask too many questions," he said, and shut the door on me.

I prowled around the room after I heard Mobius's footsteps fade down the hall, but there wasn't a single clue that could tell me who it belonged to. The bookshelves told me the owner was probably a voracious reader, for there were fantasy novels stacked atop science-fiction novels, mingled with romances and other genres that made me reevaluate my idea that the room's owner was seven. At random, I picked up a book with a unicorn on the cover, and a sudden, shrill beeping made me shout. It grew louder and louder until I took a step back from the bookshelf.

The same thing happened when I approached any of the walls.

"Are you kidding me?" I asked the empty air. With an

annoyed huff of breath, I tested the bed, half expecting the beeping to start again. Nothing happened.

I was curious to see if I could do more push-ups again since I'd eaten and refueled, but I didn't think there was a chance food would come a third time, and I didn't want to face the hunger again. So I looked at the book in my hand, sighed, and curled up on the bed. I turned to page one and began to read.

This was, I reflected when I put the book down and let my eyes drift closed a few hours later, the strangest hostage situation I'd ever experienced.

Chapter Six

THIS TIME, I had no idea how long I slept. Unicorns in-
vaded my dreams, frolicking over the shores of sleep, until
something grabbed my shoulder and yanked me back into
awareness. I tried to scream, but Dr. Mobius had a hand
over my mouth. "They're here," he said.

The darkness made it hard to see, but I could definitely
smell him. I tried to struggle away, but my legs were tangled
in the blankets, and I was still mostly asleep. "Who's here?"
I said as soon as my mouth was free. "What's going on?"

He shook his head, and his eyes looked huge in what
little light there was. "They're here," he said again. "It's
sooner than I expected."

"You were just telling me Blaze was taking too long,"
I said, but Dr. Mobius shushed me again. He let go of my
shoulder and raced to the bedroom door, peering out. I sat
up fully. Excitement began to churn through my middle.
"Wait, does that mean—is Blaze here?"

Dr. Mobius shook his head. "Not Blaze."

Something in the way he said it sent a chill through me. "Who is it, then? War Hammer?"

As he was wont to do, he ignored me. "I need to give you something," he said under his breath. "I need to give you something, I should have done this already, where is it." He patted the pockets of his lab coat. "Where is it, where is it?"

"Doc?" I asked. I kicked free of the bedcovers. "What are you—whoa." I backed up a step, mostly because he'd produced a syringe from somewhere on his person. The needle seemed to gleam like Sleeping Beauty's demented spinning wheel spindle. "Oh, no. No, no, no."

"Hold still."

When I tried to get away, I stumbled at precisely the wrong moment. Dr. Mobius grabbed me by the scruff of the neck and shoved the needle in my arm. He covered my face with his hand to keep me from crying out. A wave of nausea and dizziness slammed into me. I staggered sideways, my knee knocking against the corner of the footboard. Dr. Mobius changed his grip on my neck to grab a handful of the back of my shirt. The floor and walls unhelpfully switched places as he yanked me out of the room and down the hall.

"What did—what did you *do* to me?"

"Have you considered, my dear Girl, a little gratitude? All of this suspicion can't be healthy."

"Excuse me for being suspicious when the guy who turned me into a super-substance addict pokes me with things," I said, swallowing my gorge. "It's a bad habit."

"Sarcasm never won anybody friends."

"I don't feel like that's true." When I tripped over my own feet, Dr. Mobius hissed out an annoyed breath and yanked me back upright. "Where are we going?"

"Away. There are too many of them."

"But—" I had a hard time focusing my eyes. "But not Blaze?"

"Evidently not. It appears to me he doesn't love you as much as everybody thinks—no, no, don't lose consciousness now. There's too much to be done."

Right, I thought. Like I had a choice. We moved through the dining room and a series of rooms I didn't recognize. I was too busy trying to keep my latest meal in my stomach to really gather much detail. Another door led us to a garage with a blue sedan inside. Mobius shoved me into the passenger seat. Though I groped for the door handle, my hand missed and hit empty air.

"Gonna be sick," I said, when he climbed into the driver's seat.

"There will be ample time for that later."

"It's so charming that you think I can schedule something like this." I tried for the door handle again. It made the world wobble.

He turned the key in the ignition, and the engine gunned to life. It sounded way too loud, but I didn't have time to wonder why because he slammed his foot down. The car went backward, and the crash as it hit the garage door sounded like an explosion. My shoulder hit the dashboard, and I cried out.

Dr. Mobius stomped harder on the gas. A great, wrenching sound filled the air, and the car seemed to explode backward. I cried out again at the sound of something scraping against the car—the garage door, I realized, what was *going on*—and Dr. Mobius began muttering under his breath. I thought I heard something about "Too soon, too soon," but everything was starting to fracture and break in my head.

I caught a glimpse of trimmed green lawns, of streetlamps hanging over the sidewalks, of night. Black figures. No, men. There were men in the front yard, dressed in black. I couldn't see their faces behind their balaclavas.

They lifted guns when Dr. Mobius peeled out of the driveway. I heard popping noises, like toy pop caps being stomped on.

The window behind me shattered. Something rained down on my back.

"Girl." Dr. Mobius gripped my shoulder. He was driving, and his mouth moved for a minute, but my ears had stopped working. I wondered what he was saying and why everything felt padded in cotton floss. "—un."

"We're already running." My voice sounded slurred, the words tumbling out together. I could feel every inch the car traveled though we must have been going way faster than the speed limit. "Where's Blaze?"

"Your dependency on that green cretin is worrisome."

"He's not a cretin, he's—"

But the car slammed to a stop again, sending me into the dashboard once again. Dr. Mobius leaned over me and opened my car door. "Run!" he said. And he shoved me out.

I hit the asphalt, and it bit into both of my palms.

When I turned back to say, "Hey!" in protest, Dr. Mobius slammed the door closed behind me.

Then he stomped on the gas and drove away, leaving me lying in the middle of the street.

I rose to my feet and promptly took a knee when that made the world tilt sideways, like I was on the deck of a ship in the middle of a storm. I managed two tottering steps and looked around in confusion. I was in the suburbs. I was in a nice neighborhood in the suburbs even.

I turned around as a minivan turned around the corner, and it occurred to me:

I was about to get hit by a car.

Huh.

MY ARMS WERE strapped down, but that wasn't my biggest concern when my eyes opened. Where was I? Why were my arms strapped? Was I on the metal table? No, it wasn't cold. Something like wax paper crinkled beneath me. I was lying on a cushion with tissue paper on it, and my arms were strapped.

Above me was a white expanse: a ceiling. I could hear voices from somewhere behind me.

"I told you to take Seventh, not Bailey. You know they've got protests going on all day."

"You wanna drive? Be my guest."

Somebody had strapped my arms in. Somebody—Dr. Mobius had strapped me in once. He could have done it again.

I yanked on my right arm, one sharp, hard tug. It came

free with a quiet *snap*. After a second, I realized it was the leather breaking, not my wrist. Just the left arm to go— good. I sat up and looked around in a daze.

The drivers in the front seat of the ambulance didn't look at me. I didn't know why they were arguing or why they weren't paying attention to me, but all I knew was that I had to get away. I had to run.

Something had told me to run.

They hadn't strapped my feet down.

I climbed free of the stretcher and scrambled for the back door. One jerk of the handle and I was free, tumbling out onto the street. The stopped ambulance was trapped in a swarm of people shouting and holding signs as they walked. Its red and blue lights flashed across the brick buildings around all of us in the night, like a troop of dancers, dancing, dancing away into the night.

I stumbled away.

IT WAS NIGHT. I remembered that much. Night was when the sky went dark, and the pinpricks of stars came out to greet the darkness. Sometimes the moon came out, but I couldn't see it. I wasn't worried, though. The moon always returned.

It was night, and I was standing in front of a Kidd's Mart. My neck ached. I'd been staring at a sign, a giant green K over the door. Which was probably why my neck hurt, come to think of it. It wasn't the Kidd's right by my apartment, I discerned, looking around. So where was I? I looked around, but there weren't any street signs nearby.

With a shrug, I pushed open the door to the Kidd's and stepped onto the dirty linoleum. Usually, Kidd's was always pretty busy. The fact that it was empty except for the store clerk told me it was probably pretty late.

"Excuse me," I said in a rusty voice.

The store clerk didn't look up from his game of Cape Crush. "Finally decided to come inside, huh?"

"Excuse me?"

"You were out there for like twenty minutes. You were starting to freak me out. I thought about maybe calling the cops or something."

I knew why he hadn't; I was maybe five-two in heels. Barefoot, I didn't qualify for anything but tiny. Even with my hair at its frizziest, curliest mess, and my clothing disheveled, I was a threat to precisely nobody.

"Can—can you tell me where I am?" I asked.

The clerk looked up. He took in my bare feet and my dirtied clothing with a frown. And the fact that I had—I'd just noticed this myself, so I wasn't surprised it had taken him so long—thick leather straps hanging from both wrists. "Whoa, are you okay? You look like—"

"Where am I?" I said again.

Startled, he stammered out an address, his eyebrows drawing close together. "Are you okay? Do you need any help?"

"I'm okay." And without knowing precisely why, I turned around and left the store.

I made it about ten feet out the door. "Hey!" The clerk, puffing a little because he'd jumped the counter. "Hey, are you seriously okay?"

I looked down at the straps. "I've had worse."

"That—um, look, here." He pulled out his wallet and held out a Ventra Card. "There's only, like, a couple of fares left on it, but you look like you could use it more than me."

I stared at it like it was a foreign object. "Why?"

"There's an 'L' stop—two blocks that way." He pointed. "Maybe you should go to the police?"

I took the card. "Thank you," was all I said, and I left.

I used up what was left on the fare to get back to my normal stop. The trains were mostly empty, so I didn't have anybody staring at me. It wouldn't have mattered if I did; I felt strange, like I was in some kind of drugged haze. My feet hurt by the time I climbed the stairs down from my normal stop. I was limping by the time I reached my corner, and nearly whimpering every time I set my right foot down by the time I walked up the steps outside my building.

Grateful that I kept a key underneath the fire extinguisher down the walkway, I unlocked my door and stumbled inside. The entire world felt muffled, as though I weren't a part of it anymore. And I was more than happy to escape—and did so, flopping facedown on my own bed for the first time in what felt like years and years.

I DON'T KNOW what woke me. A noise, perhaps, the creak of my upstairs neighbor's floorboards. Maybe I'd just slept myself out. But one moment I was asleep, and the next I sat straight up in bed, eyes wide.

Something was wrong. And I was *hungry*.

Frantic, I searched my bedroom. There was my laptop on the desk with the shopping list I'd been meaning to use. My closet door was open, my rejected work outfits tossed in front of it. My cell phone wasn't on its charger on my desk, but other than that, not a single thing was out of place.

So why did it feel *weird*?

I frowned at my sheets, which had streaks of red and black, like odd, demented modern art. Where had that come from? I glanced at my feet and saw dried blood, but there wasn't so much as a scab. Very weird.

The main room was as untouched as my bedroom though the milk had spoiled so badly that I gagged and slammed the fridge closed, vowing to toss the entire thing out the window once there weren't any innocent passersby who could possibly be maimed or killed. I settled for eating anything edible in my pantry, without bothering to warm any of it up. The crackers were stale and probably past their date, but I'd worry about food poisoning later. I scooped up salsa and ate it straight with a spoon, and finally got rid of that jar of olives that had been around so long, it should probably start paying rent.

Finally, the edge of hunger dwindled, giving me a clearer head.

When I was headed back into the bathroom to shower away the layers and layers of grime that, amazingly, a single chemical shower did little to combat, I figured out what was out of place.

There was a strange smell in the apartment. Other than the milk, I mean.

Though it was familiar, it wasn't a smell that belonged in my place. Carefully, I walked around, sniffing the air. With a jolt, it hit me: somebody had been in my apartment. The scent seemed familiar, but I couldn't quite match the scent to an identity. It was like the name hovered just beyond my grasp, and if I could just figure it out . . .

I braced a chair underneath my front door before I showered.

The hot water seemed to wake my skin, sending pinpricks up and down my entire body. I stood under the stream of it for more than an hour, letting it beat over me while my brain tried to put everything together. I'd been kidnapped, turned into an addict, and . . . hit with a car. I remembered that much, but there wasn't so much as a bruise on any part of my skin. And I didn't remember anything after that. My mind was blank though I had a vague memory of red and blue lights on what had to be the roof of an ambulance.

So if I'd been in an ambulance, why am I in my apartment now? And why did nothing hurt? Had it been a hallucination?

I needed to get in touch with Blaze. Could I afford a ticket down to Miami? I winced at the thought and turned off the spray. Maybe I could just send Jeremy an e-mail on the off chance that my every instinct was wrong and he really was Blaze . . .

No. Jeremy wasn't Blaze.

I swiped a hand across the mirror to get a look at myself—and froze.

Damn. I was *hot*.

The solution Dr. Mobius had hit me with might have been killing me, but it was doing me some great favors in the process. I'd always been a little soft—one ex-boyfriend had used the term "doughy"—especially around the middle, carrying a little more pudge than I liked. I'd been one of the first girls to get a bra in middle school, and I understood the benefits of being curvaceous. But I'd always wanted to lose the extra softness. And I had. I'd traded it in for the body of a freaking Olympian: sculpted shoulders, lean ropes of muscle on my arms. Washboard abs. No extra weight on my chin, no wobble to my upper arm.

I'll admit it: I flexed a little in the mirror. Just, you know. To see.

Wrapped in a towel, I moved back into the other room and tried to turn on the TV, only to sigh. I really needed to set up my cable and internet bill to autopay for those times when I was kidnapped. Apparently, I wasn't going to be able to check the news until I could get somewhere with free wi-fi. Muttering, I ignored all my regular jeans and went straight for the skinny jeans I'd kept holed away in the back of my closet. Leftovers of either wishful thinking or a resolve to lose more weight—I couldn't remember. I pulled them on. They were loose.

With my favorite shirt bagging around my newly developed muscles, and my feet stuffed into proper shoes, I grabbed some cash out of the emergency fund and headed downstairs. My first goal was to get to the office, see what kind of damage control I needed to do, and figure out a way to contact Blaze. Late-afternoon sunlight slanted into the lobby, which made me blink.

As did the date on the newspapers at the newsstand down the street from my building. I picked one up and gaped at it.

"Gonna pay for that?" the vendor asked.

"Uh, sure. Here. Thanks." I handed over a twenty and waited for my change. According to Dr. Mobius, I'd been asleep for nearly two weeks. Adding in the day I'd been awake—or possibly longer, since time was impossible to judge in a windowless room—with Dr. Mobius, it should have still been June.

It was the first day of July. If my calculations were right, I'd been asleep in my apartment for something close to three days.

Even stranger, there wasn't a single reference to Dr. Mobius or me in the paper. I frowned at an article that mentioned a street protest against a local congressman, as the signs in the picture seemed familiar. But that was all I could find.

One of the bylines on the third page caught my eye: Naomi Gunn. It appeared that the woman who had jinxed me was more than she'd claimed to be.

"Huh," I said as I scanned her article about the new bill about superhero corporate sponsorship. Why had she told me she ran a blog called Crap About Capes when this looked like a professional, full-time gig?

At work, the security guard waved me through without looking up from his screen, so at least I didn't have to worry about my missing work badge. It was Portia, and not Adrianna, seated behind the receptionist's desk in the lobby. And she, unlike the guard, did look surprised to see me.

"Girl!" She rose on her towering heels. "I thought you quit!"

"What? No, I didn't quit. Where's Adrianna?"

"Milan," Portia said, drawing out the word to make it clear exactly how she felt about that.

I couldn't care less. "What do you mean, you thought I quit? Why would I quit?"

"Maybe because you didn't show up for work in forever? Where have you been? You look good. Did you go on that cleanse I kept telling you about? Because I am on day two, and I have to tell you—"

"I was kidnapped, Portia. I didn't go on a cleanse. Did *anybody* think to call the police?"

"You said you hated all of us, and then you left for coffee. When you didn't come back, we figured you'd quit." Portia twitched her shoulders up, then down. "I mean, it's not like you're getting kidnapped every other day now, Girl. Blaze is in Miami."

"Yeah, this guy apparently didn't know that." I ran a hand over my face, trying to gather my bearings. "Can I talk to Angus?"

"He's not here." Portia moved back behind the desk. "He's in New York, and he'll be there for the rest of the week. Fashion week's in two months, you know that. But I'll leave a note on his desk that you stopped by.

"Can't you just put him on the phone?"

"Ooh, you know he doesn't answer his phone in New York." She picked up a Post-it note and started writing, her nails scratching against the paper in a way that made my ears itch. When she looked up, she almost looked apologetic. "But, um, he gave your job away."

"What?"

"He promoted one of the girls from the mail room. And she whines less than you did, so I think he likes her more even if she's . . ." Portia bit her lower lip and her expression edged even closer to sympathetic. My stomach dropped to my knees. "She's kind of stupid? But even then, I don't think you're going to get your job back. I'll leave him a note, though, let him know you dropped by. Seriously, you have to tell me—where did you go? Secret gym?"

I had to swallow hard as hot tears threatened to build up. There was no way in hell I was going to cry in front of Portia. I might have liked her best out of the office, but I still wasn't going to give her the satisfaction. "I was kidnapped, and I'm probably dying," I said. And they'd given my job away without bothering to get in touch at all. It just figured. "Thanks a lot for the sympathy."

"You don't look like you're dying."

"Well, that's a relief," I said, and headed for the elevator. I waited until the doors dinged closed behind me before I finally sniffled and wiped away a tear. I hadn't liked the job. I hadn't liked the people. I hadn't even liked the work.

So why did losing it hurt so much?

Chapter Seven

AFTER THE OFFICE, I stewed.

Losing your cell phone and wallet during a kidnapping is always a long process, but thankfully I'd been through it before. I decided to skip the police station for now and go to an internet café not too far from my old office instead. Faint hunger made itself known by the time I paid for an hour and logged onto one of the machines in the back. I checked my bank accounts to make sure Dr. Mobius hadn't drained them like the Earl of Pain had once, and then I dug in to do my research.

Searching Dr. Mobius's name led to nothing but physics theories. There was no mention of a prison break from Detmer, no past history for the guy. I suspected that he'd given me a false name, but even searching through the supervillain database based on his looks, I couldn't find him. The only reference I found to anything related to my kidnapping was a brief blurb in a police blotter from four days ago that there had been an altercation in one of the suburbs: a hit-and-run.

I distinctly remembered that minivan hitting me. After that? Not so much.

Since the next step would be to hunt down the dispatcher who took the call, and I had other matters to take care of, I switched gears and opened up my e-mail. Jeremy's name was still listed as one of the top contacts in my book, which told me I really needed to make some new friends.

Jeremy, I wrote, *can't talk because I don't have a cell phone yet, but I need help. Please get back to me ASAP with your number so I can call.*

That was nice and cryptic, I thought with a sigh as I sent the e-mail. By the time my hour was almost up, there was no reply from Jeremy—maybe he wasn't using that address anymore?—and I'd canceled my credit cards and had started the process to get new ones. Another quick search on Mobius gave me nothing, but then, I wasn't a researcher, I didn't know how to find these people.

I did, however, know of one person who did.

I ran a search for Crap About Capes and was surprised to see that the blog was indeed real and looked pretty professional. A selfie of Naomi on the sidebar mocked me as I paged through the bio section. She was a freelance writer for a couple of the local papers, had a guest editorial spot on the Domino, and generally seemed in the know about all matters pertaining to superheroes. She had a public e-mail listed on the site, so I typed up a quick missive.

She replied in less than a minute: *omg been trying to get*

in touch. did you get kidnapped again??? that means my story won't be happening?

No, I wrote back, *and you jinxed me, you*—I backspaced before I could type several of the less-than-flattering insults that floated to mind. Taking a deep breath, I said, *You owe me for that. Can you meet me somewhere? Need help. Promise a pretty good story.*

following a lead. meet later?

I can come to you. Kind of urgent.

She e-mailed back an address, and I sent a confirmation with my last thirty seconds of time. I grabbed two gyros from a street stand and kept the hunger at bay at least a little while as I made the trip across town. The address she'd given me was a bank, one I recognized. I'd been a customer there until the fifth or sixth time some lunatic with a bomb had held the place hostage to get to Blaze. They'd politely asked me to take my business somewhere else after that.

I found her inside the bank, arguing with a woman in a nice pantsuit. The lobby was a fancy throwback to another century, with vaulted ceilings, marble floors, and an air of snootiness that was hard to fake in a newer building. Standing back so as not to interrupt Naomi, I looked around and wondered exactly what kind of story she was checking out.

As luck would have it, I got my answer comically fast.

The doors behind me blew inward from the force of a kick. Two men in camouflage and tactical vests stormed in and sprayed the ceiling with bullets. Instantly, the air filled with screams of the patrons and bankers alike. Naomi flinched, turning toward the commotion.

I'd been in far too many holdups, though, to not know what would happen next. So I tackled Naomi during a second spate of gunfire and dragged her behind a kiosk while the woman she had been arguing with scrambled for safety. Naomi looked at me with wide eyes. "G-Girl?"

"Shh," I said. I chanced a glance around the kiosk. We hadn't been noticed yet, but it was only a matter of time. Was there a possibility any of us could crawl to safety? There was ten feet of space between us and the exit, but it might as well have been a mile.

"This is a stickup!" the man on the left shouted, as both men strode into the bank like they owned the place. "Cell phones on the ground in front of you, now! Don't you dare push that." The latter was directed at a teller obviously reaching for the silent alarm.

"Oh my god, oh my god," Naomi said. She whispered it over and over. "I *knew* it."

"Knew what?" I hissed at Naomi, as we watched the men kick cell phones away from people across the bank. This really was just my luck, wasn't it? Maybe the patron saint of hostages was trying to get my attention. It was beyond ridiculous.

"It's her. It's got to be her," Naomi said.

"Her?" Both of the bank robbers looked male to me.

"Ch-Chelsea." Naomi's entire body had begun to shake. Her notepad had a picture of Snoopy on it, which seemed like a strange choice in stationery.

I gave her a long look. "I'm going to guess that's not your ex-girlfriend."

"No." She laughed, but there wasn't much humor in the noise. "Definitely not."

"We have about twenty seconds before we're discovered by the goons over there," I said, and grabbed Naomi's arm. She flinched, so I loosened my grip a little. "Who's Chelsea?"

"She's—she's a new supervillain, but nobody else is paying attention to her because she hasn't taken up a villain name yet. I keep writing about her, and I don't think she likes that too much."

"You must lead an interesting life."

She eyed me up and down, and I remembered that I had the new physique. "Same to you," she said.

Before I could reply, one of the robbers rounded the corner. I saw the gun, just a black flash of it, and my body moved without letting my mind catch up. The toe of my boot dug into the marble as I surged forward. I hit him in the thick midsection with my shoulder. He let out an "oof!"

We crashed to the marble floor together. I'd never had a gymnastics lesson in my life, but somehow I rolled right back up to my feet. It took me a second to realize it, but when I looked down, his gun was in my hand.

Naomi gaped. "What the *hell*?"

I had no idea either. The gun was heavy, not only physically, but with the thought of what I could do with it. Belatedly, I aimed it at the man. "Don't move."

He languidly reached down and pulled a pistol free from his hip, pointing it at Naomi. "Drop it," he said.

I could see rings of white all the way around Naomi's eyes. Shaking, I set my gun on the ground and kicked it away from both of us.

"Good choice," the man said. He had a faint drawl and he desperately needed a shave. A sheen of sweat covered his face. He pushed himself to his feet, warily, and kept the gun pointed at Naomi. "You, come with me."

"Wait," I said. My mouth was so dry, I was amazed I could speak at all. But I stepped forward. "I'm the one you want, right? Hostage Girl?"

"Hos—Hostage Girl?" He blinked a few times, and my stomach sank. If he was surprised to see me, he really wasn't after me. "Is that really you? What are the odds? Hey, Victor, look who we got here. We took Hostage Girl hostage!"

"What?" came from the other side of the bank. "Is she just here for kicks?"

"I dunno." The man gestured at Naomi with the gun. "You. Get up."

She shot me a "See? I told you so!" look as she pushed herself to her feet. Our captor twitched his gun to indicate that we should start walking. Hands up, we moved to the center of the bank. I saw one man near the exit look like he was eyeing the hostage takers' guns, and I prayed he wouldn't try to be a hero.

That never ended well.

The other man, Victor, squinted at our faces. Like the first man, he needed a shave. "What'd you bring her for?" he asked, pointing at me.

"She's Hostage Girl, man. This is kind of her thing."

Victor sighed. "Whatever, not my problem. The rest of you!" He turned to look at the rest of the bank patrons, all of whom were cowering in various states of terror. "Scram."

The people huddled against the ground needed no more prompting: they raced for the doors en masse. The bank emptied, leaving Naomi and me in the middle of the open lobby with Victor and his friend, whom I decided to call Gary. They didn't instruct us to kneel or put our hands on our heads, nor did they seem terribly fussed about anything though Gary kept checking his watch.

"Who are you?" Naomi asked. "Who do you work for? What do you want?"

"Shut up," Gary said. He jerked his head at me. "Watch this one. She knocked me down."

Victor snorted. "How? She weighs like ten pounds."

"I don't know, but I'm not kidding. Don't mess with her."

"Whatever. You two, move it."

Victor grabbed me by the back of the neck, shoving me toward the back offices. I saw Naomi shoot a furtive look in his direction, but I shook my head as tightly as I could. My little feat of gymnastics earlier aside, it was best not to antagonize hostage takers. My life the past couple of years had been training enough in that area.

"Ninety seconds," Victor said, and Gary acknowledged it with a nod.

"What's going on?" Naomi asked.

"Shut up," Gary said.

"Where are you taking us?"

"Naomi," I said under my breath.

"This might happen to you a lot, but this is my first time," she said. "I'm allowed to be curious."

"Your curiosity is about to get you pistol-whipped," Victor said. His grip tightened on the back of my neck. It made the world seem a little . . . off. I couldn't put my finger on how. I could smell the acidic tang of his sweat even more sharply, mingling in the air with the stale scent of an overbrewed pot of coffee from what appeared to be a break room. The light overhead hurt my eyes, like it was suddenly too bright.

When I heard the footsteps, I reacted, turning my head toward the source before any of the other three did.

A woman stepped into view. She took in the scene—Victor, Gary, Naomi looking terrified but up for anything, and me—and I felt something of a chill creep up the space between my shoulder blades. She wore all black, but not a tactical suit: simple black pants, a black top, and decently cute boots. I guessed that she was a little older than me, and she was rigidly beautiful. She must be Chelsea.

She regarded all of us dispassionately, her eyes lingering on me. "I only wanted the reporter."

"But it's Hostage Girl," Gary said, like he was being helpful. "It's kind of her deal."

"Those weren't my orders."

"But . . ." Gary frowned. "Hostage Girl."

"I hardly care what her name is. She's only another loose end I'll need to tidy up." She dismissed me with a flick of her fingers and grabbed Naomi by the upper arm. "Watch over the girl—"

"*Don't* call me that."

Her eyebrows went up a fraction, but other than that, she ignored me. "—while I take care of the reporter."

"Where are you taking me?" Naomi asked, and I hoped the police showed soon. Or, even better, somebody super. Gary and Victor were a decent threat, but something about this Chelsea—the way she carried herself, like she had every assurance that even the giant guns her hired men held were no threat to her—told me she had some kind of power. Maybe that was why my skin felt like it was trying to crawl straight off my bones.

Chelsea and Naomi disappeared around a corner.

I looked from Victor to Gary. "Um, I don't suppose you'd be willing just to let me go?"

Victor snorted.

"Worth a shot. When she said 'take care of the reporter,' do you know what she happened to be talking about?"

"Not our part of the plan. Don't care," Victor said. He'd yet to relinquish his grip on me.

I looked down the hallway. I'd only known Naomi for a grand total of five minutes, and she'd already jinxed me and gotten me trapped in the most inexplicable bank holdup of my life to date. If I had anything to say about things, this was going to be the end of our acquaintance. I could research my answers elsewhere. But that didn't mean I wanted her to die or anything.

"No, really," I said. "Any idea at—"

Down the hallway, a scream cut through the air. In a blink, I'd ducked out of Victor's grip. I sprinted down the hallway. To do what, I didn't know, but if Naomi was hurt—

Something grabbed me from behind. My stomach pitched as I was lifted off of my feet. I swung hard with my right elbow, the way I'd been taught in the self-defense class I'd taken (it had proved worthless; when your enemies have super-strength and super-speed, you're better off not even trying sometimes). Pain sang up my forearm as my elbow smashed hard into a solid surface, and ripe cursing filled the air. The arms banded around my middle let me go.

I staggered upon landing, but before I could make it two steps, Gary was in front of me, gun pointed at my collarbone. "What the hell are you?" he asked.

I looked down at my arms, which were shaking. Dr. Mobius had turned me into an addict for some kind of compound I'd never heard of, but he hadn't mentioned any side effects. And I'd say being able to take down a guy twice my size was definitely a *side effect*.

"Honestly, dude?" I asked. "Your guess is as good as mine."

And then I stepped forward and punched him.

I'd always been short and powerless, so I think both of us were absolutely startled when Gary hit the ground, hands over his streaming face. "Sorry!" I said, and leapt over him. I took off running, backward, wincing. That looked like a *lot* of blood. "Um, put some ice on it and take a couple aspirin, maybe?"

I'd been through the bank a few times during prior hostage situations, so when Naomi's scream sounded again, I knew it had to be coming from the safe-deposit box vault. I dug into the carpet, trying to push myself faster, and somehow accidentally launched myself forward. I landed, rolled ahead, and jumped right back to my feet, yelping the whole time.

What the hell was *going on*?

When I reached the vault, I rounded the corner, and it was a toss-up as to who was more surprised when I tackled Chelsea. Naomi, clutching her arm, stumbled free. Chelsea and I smacked into the wall of safe-deposit boxes and backed away from each other.

"All right," she said. "You've got my attention now."

"Goody," I said.

"Girl! Girl, look out, she's got—"

Naomi's shouted warning cut off when Chelsea raised her arm. I'd seen energy villains use their powers before, but usually they wore the garishly bright suits (they really loved blue and purple, for some reason), and they channeled the electricity through prongs or gloves. Chelsea was far more disgusting: a gaping hole opened in the palm of her hand. I gawked as yellow and green sparks poured out, forming a beam that hit me solidly in the chest.

Every molecule of my being seemed to light on fire. Thousands of bees swarmed over me, stinging every inch of my flesh. I dropped to my knees, my teeth gritted, as green and yellow oozed over my vision, blocking the rest of the color from the world. My heart pounded in my ears, but the pain went on, never ending.

I cried out, and Chelsea lowered her arm. Instantly, the bees disappeared, though I breathed through my teeth. Behind Chelsea, Naomi stared, her mouth gaping open.

"You should be dead," Chelsea said. "Why aren't you screaming?"

"What?" It took everything I had to force the word out.

"I just hit you with enough power to take down an elephant." Chelsea stepped closer, her eyebrows drawing together. She crouched a little, but I stared at the floor, trying to gather what was left of me back. Physically, my skin looked fine. It wasn't even pink. But inwardly, I knew that at any second, she could lift her arm, and the bee stings would return.

It made me want to shake. I clenched my jaw harder.

I was really, *really* tired of villains.

"Who are you?" Chelsea asked.

"Nobody special."

"You can withstand enough voltage to kill an army. You're somebody." Eyes as hazel as mine narrowed fractionally as she continued to study me. "What's your name, again?"

"Gail. What about you? You got a name?"

She sized me up slowly, then nodded once. Maybe I'd earned her respect by withstanding her special brand of bee-sting torture. "Chelsea."

It figured she wouldn't give me a last name.

"No handle?" Chelsea asked.

"That would require having superpowers."

"Pity for you. It means you won't be able to call Davenport and mop up your little mess. I'll just have to kill you."

"Davenport?" Naomi was still panting and in obvious pain, but she straightened at little. "Davenport *Industries*?"

"Quiet. The grown-ups are talking. Oh, look." Chelsea tilted her head at me. "She's thinking about trying to rush me again. How cu—"

I hit her like a linebacker.

I didn't have a plan. In fact, I hadn't had a plan since I walked into the bank, other than to talk to Naomi and see if she could get down to the bottom of the mystery of Dr. Mobius. But I had the feeling that if I could just stall, some real hero was on the way to save the day. I had to hold her off for that long. So when we landed, I tried to throw a punch like the one that had taken Gary out of commission. She dodged.

She might have been kind of slim and poised, but she had one weapon that wasn't the bee-sting zapper: fingernails. And she had no qualms about using them.

"Ow!" I said when she clawed my face. I rolled away and glared. "Knock that off. This isn't a catfight—if you're going to try to kick my ass, at least be dignified about it."

She simpered at me. "Got you off of me, didn't it?"

"Real funny," I said, flicking away the blood.

We both climbed warily to our feet and began to circle each other (while in the background, Naomi watched the two of us like we were both incredibly dangerous). I eyed Chelsea's hands, knowing that if—no, when—they came back up, I was definitely in for some pain if I couldn't dodge fast enough. Chelsea's annoyance had clearly bumped up to fury. "What are you even doing here if you're not a hero? It isn't your job to stop me. What's one idiot reporter to you?"

"Nothing, really. I just don't like seeing people taken hostage."

Something flickered across Chelsea's eyes at that: some change that I couldn't quite pinpoint or describe. It was fleeting—there, then gone. But I'd definitely seen it.

She covered by scoffing. "That's it?"

"It's more of a pain in the butt than you'd think."

"I'm sure."

"It's—" I started to say, but something to my left seemed to explode. Drywall flew everywhere, but that wasn't the problem. I was more worried about the fact that while I'd blinked, Chelsea's arm had gone up, and that green hole was opening up again in her palm.

I didn't have time to dodge, so she zapped me again.

This time, I shouted right away. The stinging hit all over, on my eyes, my scalp, in my ears and mouth. It was relentless, an eternity within another eternity within eons of nothing but agony. I curled up, as if making myself smaller could somehow minimize the pain. It didn't. If anything, it increased it. I heard mocking laughter—that had to be Chelsea—and my own heartbeat as it thudded into overdrive.

The laughter cut off with a curse, a flash of white, a blur of black. And the pain ended just as abruptly as it had the first time.

But it was already too late. My heartbeat, already racing, didn't slow. Instead, it propelled me away from the warmth of consciousness and into the coldness of that empty nothingness that had grown so familiar.

Right there in my old bank, facing a new foe, I fainted.

Chapter Eight

"I WAS JUST telling you—wasn't I telling you? Didn't I say that we were going to see another one soon? The conspiracy theorists aren't wrong. And here she is. Heavy little thing, though, for somebody who looks like a light breeze would blow her over."

"Your conspiracy theorists are a bunch of crackpots. They're right once out of a dozen times."

"Once is all I need in this case. Here, Raymond, will you take her? I need to scratch my nose."

The world tilted, just a little, but not in a terrible way. It was almost comforting, like being wrapped in some sort of cocoon. Except that the moment I opened my eyes, I would realize I was probably somewhere horrible.

Someone, apparently the unseen Raymond, scoffed.

"Need I remind you, Raymond, that I'm heiress to fashion empires galore? I do not juggle rescued victims so that I can scratch this nose, perfect as it is."

"Victoria Burroughs is heiress to fashion empires. *You*, Vicki, are a Class A. You're strong enough to hold her with one arm and scratch your nose."

Hold it. I knew that name.

Slowly, awareness leaked into the comfort. I was comfortable because there were arms holding me in the damsel position, very much like Blaze always had whenever he'd rescued me. Right away, I knew it wasn't Blaze—he smelled different, for one thing.

"Anyway," Victoria-or-Vicki said as I was apparently transferred back to her, "the theorists were right, you skeptic. Unexplained hit-and-run usually means there's a baby hero running about, new to his or her powers, and here we have our valiant little bank robbery stopper."

"She doesn't look like she's been recently hit with a car."

"It was a minivan, actually," I said, and I forced my eyes open. The face that greeted me belonged in the magazines—literally.

Apparently the name "Victoria Burroughs" sounded familiar because it belonged to Victoria Burroughs. The supermodel who had been seen in the tabloids holding hands with my ex-boyfriend and now the same woman who was carrying me in her arms like I weighed little more than a basket of laundry. She stared back, not accusing but definitely curious. Somehow, she was even more stunning in person than she was in the heavily Photoshopped ads behind the makeup counter at my local pharmacy.

"Uh," I said. "I'm confused."

"Oh, good, you're alive." Victoria Burroughs bent over and set me on the ground.

My head hurt, my body felt like I'd run a marathon without any water, and hunger was an acute ache in my midsection. Victoria remained crouched next to me, but Raymond stayed standing. Pewter-colored curls extended around his head like a halo, and he wore thick, rectangular-framed glasses. He had his arms crossed over his chest.

"Where am I?" I asked. We were in some kind of hallway though I had no idea how I'd gotten there. It was brightly lit and lacking in any decoration that might tell me where I was. Everything about it seemed rather clinical, but it didn't *feel* like a hospital. No smell of antiseptic, I realized after a second.

She tilted her head at me, considering something. "What's the last thing you remember?"

"I was in a fight?" I said. Everything inside my head felt like a blur. She hadn't answered my question. "I think it was in a bank?"

"Yeah, you seem to have discovered a new villain. And even more than that, you survived her. She packed a punch. So—what are your powers?"

I squinted at her. "Aren't you a model? And—wait, powers? What powers?"

"Modeling's the day job." A dimple popped up on her left cheek when she smiled. Photographers must have been obsessed with it. "At night, I'm, well, that's complicated to explain."

Raymond cleared his throat. "They're expecting her in Medical, Vicki."

"Medical?" I asked.

"Part of what we were getting to in a minute." Vicki shot the man an annoyed look, but he only shrugged.

Something occurred to me. "Where's Naomi?"

They shot me identical looks of puzzlement, which was really weird. "Who?" Vicki asked.

"Naomi—she was with me in the bank, Chelsea was after her. Oh, god, is she dead? I just wanted her help; I didn't want her to die."

"Oh, the reporter. She's fine." Vicki shrugged. "In the hospital, I think."

In what universe did "in the hospital" mean fine?

"She needs to go to Medical, Vicki. We're giving her too much information as it is."

"She's *obviously* not a villain, Raymond." Vicki cast her eyes to the ceiling, like she was the one sane person in a world full of weirdoes.

"A villain? Me?" My voice squeaked, but part of me wanted to laugh. I was Hostage Girl. I was villain bait, not a villain myself.

Raymond ignored me. "Not our call to make," he told Vicki.

"Buzzkill. C'mon—hey, what's your name?"

"Gail," I said.

"C'mon, Gail." Vicki pulled me to my feet, and I realized that she must not recognize me. Either Jeremy hadn't mentioned me, or the transformation from Dr. Mobius's Super-Addicting Juice had really been more drastic than I'd suspected. But it felt entirely surreal.

Not as surreal as the fact that Victoria Burroughs was a supermodel *and* a superhero, though. What the hell?

"Can you walk?" Raymond asked before I could take a step.

I shrugged. Whatever Medical was, maybe they would have food. I was more than willing to walk for that. "Sure."

"This way." Raymond jerked his head. I followed him, and Vicki followed me, and it took me a stupidly long time to realize they were flanking me like a set of guards. Since neither Raymond nor Vicki seemed inclined to say anything else, it was a silent trek through the smooth, clean corridors. Every door had a flat white panel, a little longer and wider than my hand, at about chest height right next to it, but no signs. It was unlike any place I'd ever seen. The hair on the back of my neck began to rise. Where the hell had I ended up now?

"Ah, here we go." Raymond stopped and touched one of the panels. Immediately, the screen lit up.

"Ray Goldstein and Vicki Burroughs," he said to the panel. "We've got a bogey with us in need of evaluation."

Words filled the screen: *Identify bogey. Threat?*

Raymond shifted slightly to look at me, appraisingly. Behind those boxy glasses, his eyes were centuries older than the rest of him. "Possible," he said.

The panel beeped once in acknowledgment.

"Only possible?" I said.

Vicki snickered. "Are you a threat or not?"

I opened my mouth to inform her that my track record obviously meant that Gail Godwin was a threat to precisely nobody, but I had a sharp vision of Gary's shock after I'd broken his nose. And the door opened.

It slid open, silently, like a door in any science-fiction movie. Standing there, filling the space, was one of the most gorgeous humans I'd ever seen. He was tall, and fantastically built if the body beneath the white polo shirt and blue slacks had anything to say about it. His hair was blond, a little shaggy, and his eyes were a gorgeous shade of blue.

Thankfully, I was able to pick up my chin before my tongue rolled out of my mouth.

"Ray, Vicki," the god in the doorway said, smiling and bumping his sex appeal through the roof. "Good to see a couple of Class A's in Medical. We rarely see your type down around here."

"Can't imagine why." Vicki stepped into my peripheral vision to purr at the god. "We bought you a present, Cooper."

Cooper smiled and stuck one hand out at me, ignoring my melting heart (or just not hearing it). "Lemuel Cooper."

"Gail. I have to ask: Lemuel?" I asked.

He twitched one behemoth of a shoulder. "My parents are old-fashioned. My sisters are Nancy and Nadine, if that makes you feel any better. Folks generally just call me Cooper."

Personally, I thought he got the shortest end of the stick of the three of them, but it felt nicer not to say so. Also, I wasn't sure rational speech was possible in front of him and that stunning smile. Give it time. Five years or so sounded about right.

"So you're my possible threat?" Those ice blue eyes swept me up and down, like Raymond's had just a minute before. Unlike Raymond's assessing glance, Cooper's check had my heart thudding. "Don't look like much of a threat. No offense. Little."

"Yeah, I get that a lot." I sighed.

"She took out two thugs and took an energy blast straight on," Vicki said, and I jolted as she propped an elbow on my shoulder. The smile she gave Cooper was pure flirtation, and I almost hated her for it. "We don't know the villain, and she got away before I could grab her—"

Wait, what?

"—but as far as I can tell, it was at least Class B rated energy."

"Class what?" I asked.

Vicki frowned. "Oh, right, I guess you don't know about the class system yet. A Class B—"

"Can be explained after you've been checked out," Cooper said, interrupting her while Ray Goldstein just looked tired. Cooper focused on me. "Two guards and a full hit? And you're standing to tell the tale?"

"Two full hits," I said before I remembered my motto of never telling captors more than they need to know. Vicki, Raymond, and especially Cooper didn't look like any villain I'd ever faced, but they hadn't mentioned anything about sending me on my way. I paused and decided to downplay it until I knew more. "It hurt. A bit."

"A bit." Cooper's gaze was now no longer curiously amused but direct and assessing. "You took a hit—two hits—and the only thing you have to say is, 'It hurt. A bit.'"

"Claims to have no powers," Raymond said.

"Hmm." Cooper crossed his arms, displaying perfect forearms and even more glorious biceps.

From behind him, I heard a voice call out, "All right, Coop. Room's cleared for your possible threat. Bring him in."

"Her. And you're not going to believe her size." With a surprising amount of grace for somebody so massive, Cooper abandoned the doorway and gestured to me. "After you, my nameless subject. Are either of you coming in, Vick? Ray?"

"My trainees will be back shortly. I should go." Raymond aimed a pointed look up at Vicki.

She seemed to get the message. "Not today, Coop, but if she's cleared, I'll come back for her. Later, doll." She turned to me. "See you when it's over."

Cooper flexed two fingers in a hybrid between "peace" and "bye," and turned to me. "All right. C'mon in. Time to begin the torture."

I immediately took a step back. Ray and Vicki had gone one way, but if I went the other, maybe there was an exit—

"Whoa," Cooper said. "That was a joke. We don't torture people at Davenport."

"D-Davenport?"

Cooper made a noise in the back of his throat and nudged me forward.

Warily, I stepped inside. The room was a bright, stunning white, lit by white lamps. Everything gleamed with chrome: the three desks, the white polo shirts on the men and women behind them, expensive silver equipment with odd gadgets and gizmos on platforms around the room. An eye chart like the ones they make you stand in front of with a spoon over your eye was hung on one wall, over a scale. Silver and white clipboards were piled on desks and hung from hooks on the purely white walls.

On the main wall across from the door, dominating the entire wall, was a sign with the letters "DI."

DI? Oh. Davenport Industries. I'd been carried by a supermodel who was somehow a superhero into a medical branch of Davenport Industries. Except Davenport Industries didn't have medical branches. They pretty much invested in real estate, electronics, mining, the stock market. They didn't have private hospitals like the one I'd just entered.

So what the hell was going on?

"Welcome to Medical." Cooper steered me forward, between two of the desks and into a hallway. "We've got the room all ready for you."

"What are you going to do to me?" I asked.

"Figure out how somebody who claims to be a Class D can withstand energy blasts."

There was that class thing again. We stopped by a nondescript door down the hall. "Well, it's kind of a long story."

"It usually is. You're lucky to have escaped with your life. Now"—and Cooper tapped the panel—"let's find out why you did."

He left me alone in a testing room after running my handprint on a screen. The door clicked shut after he left, with the same sort of finality I'd experienced while staying in Dr. Mobius's "care." With him, however, I'd had some idea of my standing—I was a hostage, a bargaining chip, and possibly collateral if all of that didn't work.

The room wasn't large—enough space for a bare white desk and a medical cot. No eye charts in here, I noted as I sat on the cot. I had no idea who these people were. Since when did Davenport Industries have facilities like this? I figured we were underground, as I'd yet to see a window. But underground where? And why was Victoria Burroughs suddenly a superhero, and I didn't know about it?

And if she was a superhero, why had she needed rescuing by Blaze, anyway?

The questions—and my ever-present hunger—threatened to drive me mad before the Davenport people came back for me. It wasn't Cooper, but a woman closer to my size and height, her eyes as hazel as my own. That didn't reassure me in the slightest. For some reason, she felt more dangerous though I couldn't fathom why. I rose to my feet, wary now.

"Hi. I'm Kiki. How are you doing?"

Kiki? And Lemuel Cooper? What was up with the names in this place?

"Um, I'm okay. But . . . where am I? And what is this place?"

"Oh." Kiki looked puzzled as we both sat down, her at the desk, me on the cot. "You weren't brought here by your own consent?"

"I was unconscious." Like I would be soon if I didn't eat, I thought. "I woke up here."

Kiki set a clipboard on the desk and clicked her pen—silver, I noted. "Yes, I heard you had a run-in with some energy blasts. Which would explain the unconscious part."

I shrugged. "It's becoming a habit."

"You've been blacking out?" she asked.

"Constantly."

"Hmm. We'll come back to that. I need to get some basics out of the way so that we can get the evaluation done properly. Let's see if we've got the facts correct, first. Full name is Gail Olivia Godwin, age, twenty-six . . . weight is . . ." She frowned down at her clipboard and back at me. "That can't be right."

"How do you know all of that?" I said, going cold. I pushed myself to my feet. I hadn't been weighed. That was private information, so how the hell were they getting it?

"We scanned your fingerprints and pulled your DMV records. Your last listed weight is dramatically different from your weight now." She frowned again. "And sit down." There was a suggestion, a hint to her voice that made the hair on the back of my neck prickle.

"You're telepathic?" I asked, not sitting down.

"Very minor." She waved her hand flippantly. "Nothing serious. You don't need to worry about it."

"I'm not worried." Though I was. I'd never met a psychic villain who wasn't an absolute psychopath. I'd yet to meet any of the psychic heroes. Blaze had mostly had a monopoly on rescuing me.

"Stoic. I like it." Kiki nodded her approval and turned

back to her clipboard. "Tell me," she said without looking up, "why are your listed weight and your physical weight so different?"

"It has to do with that blacking-out problem I've been having, I think. I'm not sure. I'm having a hard time concentrating. Is there any food? I'm kind of hungry."

On cue, my stomach rumbled loudly enough that Kiki's pen stopped. She swiveled in her chair to look at me.

"Okay, I'm really hungry." I sighed. "It's been a crazy month."

"Want to tell me about it?"

I sighed again. The hell of it was, I did want to tell her. I wanted to unload on somebody, even if it was a complete stranger like Kiki. So I told her about running into Naomi and how I'd woken up strapped to a metal table. I detailed what I could remember about my time with Dr. Mobius—the flashbacks, the hallucinations, all of it. How I'd mysteriously been able to do over five hundred push-ups. How I was always hungry.

"He said I was radioactive," I said, "and that in a couple of months, I'd start to crave more of this solution, whatever it was. I'm an addict. And then he pushed me out of the car and there's not anything about him in the newspaper and I don't know what to do."

"That would explain the radiation level in the room when we scanned it," Kiki said, mostly to herself. On my panicked look, she smiled a bit. "Don't worry, we damp it down. I'll take a sample of your blood, of course, to confirm your story. For the record, I believe you. Dr. Mobius was in Detmer for months. We're not sure how he escaped, honestly. He may have had help—and wasn't aware that you and Blaze were no longer, um, a thing. So his kidnapping you doesn't surprise me. His turning you into at least a Class C does."

"I don't think he meant to. He wanted something to hold over Blaze's head."

"Hmm." Kiki set the clipboard down. "And how does that explain the muscles? You're quite built."

"They came in overnight." I remembered the five hundred push-ups (well, six hundred if we were being technical), and barely resisted shuddering. "I'm told I was awake for the injection, but I don't remember any of it, so I don't know when, you know, I got these." I flexed and watched my own biceps in fascination. It still felt a bit like my body belonged to a stranger.

"I see. Here's what we're going to do. We've got the testing room prepped for you now, so I'm going to take you inside and draw some of your blood so that we can analyze it. Then we'll do the physical tests. It won't hurt, but you'll be tired later."

"Um, okay," I said. "But can you feed me first?"

On cue, my stomach rumbled again.

Kiki laughed. "We can do that. Come this way."

Chapter Nine

TRUE TO KIKI'S word, they fed me. Kiki and Cooper sat down with me at a white table in the equally silver-and-white large testing room. Once I got over my nerves at Cooper being there—he was just so gorgeous, but, I sensed after a while, completely taken. By Kiki—I plowed through three turkey sandwiches and four bags of chips before Kiki went to get more.

"When did this change of metabolism start?" Cooper asked, as I reached for a dill pickle though I hated pickles.

"Since I woke up fully in Dr. Mobius's lair. I've been starving." I bit into the pickle so emphatically that Cooper laughed.

After they'd fetched me enough food to tide me over, the tests began. They checked my heart rate and blood pressure, murmuring back and forth. I didn't bother to tell them I could hear them clearly.

When the usual tests had been completed (my leg

kicked sky-high during the reflexes test; Kiki had wisely stayed out of the way), Cooper crossed to the opposite wall and pressed a panel. A flat platform with a conveyor belt on it slid from the wall. Computer readings popped up on the wall in front of it, followed by a screen larger than my TV.

"We need to test your cardiovascular endurance," Cooper said.

I looked from the treadmill to my boots. Hours ago, when I'd been about to explain to my coworkers why I hadn't been to work, they'd seemed like a good idea. If I'd known I would be fighting henchmen or running on a treadmill in an underground medical facility, I'd have picked something a little more comfortable. If preparedness was a virtue, I made for terrible Girl Scout material.

Kiki handed me a white sack embossed with the Davenport Industries logo in silver. "There's a changing room through there," she said, pointing at the corner. "Just touch the wall panel: it'll open."

When I emerged from the little box of the room, holding my own clothes and wearing the baggy Davenport T-shirt and blue shorts, I felt like I was back in gym class. Even down to the whiteness of the sneakers on my feet.

"So what now?" I asked, eyeing the treadmill.

Cooper handed me a thin plastic strip with a cloth strap attached. "Go ahead and slip that under your shirt."

"Just under your bra line," Kiki added helpfully.

Shrugging, I gripped the hem of my shirt in my teeth while I followed instructions, trying not to flinch at the cool plastic (they'd wet it down).

When it was in place, Cooper gestured at the treadmill. "We'll start you off easy, and when I say go, I want you to press that button." He gestured at a button on the panel in front of me.

I eyed it. "What's it do?"

"It makes you work harder. If you're anywhere near as masochistic as the rest of us, you'll learn to love it."

Though I didn't think that was ever going to be the case—I loathed running even more than I hated my job—I nodded. And the test began. It started with an easy walk. The first push of the button changed that to a faster walk, then to a slow jog.

Cooper kept making me push the button until I was nearly sprinting to keep up with the treadmill. My breath scraped the insides of my lungs. The feeling of not being able to draw a deep enough breath always terrified me, which meant I'd never understood the runner's high. How could runners get past that numbing terror of what if the next breath wasn't going to be deep enough? What if the oxygen wasn't ever coming again?

I felt that terror and desperation pressing insistently against my chest and was about to call off the test, make it stop, make it stop. And something odd happened.

I took a deep breath.

I don't know if it was my lungs expanding or just the area in the back of my throat relaxing. But I took a breath, and another. My breathing began to match the pace. In through the nose, forceful exhalation out through the mouth. Repeat. Focused on that rhythm, I grew aware of other things about me.

The way my feet were hitting the treadmill, for instance. Stomping was more like it. Maybe I could vary my step, move more on the balls of my feet so that I didn't have to expend so much energy . . .

I felt my breath deepen even at that little change.

"Your heart rate has leveled," I heard Cooper say, which put a hitch in my stride. I'd been so focused on my rhythm that I'd kind of forgotten he was there. "I figure you'll want some entertainment for this part."

The screen in front of me lit up and seemed to expand and curl toward me. It surrounded me on three sides, like I was in a little running stall. When it activated, I raised my eyebrows. It really looked like I was running on the actual road.

"Neat," I said.

"We'll be at this a while. Got any preferences?"

"For what?"

"Terrain. We've got sunrise in the desert, gritty urban scenes, cornfields, suburbs, beaches." Cooper sounded amused.

"Uh, surprise me."

Immediately, a sunrise began to paint the sky with streaks of pink and purple, to my left. I was running down a gloomily lit road in the middle of the desert, surrounded by miles and miles of gorgeous red sand. In the distance, there were shadows that I supposed were mesas though I'd never seen one in person before. The sun nudged its way up in the sky.

"Hydrate." The bottle seemed to appear from nowhere. I grabbed it and took a long drink.

I noticed an immediate change. My body liked the water.

I don't know how much time passed, but I finally experienced my first runner's high, where I wanted to go faster and faster, and never stop. But the screen unfurled and moved back to the wall, and the treadmill began to slow. I blinked and slowed my stride to match.

"That's probably enough time to prove you've got endurance, Gail," Cooper said, appearing at my side. "We'll bring you in sometime for a longer run and see how long you can go."

"All right." I shook my head to clear it. "What now? Three hours of weight lifting?"

"Not quite." Cooper moved to where he could get a better look at the monitor, absently waving me off the treadmill. "Heart rate's good. You've adjusted to running better than any seasoned marathoner I've known. And you say you haven't run since . . . high school?"

"Since I had to get through the mile to pass gym," I confirmed, swiping at my brow. "And even then, I barely earned that C."

"Hmm."

"Is there any food?"

Cooper turned, surprised. "Already?"

"I'm like a human furnace on high." I said it sheepishly.

Over at the desk, Kiki nodded and began tapping away at the keyboard. Click, click, click. I scratched my ears at the noise. Had they always sounded that individual?

"This time," Kiki said, "we'll go high on the protein. You'll need your strength, and plenty of energy."

"Oh, goody. More running?"

"Not exactly. Food's on its way."

Kiki rose and collected a black apron from its peg on the wall and helped Cooper into it. Though I wondered why he would possibly need an apron that looked like the lead covers dentists put on their patients during X-rays, I didn't ask. I just wondered when the food was going to show. Standing still after my run was also proving to be a problem. I wanted to keep moving. I had liked the freedom.

"All right." With the apron strapped around his impressive frame, Cooper moved to stand in front of me. Well away from Kiki and her desk, I noted. He spaced his feet hip-distance apart, bracing himself. "Now," he said, "this may freak you out a bit, but it's okay, I promise. I want you to hit me. Right here."

He tapped a hand the size of a Christmas ham on his midsection.

"Um, I think that might break my hand."

"My theory tells me that no, it won't break your hand."

I looked hard at him. The apron he wore wasn't Kevlar. It looked like it was just heavy black cloth. But I was under no pretensions about the body beneath that polo shirt. "Dude, you're built like a rock."

"Gail, you won't hurt yourself. Just go ahead and hit me, right here. As hard as you can. No pulling your punches."

I thought fleetingly of the stunned look on Gary's face, his hand over his bleeding nose. A new fear began to nibble, not for my hand, but for Cooper.

So I looked up at him. "I hurt Chelsea's henchmen, and I wasn't even trying."

"This is a little different."

"It's okay, Gail," Kiki said. "You can hit him."

I swung my head to look at her. "I'm not going to hit your boyfriend, Kiki."

Both of them froze. Puzzled, I listened to their heartbeats speed up, almost in sync. And wondered why I could hear heartbeats now.

Kiki jolted to her feet, and said, too quickly, "We're— we're not dating! Where would you get that idea?"

I blinked back at both of them. It had seemed perfectly obvious to me. "You're not?"

"No, not at all," Cooper said so fast that I figured the gentleman did protest a bit much.

Because they looked a bit like deer caught in the headlights, I raised my hands in a nonthreatening way. "Sorry. Guess I was wrong, then. My bad."

"Girl," and Kiki now sounded both a bit curious and strangled, "why did you think we were dating?"

"Um, vibes? I don't know." I couldn't quite explain it. There'd been something subtle in the air that I couldn't have possibly explained. My gut had said they were dating, or at least were sexually involved, and I hadn't seen any reason to question it.

Cooper and Kiki shared a look that was significant to everybody in the room but me. "Pheromones?" he said.

"Sounds like. Oh, the geeks are going to have fun with her," Kiki said.

"Standing right here," I said.

"Right." Cooper shot me a sunny grin. "You still need to hit me."

"Sign a waiver first. I'm not kidding."

"Gail. Just hit me."

I sighed. At least, if I managed to do some serious damage, we weren't far from qualified medical professionals. I hoped. So I wound up with my right arm and swung it as hard as I could, right at his midsection. Midpunch, I felt my body adjust, driving power up from my legs and into my shoulder and arm. My wrist straightened out. And my fist drove right into black apron.

Thankfully, I did not punch through his stomach. Unfortunately, Cooper still went flying back. He landed with a resounding thud on the floor a few feet away.

I rushed over. "Are you okay? Damn it, you said I wouldn't hurt you!"

"Gail." Kiki stepped up. "He's fine."

And true to her word, Cooper sat up and dusted himself off. "That was fun," was all he said, and popped up to his feet easily.

It didn't take a genius to put it together. "You're superpowered!" I said, pointing an accusing finger at him.

"Guilty as charged." Cooper looked amused. "Does that change anything?"

"No, I just wish I'd known that before I hit you!"

"Why? What would it change?"

I crossed my arms over my chest. "You could've spared me the trouble of worrying if I was going to punch my hand through you!"

Both he and Kiki roared with laughter. Eventually I joined in, as truth be told, it was a little funny. Cooper had looked genuinely surprised as he'd flown back. We were still laughing when the door beeped. My sense of smell, already sharpened, made my mouth water. And rendered Kiki's announcement of "That'll be the food, then," absolutely pointless.

"We'll let you fuel up," Cooper said, "before we run a couple of more tests, then let Psych take a crack at you. They should have fun breaking you down into little bitty pieces and building you back up."

"Your pep talks kind of suck, just so you know," I said, and dug into the steak like the starving woman I was.

MUCH TO MY surprise, Vicki Burroughs was waiting for me outside Psych once I'd been cleared though I had no idea exactly what that meant. They'd bundled me into a white polo shirt not unlike those the medical workers wore, and similar blue pants, and said my mentor would be waiting for me outside. To do what, I had no idea.

So I found Vicki, slouching comfortably against the wall opposite the door. She'd changed from the black cat-suit to jeans and a baby-doll tee. Her feet, surprisingly, were bare, her toenails painted a stunning gold color.

"Wow, they really put you through your paces," she said, straightening. "You were in there forever."

"Who's they?" I asked. "What are you doing here? And what is this place?"

"Wow, lots of questions. C'mon, we'll walk and talk. Since you rank at least Class C clearance, you netted yourself a suite." Mercifully, Vicki slowed down her ground-devouring strides so that my shorter legs could keep pace.

I still had to walk pretty fast, but I didn't mind. They'd fed me pretty continually, and even better, they'd finally explained the class system everybody had been buzzing about since I'd arrived at Davenport. No powers were Class D—like I had been—and from then on, each individual power (of which they'd catalogued over fifty) was rated on a scale from A to C. Powers were apparently averaged to give somebody an overall class. Most of the heavy hitters were Class A or B, and that included Blaze.

I hadn't dared ask about him. I wasn't sure I wanted to know, but Kiki had mentioned it in an offhand way.

"Congratulations," Vicki said as we walked down the hall. "You've now become part of the superhero elite, as it goes. That's Davenport Industries. They're kind of an umbrella organization that protects us, give us a haven, whatever. A lot of us live here full-time. Trust me, you wouldn't want to see what would happen if some of us tried to live in society. Not pretty." She gave a dramatic shudder.

"I thought Davenport was into real estate and, like, everything," I said.

"They are. That's the front, though." We made a left turn. "Do you know Raptor?"

Everybody knew Raptor. He was one of the very first superheroes to show up on the scene though it was never actually proven he had powers. He was, simply put, legend. "What about him?"

"Now, you'll have to keep this quiet when you're not in DI, but Raptor? Kurt Davenport."

I stopped to gape at her. I'd had the weirdest day possible. Nothing should be able to floor me now. But this did. "Kurt Davenport is Raptor?"

"Crazy, I know." Vicki grinned.

"Kurt Davenport's dead," I said. The playboy and founder of Davenport Industries had passed away nearly three years ago. "But Raptor's still around. I saw him on the news just—well, before I was kidnapped, however long ago that was."

"It's complicated. Like most of us with our origin stories. You'll pick them up as time goes on. Maybe I'll even tell you mine someday. It'll be fun. I've never had a mentee before."

"Mentee?" I said, still marveling at the fact that Kurt Davenport, whom everybody in my parents' generation adored, was the skulking superhero who kept New York City free of criminal dirt. Or had been, before he'd died. But the Raptor was still around, wasn't he?

"Yup. I'm your mentor. I'm supposed to show you the ropes." Vicki flicked her fingers. "I'm not supposed to get a mentee for a couple of more years, but since I brought you in, they did me a favor. Exciting, right? You get the one and only Plain Jane as your mentor!"

This time I didn't stop to stare. I was learning to take things in stride, apparently. "You're Plain Jane?" I asked.

"Yup." She trailed a hand through her dark locks.

"Um, hate to be the one to break it to you, but you're not plain."

"I know. I think it's called irony." She grinned, her face lighting up with a side that very few cameras got to see.

And on that statement, we burst from the maze of moss green corridors and into an area as white and minimalist as Medical had been. The hallway widened, brightening as the light changed. Doors on either side of us were now a royal blue color and they, unlike the doors we'd been passing, had regular doorknobs. The screens displayed different names. I eyed a few surreptitiously.

"And this, my new mentee, is the main compound of the Davenport Industries Superpowers Complex," Vicki said, as we sauntered along. "Medical and Support are all located in the secondary compound, which is where we just were. In a while, I'll get you acquainted with a map. They tell me you've got some sensory talent, so I can just show it to you, and you can memorize it. Saves time, I've gotta tell you."

I blinked at that. I'd never had an eidetic memory before. Sensory talent? Just because I'd sensed pheromones between Cooper and Kiki? And . . . heartbeats, I realized. And changes in the air, like the strange-yet-familiar smell in my apartment.

Okay, so I had sensory talent.

"I'm jealous," Vicki said, leading me into some sort of indoor courtyard that teemed with greenery. A man-made pond gurgled close to the opposite wall. Overhead, giant lamps simulated sunlight, but I got the feeling we were still underground. My companion didn't seem to notice the indoor forest; we strolled through it, Vicki occasionally nodding to those we passed on the path. Like Vicki, they were dressed casually. "I can't remember directions to save my life. Which is why I'm glad I ran into Raymond when we did. We'd probably still be looking for Medical."

"Uh-huh." This was Plain Jane, ranked something like seventh in the world as far as super powers went. Jealous of me. What?

"Now," and Vicki launched into lecture mode once more as we skirted the pond on a little brick path, "we have the Indoor Arboretum. I think it's pretty much a getaway for those of us who don't want to go topside. Especially those still getting used to powers. It's not far from your new room, which is right down the hall from mine, actually. We're going to be neighbors. Isn't that exciting?" She shoulder-bumped me.

"Um, yay." I was going to be staying here? For how long? I mean, it was a relief, what with no longer being able to afford my apartment until I could find a new job, but I was a little creeped out by just how quickly everything was happening.

"Yay is right," Vicki said. "It's this way."

We made a left out of the Inner Arboretum into yet another hallway. White walls, gray carpets, though this hallway was wider and a great deal more populated. A few people gave me curious looks, but they didn't say anything.

"So, back to the story. You remember the Feared Five, right?" Vicki asked.

"Raptor, Phantom Fuel, Invisible Victor, The Cheetah, and Gail Garson? My mom named me after GG. I think a lot of drugs went into that, though, because I'm nobody's hero."

"You held this Chelsea person off, and she was strong. One of the strongest I've faced, certainly," Vicki said.

"Really?" I asked.

We headed up a set of carpeted stairs. "I wouldn't have gotten to your friend Nicole—"

"Naomi."

"—in time if you hadn't held Chelsea off the way you did. So chalk that one up on the saves list."

"Okay." Warmth spread through my midsection. Pride, I realized. I was proud of something I'd done.

That was a first in a long, long time.

"But anyway," I said, clearing my throat, "what about them? The Feared Five?"

"They started this place. And Detmer, too, while I'm thinking about it."

"No, that can't be right." I hadn't actually paid attention in history, but I did remember some things. "Everybody knows the Alliance of Ten set Detmer up."

"Nope. History tells it wrong, but I don't think Davenport really wants people knowing that, so they let it slide. Because, you see, Kurt Davenport was married to Fearless, whose alter-ego was Rita Detmer."

I gaped. "Davenport named the prison after his wife?"

"And his mortal enemy, though history books gloss over that part. See, Rita—Fearless—had VS."

"VS?"

"Villain Syndrome." When I gave her a blank look, Vicki squinted back at me. "Have you been living under a rock? It's a pretty common form of the sociopath. Villains who can't help themselves. They want to save the world, but it means burning it down first? You know?"

"Oh, that type of psychopath. Yeah, I've met one or two of those before."

"Where on earth would you—never mind, we'll get to life stories later. Anyway, Davenport set up a really nice wing at Detmer for VS rehabilitation."

Our rooms were apparently quite a distance from Medical. A month before, I would never have remembered the route, but now it was like I could memorize it by a series of distances—how many steps from one doorway to the next, how many feet between the wall and me, how high the ceilings reached. As we walked, Vicki divulged more than the history books had ever recounted about the Feared Five. Kurt Davenport, in addition to being a shrewd business mogul and a masked crusader for justice, had possessed quite a bleeding heart. He'd sympathized with his less conventional superhero friends' struggle to adjust to everyday life.

"So he started this facility," Vicki said in conclusion, "as a sanctuary. Water-breathers get their own wing underwater, the deeply messed-up-in-the-head have the underground bunkers, and for those of us who choose to keep up appearances with our alter egos, this is just a crashing pad every once in a while. I live here when I'm not on location. It's easier. I like to avoid the stalkarazzi."

"Not all the time, apparently," I said under my breath, thinking of all the shots I'd seen of Jeremy grinning, his arm around Vicki's waist.

Vicki gave me a strange look for that one.

"So what happens now?" I asked to change the subject, as I was really too tired to get into it.

"Well, they haven't given you a schedule for your adjustment period yet, but I imagine tomorrow you'll be put with a trainer. If you want to stay, I mean. You could go back to your life and sort out your adjustment period on the outside." Vicki looked doubtful. "But a lot of people, even Class Cs, have trouble with it."

As would I, I realized. With my luck and my changing abilities, I'd likely run into every supervillain in Chicago by accident.

"After your adjustment, you can stay here as long as you contribute something," Vicki said. "You know, being on call for other heroes if you don't want to be one of the headliners. Some of them are looking for partners right now. So that's something to look into. Since you're a Class C."

"By partners, you mean sidekicks, right?"

"We call them partners." Vicki grinned. "C'mon, our rooms are up this way."

We headed down yet another hallway. How big was this place? I pushed that thought aside to ponder over later and aimed a sideways look at Vicki. "You're not looking for a sidekick, are you?"

"Darling, I work alone. But I appreciate the thought."

"That's probably a good thing. I think you got the short end of the stick if you were waiting to get a mentee." I stuck my hands into the pockets of the pants they'd given me. "I'll probably be dead in a couple of months if they don't find Dr. Mobius."

"Huh. Fatalistic much?" Vicki said, surprised.

"He turned me into an addict for a solution only he can make apparently. I've got an expiration date."

"Nonsense, Medical will figure out what it is. If they

can't make the exact stuff, they'll give you enough of a substitute to get by."

"Really?"

"Outside, you might be considered special now, but here at Davenport, you've got nothing they haven't seen twice over," Vicki said. "You're not dying on Davenport's watch."

It seemed absurd to feel hope, but the entire day had been so weird. I felt my spirits pick up. They'd drawn a sample of my blood. Maybe they could reverse engineer something.

"Right." Though doubt still ruled, hope edged its way in.

"Oh, here we are," Vicki said. For the first time since we started walking, we reached an actual door, and Vicki pressed her hand against the panel beside it. The hallway on the other side, for once, looked like one you might find in an actual apartment building. "We'll take the elevator instead of the stairs. It's just around the corner, and it practically leads right up to your room. How's that for awesome?"

"Awesome," I agreed, inwardly marveling. This woman was Plain Jane, protector of Miami. She regularly flew around buildings, and when she was in a hurry, through them (though I heard the building owners always received checks for the damages). She fought bad guys in one of the best superhero uniforms out there, with a creepy white mask. And she was excited about the fact that the elevator was right outside my new room. It takes all kinds.

We rounded the corner, and, as predicted, the elevator

lay ahead. Its doors were already open, and two people were climbing on. Two tall, well-built people. One of whom wore a skintight green shirt and black pants with black, scuffed boots. There was a small cartoon of a flame on his shirt.

"Hold the elevator?" Vicki called.

The two men turned, and I saw, quite clearly, my ex-boyfriend Jeremy.

And standing next to him, wearing Blaze's uniform, was none other than my old coworker, Guy Bookman.

They both looked as stunned as I felt. The elevator doors slid closed.

"Well, that was rude," Vicki said.

I couldn't think of anything to say to that besides the obvious: "What the *hell*?"

Chapter Ten

IT TOOK VICKI a few seconds to catch on. She looked back and forth between the closed elevator doors and me quickly a few times. "Wait a minute," she said. "You're that Gail? You're Jeremy and Guy's Girl?"

"How many Girls do you know?" I asked, and cursed when I realized how it sounded.

But Vicki didn't seem to notice. "Wow," she breathed, really looking at me now. "Wow. It's such—it's such an honor to meet you. Wow."

I blinked at her. "Why's it an honor to meet me?"

"You're a legend."

I opened my mouth to demand what was so legendary about a workaholic with a tendency to stumble into bank holdups, but a *ding* stopped me. Looking up, I saw that the elevator had stopped one floor up. "What's so—?"

The door beside the elevator, the one that apparently led to stairs, flew open. I only had time to register a green blur before I found myself locked into a crushing hug. The arms around me were familiar, and the smell—

"You're okay!" Abruptly, I was pushed backward and craned my neck to stare up into Guy Bookman's handsome face. "You're not hurt! I was worried—"

"You were in my apartment," I said, as I realized why the smell had been so familiar. "You went through my apartment."

Immediately, Guy looked abashed. "I called to talk to Angus, and Portia mentioned you hadn't been at work. I was worried, so I thought I'd check—"

"You're Blaze," I said. "You. You're Blaze. You're not Jeremy. Jeremy is not Blaze. You are—what?"

"Um." He went still and suddenly looked sheepish. "Yes, yes I am."

"You didn't know?" asked a voice behind him, and I saw Jeremy leaning against the doorjamb of the stairwell. He looked, as always, confident and a little bit dangerous even though I now knew he wasn't Blaze. "Figures."

"Hey." Guy reared up to his full height, which was, as expected, exactly the same as Jeremy's. Standing next to each other, they could have been twins in everything but coloring. Jeremy wore a white muscle tee and blue jeans. But he was much darker in complexion than Guy's bronze hair and green eyes. "It wasn't like I was giving her a lot of clues to go off of."

I ignored him for a second because I had a feeling that if I tried to wrap just one more surprise into my expanding brain, it might very well explode. Jeremy was safe. Jeremy was a known quantity. "What are you doing *here*?" I asked. "You're—you're not War Hammer, are you?"

When Vicki began to laugh, genuinely, like that was the funniest joke she'd heard in a long time, I suspected otherwise. Jeremy shook his head and sketched a little bow. "Class D. Just like you."

"Oh. Uh, about that . . . never mind." I turned on Guy, who took a step back as if he had just realized he was violating my personal space. Since the guy had rescued me countless times, I wasn't inclined to care about that. But the rest of it . . . "You're Blaze. *You're* Blaze."

But Guy frowned at me. "What are you doing here? Did Eddie bring you here?"

"Eddie?" I said, confused.

Vicki stepped between us. "As fun as this little reunion is, the walls around these parts have ears." She pointed down the hall at several doors. "Let's take this inside somewhere."

"Right." Guy actually sounded strangled as he backed up. He couldn't seem to decide what to do with his hands. He rubbed his hips like he was hoping the Blaze uniform would have pockets. "Let's, um, do that, then. My place—"

"Way too far," Vicki said. "Mine's fine. So, boys, Gail here will be just down the hall from me. Isn't that lucky?"

Jeremy had a frown on his face, and I realized he was checking me out under the shapeless Davenport clothes. "How'd you net a room on the powered floors?" he asked.

"I don't want to talk about it here," I said, which was about all I felt comfortable disclosing. For some reason, Vicki's statement about the walls having ears stuck in my head. It couldn't be literal, right? I was beginning to accept that there was a secret world of superheroes, and, oh, right, that my coworker who I had barely spoken to *regularly donned a mask and saved my life*, but the walls with actual ears? No thanks.

Silently, we climbed onto the elevator, and Vicki pressed the button for the seventh floor. I stood back from both Jeremy and Guy. Vicki seemed like the safer choice. If she noticed what I was doing, she didn't remark on it. When we disembarked, she jerked her head to say that we should follow her. I wondered briefly if our rooms, since they were on the same floor, were at all alike.

Probably not. For one thing, I don't own nearly as much S&M equipment as Vicki does.

"I collect it as a joke," she said when I stared, dumbfounded, at the leather crops and whips artfully arranged on one of the stark white walls of her apartment. The black leather couches with the bright red pillows made me do a double take, but it was the white bust wearing a full leather mask on the coffee table that really made me goggle. "Designers send me the weirdest things, so I collect some of them. That's Peaches Franklin."

"You named your S&M mannequin head?" I asked.

"You'll get used to it," Jeremy said as he dropped onto the couch.

Guy waited until I'd seated myself on the couch opposite from Jeremy and Vicki before he sat down. Next to me. Tension coiled through every line of him, from the way he sat straight up without touching the back of the couch to the way his hands fisted on the black knees of his uniform.

"So . . ." Vicki shrugged. "Who wants to start?"

"I say Gail goes first." Jeremy tilted his head slightly in challenge, and I narrowed my eyes right back at him. I remembered this plan of attack well. He was hiding something—that much should be obvious since we were literally in a secret superhero compound—and was planning to antagonize me until I forgot about it.

"We're all dying to hear how you got hot," he said. "I mean, not that you weren't hot before. But now—took a few steps up the babe scale. How'd that happen? Did you burn off your sadness for me on the treadmill?"

I gave him a tired look. "Do you have to be a pig right now? Seriously?"

"Old habits die hard." He leaned back and spread his arms on the back of the couch, his legs crossed at the ankles in front of him. Jeremy in repose.

"It's not a habit, you're doing it on purpose. Quit being an ass."

"Ohh-kay," Vicki said, holding her hands up in a time-out position. "Clearly there's some history here."

"Yeah, he's my ex, who dumped me while I was in the hospital," I said. I looked between them. "That didn't come up on one of your dates? Usually a discussion of the exes is par for the course."

"One of our . . . oh, huh. Does she not know?" Vicki asked Guy and Jeremy.

"Well, considering the ruse was to fool the entire world, and not just her, I'm going to guess no," Jeremy said, and why he glared at Guy as he said that, I had no idea.

"What is everybody talking about?" I asked.

From beside me, Guy spoke quietly. "I'd rather hear

what happened to you first, if that's okay, Gail. We can explain everything else since it's all tied together."

I wanted to know more about the ruse, actually. "You have to promise me you'll tell me what's going on. *Everything* that's going on. I've been in the dark for far too long."

Guy nodded. "That's fair. You go first?"

"Okay." For the second time that day, I ran through the entire tale of my time with Dr. Mobius, from beginning to end, stopping only when Vicki or Jeremy asked a question. Guy remained deathly quiet. The tension never faded from his shoulders; nor did he look at me. He stared at a point on Vicki's black coffee table, never looking up. The look on his face grew grimmer the longer the story went on.

"Wow, quite an adventure," Jeremy said when I finished my rundown. "Trust you to stumble into a bank holdup on your first day awake, though."

I cracked a small smile at that. It was either laugh or cry at this point. "Well, you know. Habit."

Next to me, Guy was nearly vibrating like a plucked string. Though it seemed glaringly obvious to me, neither Vicki nor Jeremy seemed to notice. "I left," he finally said, "so that you would be safe."

Jeremy levered himself off the couch and crossed into the kitchenette area of Vicki's apartment, obviously very at home. "Well," he said over his shoulder, "that didn't work now, did it?"

"Jeremy," I said.

Jeremy shot an "Ain't I a stinker?" smirk over his shoulder.

"So what about you three?" I asked, mostly hoping to put Guy more at ease. His tension was making *me* tense.

"Witness Protection," Jeremy said, grinning.

"That's just what he calls it." Vicki folded her yards of leg beneath her. "We were tired of staking out his apartment when the villains decided once and for all that he was Blaze. So we moved him here and inducted him into Davenport society."

I remembered something Vicki had said in the hallway. "So how do you contribute?" I asked him, suspicious. What on earth could a Class D add to Davenport Industries, which was obviously lousy with superheroes?

"Superior gaming skills." Jeremy returned with a bottle of Pellegrino. "I run the simulators."

"The slower ones," Guy said, earning a laugh from Vicki and a scowl from Jeremy. For a second, the corner of his lips pushed upward in something close to a smile, like he was pleased with himself for the burn. But he schooled his features back into the regular Guy face I remembered from the office. "Sorry, Jer."

Jeremy grunted at him. "Slower ones, my ass."

I knew so little about the man who sat next to me, which felt incredibly unfair, given the number of times he'd swooped in to save the day. So I turned an expectant look on him. "And you? I think you owe me your story now that you know what happened to me."

"I'm not going to start at the beginning," Guy said. "We'll be here all night, and . . ." He cast a look at Jeremy.

My ex twisted the cap to the water bottle. "They don't share origin stories," he said. "Not with Class D freaks like me. Can't have the plebes wandering around with all of their big secrets. Bunch of whiny babies."

"Anyway," Guy said, "when it was obvious to me that the villains weren't going to leave you alone, I hatched a plan. I'm sorry I couldn't tell you about it, but for it to work, you had to seem fully broken up with Jeremy and with Blaze."

And he launched into a story, the most I had ever heard him talk. Jeremy and Vicki interjected a few details, but the story unfolded about how Guy had used his Bookman influence to convince Jeremy's job to move him to Miami. How he'd enlisted Vicki to stage a meet cute at a bar down the street from Jeremy's new pad so that that public would know that Jeremy Collins and Gail Godwin were no longer a thing. And once the two of them—Jeremy, it appeared, had been in the dark—were sure that everybody knew about the newest It Couple, they'd arranged a very public rescue of Vicki, cementing it for everybody that Jeremy Collins was truly and forever Blaze.

"Of course, the villains started going for him," Vicki said, grinning. She ruffled Jeremy's hair when his scowl deepened. "So it became a full-time job for both Guy and me to keep him safe. We had to tell him. Eventually, we decided just to move him here."

"So, that's it. That's the story." Guy wouldn't look up from his hands.

"How did you know that the villains were going to leave me alone?" I asked.

"Eddie," Guy said.

"Who?"

"Eddie Davenport. He came to visit me that day in the office—when he met you—because he wanted to get a look at you. At the, uh, the girl I was giving Chicago up for."

I could think of absolutely nothing to say to that. My feelings were all still a jumbled knot in my stomach. I needed a sandwich and about twelve hours of sleep to begin processing any of it, so I just stared. "Eddie Davenport was there to meet me?"

"Yes." Guy finally looked up and met my gaze. "And he pulled some strings, so supervillains would really believe that you and Blaze were through. Until . . . Mobius."

"Meanwhile, others got to pay the price," Jeremy said, and the bitterness in his voice made me look at him fully. So that was what he'd been trying to hide. His fingers fidgeted with the cap of the Pellegrino bottle.

"I'm sorry," I said, since there wasn't anything else I could really say. Sorry for what, though? None of this had exactly been my fault.

For a moment, I didn't think Jeremy was going to say anything. But he sighed and pinched the bridge of his nose. "It's water under the bridge," he said in a way that sounded like he was trying to convince himself. "Can't do anything about it now."

"Kids," Vicki said, and all three of us looked over at her. I'd kind of forgotten she was even there, which was a bit surprising, given that we were surrounded by her collection of kinky sex gear. "I hate to be the buzzkill, but I've got an early-morning photo shoot, and if I show up with bags under my eyes, Denise will simply murder me."

"Denise?" I asked.

"My makeup artist. She's a genius, but she likes an untouched canvas." Firmly, Vicki ejected us from her suite, promising that she'd take me to Testing in the morning before she left, if she could. I began to see why they hadn't let her have a mentee before. Right before she closed the door, she turned to the guys, "Will one of you take her to her new room? Suite 704."

"I'll do it," Guy said before Jeremy could pipe up.

The latter raised his eyebrows. "Okay. I'm going to get a few hours in on *Call of War*." He did a really geeky hang-ten sign with his right hand. The move felt old and familiar in a way that had tears gathering unexpectedly at the back of my throat. "Got a level-42 druid requesting a private meet-up."

"I hope she's female this time," I said.

"Get catfished once, never live it down." He peered at Guy for a moment, shrugged, and gave me a sunny grin. "See ya, babe."

I gave him a smile because it was simpler than giving him the finger. He knew I'd always hated that pet name. "Good night."

Once Jeremy had strolled off with his hands in his pockets, Guy turned to me. "He grows on you," I said.

"Yeah, he has his moments." Guy pushed his shoulders back, and I thought of all of the times we'd stood like this, waiting for the police to show so they could get me to safety. Only then his mask had been on rather than crumpled up in one of his hands. It made me want to ask a thousand questions. Why me? What is it about me that the villains came after me and not somebody else?

I wasn't sure I was ready to know the answer to that one yet.

"C'mon," Guy said, clearing his throat, "your room's this way."

"So, Vicki," I said to break the quiet as we walked. "She's interesting."

A line appeared between his eyebrows as he gave the matter some thought. "Don't always believe what you see with her. You'll be hanging around with her a lot, and what she presents and who she is, they're . . . not the same."

"You're close?"

"She's a good friend. We came to Davenport at the same time."

"You did?" That was a surprise though I had no idea why it should be. After all, I knew nothing about Guy Bookman. Blaze, I could quote you chapter and verse about. But the man behind the mask, to put in it in cliché form, he was a mystery.

"Yeah. I'll, um, I'll tell you about it sometime." We stopped outside of Room 704, my new home. "After all, it's the least I can do."

"For what?" I asked, puzzled.

"For . . ." Guy looked away. When he looked back at me, his stare was as intense as it always had been behind the mask, whether he was pulling me out of a flaming volcano or fighting off the latest death-ray-wielding supergenius. No wonder I'd never noticed his eyes as Guy, I thought distantly as I waited for him to control himself. They'd always been hidden behind glasses. With those out of the way, I could see every fleck of gold and brown in the brilliant green.

"It's all my fault," Guy finally said, and I blinked, drawn out of the trance his gaze cast over me.

"What? What is?"

"This whole mess, that's what." Where others might have tried to pace, Guy stayed entirely still. "Every time I saw you at work, I wanted to apologize, to beg for forgiveness. But I couldn't. Not without giving up my secret."

"Whoa," I said. "Bl—Guy, what are you doing?"

He gave me a pained look. "I'm trying to apologize."

"Well, stop trying. I don't want your apology." I also didn't want his intense gaze focused on my face like that. Even with my new muscles and body, it made me feel oddly vulnerable, and I really didn't like this feeling, on top of everything I'd been through.

"But it was my fault," Guy said.

"Really? Did you tell all those villains, super-geniuses, and madams of evil to kidnap me?"

"No, not exactly—"

"Then you don't owe me an apology. If anything, I owe you my gratitude."

"You don't," Guy insisted.

"We could probably stand here arguing this all night," I said, and looked at the door. Guy's intensity was the last thing I needed on top of this unending day. I wanted to get horizontal and stay that way for a few hours. And even more, I wanted to get away from the intensity of Guy's stare. "But I'm a little wiped out. Would you be terribly offended if I declared a temporary moratorium on this conversation until I'm better able to handle it? My brain's swimming as it is."

Instantly, Guy took a step back. "You're right," he said. "I'm sorry. I shouldn't be pressing the matter. I imagine you're tired."

Bone-weary was more like it, but I just nodded. "I could use some sleep. It's been a long day—hell, a long month."

"Right. Right. I'll, um, I'll let you get some sleep." Guy took another step back. "Good night, Gail."

"Good night, Guy."

Guy looked like he might have liked to go in for another hug or a handshake or something, but he chose just to nod at me and walk back the way we had come. I deliberately turned away as well, to face my door.

"Um, Guy?"

Immediately, he stopped and looked back. "Yes?"

"No, um, just there's . . ." I gestured at the door, a blank white expanse. "There's no doorknob."

"Oh." Guy smiled, and the effect was instantaneous, transforming his whole face into handsome lines. "Just put your hand on the screen. It'll let you in." With a final dazzling smile at me, he turned and left.

With a shrug to myself, I placed my hand on the screen. It heated for an instant, then words began to scroll down the screen, as they had outside Medical. Fascinated, I leaned closer and realized they were listing my statistics, name, age, weight, class.

Wow. Was that going to happen every time I touched a screen in this place? Good thing I didn't have anything to hide.

I would have liked to explore my new place, to poke

through cabinets and see exactly what it was that Davenport Industries issued to a newly minted Class C. But my body had other ideas. With Guy out of sight, I no longer had to conceal my exhaustion, so I dragged myself through the suite until I found the bedroom. I toed off my new sneakers and fell face-first onto the bed. Even with the fountain of new knowledge in my head begging to be reviewed, I was out before the mattress had even settled.

Chapter Eleven

"THE GOOD NEWS, Girl, is that you're dying."

I looked up from the glossy introduction packet I'd been handed and gawked at Cooper. My heart began to pound. Maybe I'd just misheard. "I b-beg your pardon?"

Cooper swiveled a computer screen toward me. All I saw on it were a bunch of graphs and charts with words that meant nothing to me. He tapped one finger against a graph in the corner. "Your dying rate."

Oh god, I hadn't misheard.

"You're dying, yes," Cooper went on, "but the chances are you'll live a nice long life before that happens."

Again, it took a few seconds for the meaning to cut through. "Are you messing with me?" I asked, putting a hand over my chest as if it could possibly hope to calm my heart rate.

"A little." He smiled, and I sagged back into my seat.

I was back in Medical on my second day at Davenport.

About ten minutes after I had woken up, Vicki had shown up outside of my new apartment to escort me on the long trek back. I'd been brought to Cooper's office, which was mercifully a lot darker than the rest of Medical, where they had the lights set to full glare. Cooper been hard at work on three different screens, all of which had something to do with me. And as amused as he had seemed during our testing session the day before, I could already tell he was in his element, surrounded by all of that data.

So cute, and so very much a geek. Neither of which took away from the fact that he was also a sadistic bastard.

I cleared my throat and glared at him, unimpressed with his little stunt. "A long life? How is that possible? Dr. Mobius was pretty clear that I'd wither away without the, um, 'upgrades' as he called them. I've got the stuff in my bloodstream, don't I? It didn't magically vanish."

"It didn't." Cooper swiveled the screen back toward himself and moved another one to where I could see it. "When we took your blood, I had no idea it would be this fascinating. I've never seen anything like this."

"What's so fascinating about it?" I asked.

"I don't know what Mobius was trying to do to you, but it clearly didn't work the way he wanted it to." Cooper pulled on a pair of wire-framed reading glasses, peering over the top of them as he typed. He never slowed or stopped talking. "From what you've been telling us, the end goal was certainly not to make you a superhero. I haven't run enough tests to be sure, but you're now on the cusp of Class B. Not quite there but still, either way, it's neat. Congratulations."

"Um, thanks."

"Now, what Mobius didn't take into consideration is that whatever he used in this solution of his had some sentient properties." Cooper rolled over to the other side of his L-shaped desk. "According to his file, he was held in Detmer for twenty-two months. The day after he escaped, you got kidnapped. So that tells me he didn't have time to whip up a new batch of his Solution of Doom. Which means either he had a partner or you got the two-year-old compound that had been sitting in a rotting, dank lab for all that time."

"He gave me expired junk? Ugh." I shuddered. I'd never been overly careful about what I put in my body—I liked cheeseburgers and caffeine a little too much for that—but the idea that there could be rotting, foul chemicals in my blood made me want to squirm. And then it caught up to me, the rest of what he'd said. "Wait a minute. Sentient properties? Coop, are you saying the stuff inside me has a *brain*?"

"Not a brain, exactly." Cooper's lips quirked into a smile, but he didn't look away from the computer screen. "No reason to freak out. The 'stuff,' as you call it, doesn't have a brain. But it has a survival imperative, and we found out by studying your blood sample that it's self-replicating at an intriguing rate. In fact, it's taking over for the carbon in your body."

I stared at him. "It's doing what? That means it's reproducing on its own, right? Like, I won't have to worry about an injection from Dr. Mobius again?"

"Chances are, you wouldn't have had to worry about

injections anyways. Even if you hadn't gotten powers, Davenport would have reverse engineered the formula for you." Cooper shrugged, a twitch of his massive shoulders. "It would have been a challenge, but I'm confident we would have been able to. Might've gotten a good paper out of that to present in Fresno at the Superhero Convention next year."

"Sorry to deprive you of the opportunity," I said.

"I have a feeling that I can get a good paper out of your, er, more interesting properties anyway."

"Why's that?"

Cooper rolled over to swivel the original screen at me again. This time when I saw the graphs, I immediately understood them, which gave me some pause. Science had always been my worst area in school. There was a simple BMI chart, EKG and EEG readings, the results for the lie detector test I'd taken in Psych the day before. A graph charting my heart rate during my run. And, of course, in the corner, my death-rate chart.

"You're human, Girl, but you're . . . extra," Cooper said. When I gave him another blank look, he smiled indulgently. "It's like this. We'll use your, ah, friend Guy as an example."

I wasn't surprised that his tone implied there was more between Guy and me than just friends. I was used to it. The name being Guy and not Blaze, though, that was new to me.

"He went through a pretty typical experience to become Class A. The explosion that changed him caused a change at the molecular level, altering him to be pretty damn near invincible. You're going through a similar molecular change. This semisentient isotope is altering your molecular composition."

"Altering *how*?" I asked. "Is this thing going to take over?"

"I don't think so. It's not that smart. I think, and this is just a theory, as we'll need to keep a close eye on you—it just wants an enhanced host, so it's replacing all of the carbon in your body with Mobium, which is stronger and denser."

I felt a bit like retching, but I forced myself to nod. A host meant that the thing in my bloodstream was a parasite. "But it's not controlling me. I'm still me, right?"

"You're still you. But a better you. Right now, you're in the best shape I've ever seen. Your brain is operating incredibly efficiently—but your thoughts are still your own! No worries there. Every sense you have is heightened: hearing, sight, smell, everything. You're still transitioning, so it'll take you a little while longer to be at full capacity. But when that happens? I can't wait to run those tests."

"I'm sure." I wasn't entirely sure I quite understood, but I had Cooper's packet of information. I could always read it later.

"Even better is that you're going to have muscle memory like none other," Cooper said. "We teach you something once, and you're going to know it forever."

"Makes me wish I could go back and retake all of those high school classes I barely passed." I leaned forward, set the packet on Cooper's desk, and rested my elbows on my knees. I gave him a look. "You said good news."

"What?"

"At the beginning, you said the good news is that I'm dying. Good news implies that there's bad news, too."

"Oh, pessimism." Cooper swung away, back to the other desk, and tapped something into the keyboard very rapidly.

"Try living a day in my life sometime, and you'll see why pessimism is a necessary survival skill. What is it? What's the bad news?"

"Well, it's not terrible news, but . . ." Cooper pushed his fingers together in a steeple and met my eyes. "You need to promise me that you'll remain calm."

"You started this conversation with 'you're dying, but that's okay!' I don't see what could be worse."

"Gail, we found traces of cancer."

I stared at him, once again positive I'd misheard. Cancer? I had cancer? The words felt like a punch to the gut from Chelsea's bee-stinging powers. Where had all of the oxygen in the room gone? I grabbed the edge of the desk. "You just said I'm in the best shape of my life," I said.

"Yes, and that's true, but—"

"You *also* said I was going to live a good, long life!"

"And chances are, you will." Cooper held my gaze. "It's not your typical situation with cancer. You're a special case."

"Special case, how?"

"Gail, this cancer isn't dangerous. Not to you. Because it's coming from the solution in your bloodstream."

"The one that's making me healthy," I said.

"Right. And while it's making you as superhuman as they come, it's also giving you cancer. It's a cycle."

The knowledge was a lump in my chest, a lump that sat heavier and heavier and refused to dissolve. I whispered around it. "What kind? What kind of can . . ." I had to swallow hard to keep going. "What kind of cancer?"

"It's called Chronic Myelogenous Leukemia, and there are a few articles about it in that packet I gave you. The thing you need to know, Gail—Gail, look at me."

I lifted my gaze up from the shiny packet of information on my knees.

"Gail, you're going to be fine."

"How? It's *cancer.*"

"Yes, it is. And it's serious business. But you've got the symbiotic parasite in you, and that's not going to let you die of cancer." Cooper leaned a little closer, his eyes just a little more emphatic. "There's a chance that once you've fully absorbed this solution inside of you, it'll eradicate the disease completely. In fact, it's likely."

"And if that doesn't happen?" I asked, feeling hope begin to trickle through the numbness.

"Then there's just a balance to find. The isotope wants to keep you healthy because of the survival imperative. So it will do its best to keep you alive."

"And if it's not good enough?" I asked, my stomach slowly creeping downward.

He shrugged in a way that indicated he wasn't going to answer that.

I leaned back and took a deep breath. "So I've got

cancer." Saying it aloud gave it a potency that made the air feel colder; I shivered.

"Yes, you do. But we're going to do everything we can for you, so you don't have to worry."

"How?" I asked him, feeling blind and desperate. "How will we do that?"

Cooper smiled and pressed a button on the panel on his desk. "You're going to like this next bit."

The door, which was only a few feet to my right, opened. I blinked as light from the hallway flooded in, silhouetting a woman in perfect shadow. "Wow," I said before I could stop myself. "Dramatic."

I couldn't be sure, but the woman might have smiled. I squinted, but she wasn't looking at me. In turn, she was squinting at Cooper. She reached her arm out and—

I yelped as the overhead lights flared on. My eyes adjusted almost instantly, but Cooper looked pained. "Must you do that every time?" he asked.

"It's dark in here," was all she said.

In the light, I got a much better look at her though the main impression was a study of contrasts. Obvious muscle that spoke of a true dedication to the gym rippled under her olive-toned skin. Her ink black hair was pulled back into a severe ponytail. But her dark eyes flashed with amusement, and she wore tiny silver hoops in each ear.

"It was dark in here for a reason, Angélica," Cooper said.

Angélica crossed her arms over her chest in amusement. "Yes, but how else will the rest of us get to see your pretty face?" Abruptly, she shifted her attention from

Cooper to me. She looked me up and down once. "Are you my victim?"

"Gail," Cooper said, "this is Angélica. She's going to be your trainer. Angélica, probably not a good idea to bring up torture."

"Got it, leave the thumbscrews at home." Angélica's smile wasn't exactly reassuring. She looked about my age, but she exuded an air of authority that I could never achieve. "You done with her, Coop?"

"I'm leaving her at your mercy," Cooper said before he flashed me a grin. "Good luck."

"Thanks." I rose to follow Angélica out, not certain about what was going to happen to me next. I stopped in the doorway. "Cooper?"

"Hmm?" He'd already turned his attention to the computer screens and away from me. But now he swiveled to look over at the doorway.

"Tell me one more time—"

"You're going to be fine. Just listen to Angélica. She's never steered one of her trainees wrong."

ANGÉLICA LED ME into another part of the complex, and I did my best keep up. It wasn't hard: Angélica was only a couple of inches taller than I was. She wore workout clothing, which made me wonder. Did she train other superheroes? Did Guy and War Hammer (whose real name I still didn't know) have to go through sessions with trainers? Maybe they still did. What exactly did trainers do, anyway?

"Big place," I said when I was tired of the quiet. We'd been walking for a good five minutes in absolute silence.

"Davenport's huge," Angélica said amiably. "And growing all the time. Medical sent me your folder this morning. How do you feel?"

How did I feel? Overwhelmed. But not like I had cancer, and not like I was being built up by a weird chemical parasite. I shrugged, dithering between confessing and my usual hang-up about revealing information to people I didn't know well. "I feel okay, I guess. Surviving."

I began to suspect that Angélica might have had psychic powers, for she asked, "Hungry?"

"A little. How'd you know?" There had been three breakfast sandwiches in my refrigerator, which I'd had time to wolf down before Vicki had shown up. But they felt like a distant memory already.

"It's my job to know." Angélica dug into the satchel she wore slung over one shoulder. She handed me a candy-bar-sized silver package. "Go ahead, eat that."

"What is it?" I unwrapped the silver and wrinkled my nose at the nut brown lump it unearthed.

"All you want to know is that it's healthy." She mimed biting into it. "Chomp-chomp."

She was right; I didn't want to know what was in it. Because it tasted a bit like I imagined licking the bottom of a dumpster would. But with Angélica watching, I had no choice but to choke it down. Wordlessly, she passed me a water bottle, and I chugged deeply.

And miracle of all miracles, I felt full for the first time in days.

"We call them crap-cakes among the training staff," Angélica said, taking the water bottle back and stowing it in her satchel. "For a regular human, you could eat that when you first wake up in the morning, and it would release nutrients over the course of twelve hours. So you wouldn't have to eat."

"And for me, how long?"

"With what we'll be doing today? About two hours, so look forward to a lot more of these." She moved her satchel to where I could see inside, and I groaned. It was full of crap-cakes.

"Training Room Fourteen, that's us." Angélica stopped and touched her hand to the screen. The door slid open, and she gestured for me to go first.

"Okay," I said, "but what exactly—"

I never got to finish my question. Mostly because I was too busy dodging the fist that came through the door. I don't know how I sensed it, but in a split second, I'd thrown myself backward, straight into Angélica. Graceless, both of us tumbled back into the wall. I sprang immediately into a low crouch. To do what, I had no idea. But when the owner of the fist came through that door, I was going to be ready.

Nothing of the sort happened. Angélica merely rose, as graceful as I'd been awkward, and adjusted her bright red muscle tee. The door slid closed. "Hmm," she said, looking me up and down again. "That was the most interesting reaction yet."

"Was that on purpose?" I said.

She grinned. "Welcome to training, kid."

My mouth dropped open. "It was! It was on purpose!"

"What, did you think training was going to be a bunch of time on a treadmill?" She laughed.

"Well, probably not," I said, considering I hadn't even really been aware that there would be training at all. "But one can hope."

"We put all of our trainees through the doorway test," Angélica said, touching the screen on the door again. This time, it showed a number pad, and she tapped a sequence of numbers. "Just to see how they react. It's amusing. Most of them get hit in the face."

"What's so amusing about that?"

"Oh, the cursing, usually." Angélica bounced from foot to foot. "Some of the people we get are already honed to the point where they fight back. They've actually gotten some critical hits in on our trainer on the other side of the door. You're the first person to successfully dodge."

The door slid open, and I blinked up at Cooper's massive frame. "Hey," he said. The phantom fist, I realized. He'd been the one behind the door.

"How on earth did you beat us here?" I asked, gawking at him.

"Took a shortcut." He gave me a quick grin. "Angélica, need anything else?"

"I can handle it from here, Coop. Thanks."

Cooper tapped two fingers to his temple in a salute and sauntered off.

"So, you passed the doorway test," Angélica said, and gestured once more for me to precede her.

I crossed my arms over my chest. "After you. I insist."

"Suit yourself." She slung the satchel off of her shoulder and moved into the room.

I stepped forward on high alert, waiting for another attack. If they were willing to try to punch me for walking through a door, what could possibly be next? I had no idea what to make of Davenport, but it didn't take a genius to realize that they employed some rather sadistic people.

Angélica, it turned out, was a lot faster than Cooper. I didn't even sense movement this time before she had both fists clenched in the front of my shirt. She picked me up off the ground as though I weighed little more than a sack of potatoes.

I held very, very still.

"Now," she said, holding me up effortlessly, "time to find out some of your bad habits. What's your fighting experience?"

"Besides shoving somebody at the coffee shop when he got between me and caffeine? Geez, nothing. Let go."

To my surprise, she laughed and dropped me. Instincts I had absolutely no control over kept me from landing flat on my ass.

"I can already see this is going to be fun," she noted.

I straightened my shirt. "Fun for whom?"

Angélica just smiled and raised her voice. She reeled off the date and her last name—Rocha—and a string of numbers that meant little to me. She ended the whole spiel with, "Subject, Gail Godwin, Day One."

"Who're you talking to?" I asked, even as the screen on

the inside of the room, right next to the door, flashed and beeped once. Oh. Some sort of recording device. Great. They were going to be taping the humiliation I was about to endure.

"And now," Angélica said with a gleam in her eye that I was beginning to understand boded ill for me, "we begin."

And she rushed at me.

Chapter Twelve

"Owww."

Every muscle, every tendon, every sinew, every bone, every molecule in my body ached. Not a constant ache, either, but a dull, throbbing pain that ebbed and flowed into my consciousness. In one moment, my body might be completely fine. The next, I would find myself contemplating simply lying down on the mats and quietly dying.

Davenport Industries did not believe in regular physical therapy and training, evidently. Their idea of teaching me how to deal with my new abilities and the fact that I had cancer was to beat the bloody daylights out of me.

Angélica had come at me, forcing me to dodge and fight back. Against Chelsea's henchmen, I hadn't had a problem, but I was starting to realize that Chelsea's henchmen were idiots with no martial skills. Neither of these things applied to Angélica, which was why my body felt like one gigantic bruise.

She'd wanted to see what I knew how to do already, fighting-wise, and that apparently meant letting me rush her over and over, trying to take her down. She either blocked or hit back, depending on whatever move I tried. By the end of the day—a day filled with breaks every two hours so that I could replenish my fuel supply—I'd begun to anticipate some of her moves, but by that point, the damage had been done. She was sneaky, and more than a little mean, and while I enjoyed her sense of humor, I also hated her deeply.

"All right," she said a few hours later, while we both chugged water like shipwreck victims, "I've got a firm grip on your fighting style now. What we'll need to change and tighten up, and outright get rid of. You've already developed habits."

"How?" I said, shoving my hair out of my face. "I'm not a fighter, I haven't fought anybody. The line about the guy in the coffee shop was a joke."

"Movies, television, even books if they were descriptive enough. Don't worry, though, we'll fix all of that."

"Great," I said.

Angélica laughed. "Oh, come now. Get excited. Hostage Girl is learning to fight back."

"But why?" I asked. The use of my nickname made me want to flinch, and it all came rushing down on at me at once. Because I was Hostage Girl, I'd been kidnapped again, and now I had the isotope in my bloodstream. "Why are you teaching me this? Why start with fighting? I have—I have cancer."

"Technically, you do. But unlike most people, you're

not going to have to worry about chemo treatments unless something goes wrong."

I stared at my hands. Leukemia. There was a cancer-ous . . . actually, I didn't know anything about how cancer worked. It was the big C-word that loomed as a constant threat on the horizon, the one you secretly hoped happened to somebody else. But I had it, and it wasn't something I was supposed to worry about because the thing in my blood-stream would just magically keep curing me, apparently.

Maybe I was a little slow for not having arrived at the conclusion sooner, but it had been a stressful few days. I'd faced and sort of held my own for the first time against a villain, I'd been essentially dosed by accident with super-steroids, I'd seen Blaze without his mask and solved the biggest mystery in my life, and I had cancer. I lowered the water bottle slowly. "They can't take it out, can they."

Angélica shook her head. "I was wondering when you were going to figure that out."

"I'm stuck with it, whatever *it* is."

"This is your life now, Gail Godwin." She jumped to her feet and pulled me to mine. There wasn't an ounce of pity on her face. "Welcome to Davenport."

This time, when she rushed me, I at least knew it was coming.

After she declared that I'd had enough for one day, she walked me back to my suite. "We'll do more orientation tomorrow," she said, handing over a bag of crap-cakes. "Right now, focus on getting some rest, read over the stuff Coop gave you. If you have any questions, I'll be by in the morning."

An hour later, I'd showered off the sweat and slid, boneless, onto my new couch. Hunger gnawed semi-insistently at my belly, but I didn't have any food in my suite, and there was no way I was reaching for one of the crap-cakes Angélica had sent with me unless it was life or death. Which, I remembered, it might be. Until we knew more about the thing in my bloodstream, it was safer to eat when I was hungry, rest when I was exhausted, and do everything I could to prevent the isotope from going into overdrive, as that might make the leukemia worse.

Since I really didn't want to think about having leukemia, I looked toward the door. Did I care enough to haul myself down to Vicki's suite? She'd have food. But since the alternative was a crap-cake . . .

I tensed; a second later, somebody knocked on the door. I didn't move. I just listened. The heartbeat, the breathing. The scent.

Guy was at my door.

I was tempted, after last night's intense session, to remain where I was, to let Guy just keep walking. It had yet to settle that somebody who had once been a coworker was the one to beat down doors, to retrieve antidotes whenever I was poisoned, to save my life time and again without wanting any gratitude for it. Those actions spoke of love. When I'd been pretty sure Blaze was Jeremy Collins, I'd been okay with that. We'd been together. The L-word had even been tossed around a couple of times.

But all of those feelings from Guy, whom I barely knew? Emotional overload.

"Gail?" Guy asked when I remained silent. "It's me. Um, Guy."

Another scent hit me just as he announced, "I brought food."

Instantly, I was on my feet and across the suite, tapping the panel to open the door. "You officially have my interest."

"Yes, Angélica said that you get hungry. So I brought this." He held up the brown grocery sack he carried. "Still hot. There are some advantages to being as fast as the wind."

"I bet." I stepped aside to let him in. He wasn't wearing his uniform, so he was closer to the Guy I remembered. Khaki shorts and flip-flops with leather straps, and a designer tee that accentuated his assets almost as well as his uniform did. "You talked to Angélica?"

"Yeah, we're good friends. She trained me, once upon a time." He smiled indulgently, almost fondly. "Has she shown you her powers yet?"

"Besides a freight train of a right hook?"

"Her left hook's worse." Guy set the bag on my kitchen counter and began to unload it.

"Well, if the right hook's not a listed power, it should be," I said, deciding I was too tired to try to play hostess. When Guy gestured at one of the stools at my kitchenette island, I didn't hesitate to take him up on it, and sat. "It gave me this, after all." I touched my left cheekbone, where my eye had been throbbing all day—

And felt nothing.

Guy finished unloading the sack and folded it up. "The reason you're burning through food so fast right now is because you're healing yourself," he said. "Cooper should have explained that to you."

"He, ah, gave me some information to read. I was going to do that."

"Well, *et voilà*." Guy pulled out a full rotisserie chicken and presented it with a flourish. He leaned over to open a cabinet and pull out a couple of plates.

"How do you know where everything is?" I asked him. I'd poked through them, so I knew there were plates in there, but I was pretty sure X-ray vision wasn't part of Guy's listed powers. Unless he'd been keeping that a secret from the public and been checking out what was underneath my clothing for years.

The thought made me just a little uncomfortable.

But he quelled my doubts with another one of his smiles, a lazy one this time. "All the apartments are set up the same way."

"Ah. Do you live here, too, then?"

"No." Guy began to dish food onto the plates quickly and efficiently, which lessened my guilt about not playing hostess. "I live topside, in Miami, but we keep an apartment at headquarters. My brother and I do, I mean. It's on the other end of the complex, though. Quieter. Fewer of the new folks around, discovering their powers day and night."

"Discovering their powers?"

"Yeah. You know. We all get our powers differently, and it can get loud." Guy prepped a second plate, and I found myself watching his hands. There was the grace I recognized from Blaze, who'd always fought a little bit like a dancer. Jeremy was good with his hands, too, but it had seemed different. Not as tightly controlled, I thought. "Especially if they're pyro. Things tend to melt around pyros, especially at first."

"Am I going to get to meet any superheroes, other than the trainers?" I asked, wondering if I'd have to avoid the pyros. I'd never been a fan of my eyebrows, but I kind of liked having them.

"You will," Guy promised. "They're around. There's a community, I guess is how you'd put it. We go topside to live our alter-ego lives, but down here, it's nothing but the truth."

"And the truth about you is . . ." I prompted, suddenly avidly curious about this man. After all, he'd rescued me from countless situations, so he'd seen every side of me there was—and, after the Trouble Twins ambushed me in a satin negligee, quite a bit more than he'd expected. It turns out satin doesn't stand up well to flying at high speeds, running through the woods at night, or class-three rapids. Looking back at that night, I remembered practically getting a sunburn from the force of Blaze's blush, even through the mask.

Now, he smiled, the blush nowhere in evidence. "Rain check? You've had a long day if I remember my own training with Angélica right."

I sat back, slightly disappointed that he wasn't willing to share. He placed a plate in front of me. His own held a lot less, I noticed right away, but I was too busy trying not to attack the food like a starved wolf to be bothered about that. I managed not to slurp, but Emily Post would still not have approved.

Guy didn't comment. "So, I wanted to apologize."

"For what?" I asked warily. We weren't going to have a repeat of last night, were we? Even buoyed by the meal as I was, I didn't think I could handle another punch of Guy's emotions, strong as they were.

"For last night. I, ah, I came on a little strong."

I side-eyed him. "A little?"

He flushed. "Okay, more than a little. I was just so surprised to see you, and it threw me off. I didn't even think about what kind of day you must have had. You were just *there*. And I probably should have tried harder to contain myself."

"It's no big deal," I decided, helping myself to more corn. "We'll forget it."

"I didn't get any sleep last night," he went on, "because I was pretty sure I'd freaked you out, and now you were going to run away or hate me and—"

"It was a crap day all around," I said as I began piling round two of dinner on my plate. "I think all actions are forgivable. I fact, I'm calling an umbrella forgiveness on everything that happened yesterday."

Guy rose to rinse his plate off. "Is Jeremy included in that umbrella forgiveness? He was pretty much being an ass to you."

"It's rough on him," I said, slowly. "Being here. Isn't it?"

"It's not a picnic," Guy said. "He always has the option of reconstructive surgery."

"Surgery?" I actually stopped eating. "Plastic surgery?

Jeremy would never do that. He's way too vain about his looks."

"Probably. I'm sorry he dumped you while you were in the hospital."

"I kind of pushed him into it. Not that that makes it okay, but either way, I'm mostly over it." Apart from a little lingering flame of resentment, but really who had time to stir the fire when these people enjoyed making my life so confusing? And pounding the crap out of me?

"You didn't—" Guy began, but stopped himself. "Okay."

Silence fell as Guy stared at the table, and I continued to load food in. I began to wonder if this was why he'd never talked directly to me as Blaze. Maybe he just didn't have anything to say. The quick looks he kept sneaking at me, however, told me it probably wasn't like that.

"You eat a lot," he finally said, smiling across the island at me.

I grunted. "Well, I'm eating for two now."

Guy's smile vanished. "W-what?"

"Me and the isotope. What did you think I meant to— oh, for the love of—I'm not pregnant. Though god, would that put a cap on this crapper of a week or what?"

"Amen," Guy said.

"Pass the chicken, will you?"

ONCE WE'D FINISHED dinner (well, really, once I'd finished dinner), Guy considerately helped me with the dishes and hunted down containers that let me stow the food in my otherwise-empty fridge. He bade me a polite good-night, and left.

I remained sitting at my kitchen island and watched the door for a good ten minutes after he was gone, trying to puzzle it all out. I'd spent a lot of time wondering who Blaze was, under that mask. Waiting in the elaborate traps the villains liked to build around me had led to more downtime than most would think. After a while, you stop seeing your life flash before your eyes, and your mind wanders to silly little questions. Like, was green his favorite color, or had he picked his costume because of his eyes? Who designed the uniforms?

Now that I knew there was a secret superhero society with a hierarchy and everything, I guess that answered some of my old questions.

When I'd wasted enough time thinking about Guy and his cute blushing, I dragged myself back to the couch and curled up with the glossy packet of materials Cooper had given me. It included the same charts I'd seen on his computer screen when he'd been explaining things to me, as well as detailed breakdowns of what they meant. Side-by-side graphs of what my body could endure versus what a normal body could endure. It was detailed enough to include words like "mitochondria," which I vaguely recalled from biology in high school, but it beat me what it actually meant. And my room didn't come with a computer or a way to access the internet, so I couldn't check Wikipedia.

It looked like I was cut off from everything. At least there wasn't anybody out there to worry about me. Mom and I had run out of things to say to each other before I'd turned fifteen, Dad had never been in the picture, and I had more than enough evidence my coworkers, the people I spent the most time around, would barely realize I was gone. Davenport could keep me for years, and the only one who would notice was probably Naomi Gunn whenever the next big anniversary of my not being kidnapped came around.

It was a little depressing to think about.

There was also a printout of a few pages, stuck in the back, on the types of leukemia. Curious, I flipped through, seeking "Chronic Myelogenous Leukemia," and began to read.

I fell asleep reading what was probably the scariest information of my life.

Even in sleep I was apparently healing, for I woke abruptly in the middle of the night with a growling stomach. I eyed the fridge and decided instead just to bite the bullet. After I choked down another crap-cake (what would become one of many, I feared) and washed it down with two glasses of water, I stumbled back to the bedroom and collapsed into the bed.

Angélica woke me up this time.

She poked me in the shoulder. Awake before I was even aware of it, I scrambled away from her. I opened my eyes to find myself across my bed and staring into the smiling face of the woman who had beaten me to shreds the day before.

"Ready for another day, kid?" she asked brightly.

I squinted up at her. "You're in my room."

"That is where I am, yes."

"Why? Why're you in my room?"

"Because it's time for you to train," Angélica said, as though it were obvious. She smiled down at me, a happy smile that hid the sadism. Today's ensemble was a blue muscle tee and black stretch pants with a blue stripe over the knees. She crossed her arms over her chest. "Out of bed."

Automatically, I glanced around for a clock, but the room lacked one, and my cell phone was gone, lost to whatever had happened with Dr. Mobius. Since Davenport Industries didn't seem to believe in posting clocks everywhere, I was once more stuck in a strange, timeless world.

And that wasn't even my biggest problem. I gave Angélica a long look, sizing her up. "How do I know you won't just attack me?"

"You don't, but I could attack you right there. You'll have to take your chances."

"No thanks," I said, pulling the pillow back over my head.

It was snatched away a second later. "Two minutes."

"Or what?"

"You don't get breakfast."

That was enough to get me moving. I rolled out of bed. Whistling a cheerful tune, she gave me a gleeful wave and left. Two minutes later, freshly changed into workout clothes, I walked into my kitchen to find her scrambling eggs.

My mouth immediately began to water. "Oh, thank god, it's not a crap-cake."

"You get real food today, at least for a little while. I don't plan to beat on you until this afternoon." She grinned over her shoulder at me. "And that'll be fun."

"I'm buying you a dictionary with the proper definition of 'fun' in it," I said. I pulled down plates. "So what's on the agenda for the day, then? If you're not going to spend it beating me to itty-bitty pieces of Gail?"

At that, Angélica chortled. She had a genuine laugh, I'd noticed the day before. Just like she had a genuine hug. When we'd both finished fighting—by the end of the day I'd gotten a few hits in as well—Angélica had grabbed me in a one-armed hug and declared herself proud of my progress. "We're going to make a hero out of you yet," had been her words.

Now, standing at my stove, she grinned. "I think I'm going to like you."

"Does that mean you'll stop beating on me with regularity?"

"Probably just means I'll beat harder."

"Oh, joy." I took a seat on the stool since it was obvious I couldn't do anything.

I was wrong there, it turned out. "I brought orange juice with me," Angélica said without looking at me—I was beginning to suspect that she had eyes in the back of her head. "And you could make some toast."

"Aye-aye, sir," I said, and hopped off the stool to put bread into the toaster I didn't even know I had. I poured both her and myself tall glasses of orange juice. She set hers aside; I gulped mine down and went for more.

"Water, too," she said, nodding at the drinking-water

faucet in my sink. "First thing you should do in the mornings is drink a huge glass of water. Rehydrate what you lost in the night."

"With my metabolism, I should probably drink an entire swimming pool," I said, but I obediently filled my glass with water and drained that, too.

Angélica smiled. "You know, people have to work out for hours and hours to get the kind of body you've got now. Just think of that whenever you're—"

"Regularly eating amounts that most people only attempt at Thanksgiving?"

"Exactly."

When she'd finished cooking, we sat down together at my island, just as Guy and I had the night before. I wondered if it was going to be a habit for people to bring me food. I didn't mind, but it would also get tiring living on the good grace of those around me. I really needed to figure out a better food situation at some point.

"We'll review the log from yesterday," Angélica said before I could ask about that, "and you can get a good look at your form, and mine. We'll break for lunch, then head back to the training room and get started breaking some of those bad habits of yours."

Since I imagined breaking those bad habits involved throwing me onto the floor, repeatedly, I slumped. "Goody."

"We're going to start teaching you training stances and katas. And I may have one of the other trainers come in and teach you some yoga stretches to improve balance and standing strength."

"I thought the isotope stuff was keeping me as strong as I can get," I said, pausing between inhaling mouthfuls of scrambled egg.

"It isn't yet," Angélica said. "It'll be another week before you're at your full potential. Your body has muscle memory, and disciplining that muscle memory is the best thing you can do before you join the fighting ranks."

"That's an option?"

She eyed me. "For you, a strong one. Kiki told me what happened at the bank."

I wrinkled my nose at her. "I got my ass kicked?"

"Took on a couple of guys with guns."

"I think I got lucky."

Angélica waved her fork at me. "And facing down Chelsea?"

"I . . . don't know." I frowned and scooped up more eggs. "I don't like to see people in pain, after all that I went through, getting kidnapped so much and having Blaze—Guy—rescue me. Which is also something I'm not sure I want to think about yet, so if you're going to ask, um, please don't."

"Fair enough," Angélica said. "But I think you did it because you're hero material."

I snorted. "Hardly. I'm Hostage Girl. My shtick is getting kidnapped. That's all."

"No, you're Gail Godwin, Class C. Now what you do is train to be a hero. Are you done with your eggs?"

I forked up the last bit and swallowed quickly, lest Angélica should decide that putting distance between food and me was part of my training. "So where're we going now? Back to the training room?"

"There." Angélica pointed at my couch. "Might as well be comfortable while I tell you every single thing you're doing wrong. Then, we go to the training room."

"You know, I had a feeling when I woke up that this was going to be a very painful morning."

"That's not from waking up, that's from seeing my face." Angélica slung a friendly arm over my shoulders as she led me to the couch.

"Um, Angélica?"

"Yes?" She licked her thumb and turned the page.

"I know you said I'm supposed to trust you implicitly."

"You are." Another page turned.

"And I do, I guess. But I'll admit I'm confused."

Now Angélica actually looked up from her magazine. "About what?"

"About this?" I gestured at my feet. "About why I'm standing here. Like this."

"It's about standing strength. You're relying too much on your upper body—not surprising, since I imagine the only time you've seen fighting is when it's TV actors going at each other with poor choreographers. Even though you're better than most beginners about using your legs to drive you, we want you in optimal condition. So . . . you get to stand like that."

"Lucky me." I looked down at my feet, which were spread wide, toes pointing forward, putting me into a squat. As per Angélica's instructions, my shoulders were back, my sit-bones (her words, not mine) tucked under. I kept my head up straight.

I felt ridiculous.

"Can't I at least have something to read, too?" I asked, wanting to shift my feet. I knew better; the last time I'd tried, Angélica had risen to her feet specifically to rap my knuckles. I was beginning to suspect that underneath that trainer's body beat the heart of a fussy old schoolmarm.

"If you're busy reading, you're not concentrating on your form," Angélica said, returning her attention to her reading. "You should be thinking of each muscle in your legs, one at a time. Individually, and how they work together. What they can do for you."

"Oh, now, when you put it that way . . ." I made a face.

Angélica's watch beeped. "My favorite part," she said, smiling. "Deep breath. Deep, deep breath."

Slowly, I drew air into my lungs, copying the hand movements she'd showed me after lunch. They helped me focus though I wasn't going to admit that and prove her point. Not when she got to read magazines while I stood in awkward positions all afternoon.

"And now exhale," she said, "and sink deeper into your legs."

I did so, lowering my sit-bones even closer to the floor than they had been. "If I were a vindictive person," I said once I'd finished my breathing exercise, "I'd get a dartboard and put your picture on it."

She smirked and twitched a shoulder but didn't look up from her magazine. "It wouldn't be the first time."

Chapter Thirteen

THERE WASN'T A lot to do after Angélica let me go for the night. I had a very restricted list of people who could see me, and my suite didn't come with any books or a new cell phone. Davenport apparently believed in keeping new superheroes in an anti-media bubble away the world. I had no idea what was going on outside of Davenport. Angélica had handed me a big stack of papers that Cooper had given her to pass along to me, but after about ten pages of scientific nonsense, I'd given in and taken a nap on the couch instead. My brain might understand science now, but that didn't mean I found it any less boring.

I woke up from my nap to the sound of light tapping on the door.

"Hey-hey," Vicki said when I opened the door. She pulled me into a one-armed hug. "Guy says you eat a lot, so we brought dinner."

Jeremy nudged past us, holding a full grocery sack of

something that smelled delicious though I hadn't officially invited them in. "Lasagna still your favorite?"

"Always and forever." I raised my eyebrows, surprised that he remembered.

Vicki sashayed into the room, immediately taking one of the island stools. Since I had the energy and inclination to play hostess, I quickly unloaded the supplies and began dishing it up. "What are you two up to tonight?" I asked.

"Just got off work," Jeremy said, tugging at the collar of his polo shirt. "Went a few rounds with Striker, for old times' sake. He designed the original simulators, and I've made a few tweaks. He liked them."

"Wow. Busy day." I wondered if it was as rough on Jeremy as Guy and I had supposed. After all, he had achieved his lifelong dream of playing video games for a living. There were worse fates to be had. I turned my attention to Vicki, who was idly swinging one leg back and forth. "How about you? How'd the, ah, shoot go?"

"Stupid outfit, dumb expression. The photographer swore up and down I wouldn't look like an idiot, but . . ." Vicki twirled one hand as if to say, 'What can you do?'

"Can't be as bad as that shoot you did for *Beautiful Woman* last month," Jeremy said.

"Yuck, please, let's never talk about that ever again," Vicki said. When she saw my curious look, she sighed. "The photographer had a tulle fetish. And I still had that awful red hair." She fluffed a hand through it. "Girl, do me a favor. If I decide that I'd like to be a redhead again, send me down to Psych so that they can fix whatever's wrong with me."

"I can do that," I said, and slid plates across to them. The model wannabes at my old office had been on a never-ending list of diets, but Vicki dug into the lasagna with gusto, ignoring the salad. I had to figure it was probably different for supermodels when they moonlighted as superheroes. I fixed up my own plate and took a seat. Angélica had warned me to stay away from alcohol for a little while, so I stuck to water instead of the beers they'd brought with them. Something that I'd thought about before my nap flitted to the top of my mind. "Vicki, I've been wondering . . ."

"Hmm?" She leaned over to break off a piece of the garlic bread.

"You said something a couple of nights ago about my being a legend?"

To my surprise, Jeremy snorted into his beer. Vicki nudged him with an elbow. "What about it?" she asked.

"What did you mean?"

"You haven't been down to the Nucleus yet," Vicki said.

This did not seem like an answer to my question. "The what?" I asked.

"The Nucleus. It's the main office for this place. And there's a chart on the wall."

"Of what?"

"Of how many times you've been kidnapped and your odds of surviving the next bout with the villains."

My jaw dropped. "You're kidding."

Vicki had the grace to at least seem embarrassed. "You've got some pretty long odds going on there."

"I placed a bet on you," Jeremy said, tipping the mouth of his beer bottle toward me in a weird toast. "For you to survive, that is. Call it sentiment or something."

"Or something is right," I said. "They *bet* on if I would live or die? Is *everybody* in this place secretly an asshole?"

Vicki gestured with her beer bottle. "It's just the way we operate sometimes. A lot of the active heroes have seen so much . . . so much bad stuff, you know? Botched kidnappings, random acts of evil that will make you sick for a month just thinking about them. So we're all a little morbid because it helps us get by."

That was my life—my overworked, unimpressive life— they were betting on, so the sympathy wasn't exactly flow-ing. One particularly philosophical villain had spent the time we waited for Blaze to loudly debate with himself about the minimal differences between superheroes and supervillains. He'd been attempting to use rat poison to kill off the population of half of Chicago at the time, so I hadn't exactly thought the line of morality was as murky as he had claimed.

Maybe I had been wrong.

"Did Guy ever bet?" I asked.

"Never," Vicki said. "The first time he saw the chart, he tore it down and kicked Sharkbait's ass."

"Um," was all I could say to that. "Wow."

"Yeah. Sharkbait had it coming."

"Sharkbait's kind of a dick," Jeremy said, nodding.

"But since he's Guy, he apologized about the ass-kicking thing. Eventually."

"Does he get ribbed a lot? For all the times I get kidnapped?" I asked. "Or I guess you could say 'got kidnapped.'" I crossed my fingers.

"Some." Vicki returned her focus to her lasagna, digging in with renewed gusto. "But everybody gets teased for something down here."

"Speaking of 'down here,'" I said.

"What about it?"

"I mean, it's great that I have people looking out for me and making sure I don't die of cancer and all, but what do I do about my apartment? I mean, I can't exactly afford rent there, but I need to go pack everything up so that I have stuff here."

"If Angélica deigns to give you a day off, I'll take you topside, and you can pack up your apartment. You can put it in storage. Davenport'll cover it."

A cell phone burst to life with a mambo ringtone, making me jerk and reach for my butter knife. Jeremy noticed and gave me an odd look, but it sailed completely over Vicki's head as she freed her phone from her pocket. Her eyes lit up. "It's Sam!"

And before I could ask who that was, she danced out of my apartment.

Jeremy's look immediately soured. "Great," he said. "*Now* he calls her."

"Who's Sam?" I asked.

"You know him better as War Hammer. Your new boyfriend's brother."

"My new boyfriend?" Oh, I realized. He meant Guy. "We're not dating. And *what*?"

"War Hammer is Sam Bookman."

"Blaze and War Hammer are brothers?" I asked. Guy had a brother? He'd said it last night, but it hadn't quite sunk in. I was pretty sure Guy had never mentioned him at work, but maybe I simply hadn't noticed. For as little attention as Guy had apparently paid me, I'd given him very little mind.

It made me wonder just what he saw in me.

"You really didn't know," Jeremy said.

"What?"

"About any of it." He studied me with narrowed eyes, idly playing with his beer. "You didn't think I was Blaze, but you didn't know *he* was, either. Tell me, how's it feel to be such a genius?"

"I don't know. Let me ask the moron who dumped me while I was in the hospital."

His shoulders immediately drooped. The hit had apparently struck true, for he ran a hand over his face. "I said I was sorry about that. I tried to avoid it, but it's impossible to keep secrets from you. Especially when you know something's up. You're like a damn dog with a bone."

"Thank you," I said in a frosty voice, "for that flattering portrait of me."

"You know what I mean." Jeremy scowled. "I felt bad. I still do, actually. It wasn't fair."

It was nice to have that vindication even though it was months late. And I'd come to realize that even though I might be super-powered now, I was still in a strange environment and surrounded by a new group of people, Guy included. Having a familiar ally in my corner, even if it was Jeremy and his attitude, was more valuable to me than being right or winning a stupid argument. So I shook my head. "You know what? It's in the past. Let's move on. But I have to ask: why are you being such an ass about Guy?"

"I dunno." He shoved his hands into his pockets and leaned back against the counter. "Maybe it's nice to have something on the ever-perfect Blaze for once."

"Fair. Do me a favor, though. If you're going to needle Guy, don't use me as a conduit. I want nothing to do with it."

"Sorry," Jeremy said. His lips twitched in the way I remembered they did when he was trying not to smile.

I scooped up my final bite of lasagna and carried my plate to the sink. "So they really have simulators here? Like what pilots use?"

"Better." Jeremy gave me a nerdy grin. But he didn't, as I'd feared, launch into a long stream of chatter about coding and other undead geek languages. "The interface is just—we can do so much with it, and it's light-years ahead of everything, you know? We can implant images and sensations directly into your brain with these headsets, make you feel like you're flying, things like that."

"You could really make me believe I was flying?"

"With one of those headsets on you, I could make you believe you'd died and come back as a chicken," Jeremy said. "A purple chicken."

"There are worse fates."

"Want to try it out? Not like either of us have anything else to do right now."

I eyed Vicki's plate, which still had half of her food on it. "What about Vicki?"

"Bet you anything that in about two minutes she comes back in here and tells us she has a hot date." Jeremy lifted his beer to his lips and eyed the door, which had not yet opened.

In turn, I studied him, my eyes narrowed. "Oh for the love of—you've got a thing for her, don't you?"

"Shut up!" he said. When I gave him a puzzled look, he mouthed, 'She's got ears like a cat!'

"Oh." I lowered my voice. "How long?"

"I can't talk about this. Not with you." Jeremy gave his beer bottle a broody look. When he saw my steely-eyed look, he sighed. "Fine. But not here? Away from . . ." He trailed off and jerked a thumb at the door.

My ex. In love with Plain Jane.

Somehow, the thought of Jeremy and Plain Jane together was even weirder than seeing all of those paparazzi photos of him with Vicki Burroughs, supermodel.

"So I'm guessing she has no idea?" I asked.

He mimed zipping his lip and throwing away the key just as the door opened, and Vicki bubbled back into the room. "I'm going to have abandon you," she said without preamble. "Something came up."

"I bet it did," Jeremy said.

I shot him a look, hoping to express that sarcasm wasn't going to win him any favors from the girl he was crushing on. He ignored it.

"Is it okay if I take a rain check?" Vicki asked me, ignoring Jeremy as easily as he ignored me.

"Sure, it's no problem." I gave her a smile and a little wave. "Go on, enjoy your 'something.'"

"Oh trust me," she said, "I will."

She sailed out, leaving a cloud of jasmine perfume in her wake.

Jeremy polished off his beer with a final scowl at the door. "Let's go play with the simulators so that I can get my mind off her always being at that dumbass's beck and call. What's *with* you women, anyway? Why do you always go for losers?"

"Do you really want to get into that conversation with *me*?" I asked.

He considered that. "Point taken."

DAVENPORT ENJOYED CONSTANTLY subverting my expectations. After the futuristic training rooms, with their quiet tech, I expected the simulator rooms to be dark, full of green and purple light, and possibly filled with obstacles. Instead, Jeremy led me into a spacious, well-lit room with curved walls. There were mats on the floor.

"I know," he said without looking at me, "you'd think it would be some sci-fi junk or whatever. Nope, this is it." He jerked his head at the wall. "Eternity walls. Trust me when I tell you that once I start programming bad guys coming at you, you'll appreciate not smashing your face into a corner."

"I thought I was here to fly," I said. I'd had more than my share of bad guys.

"You are," Jeremy said. "But, you know, if you get bored and want to fight some bad guys . . ."

"And have Angélica tear me to tiny little pieces when

she finds out I've wrecked the form she's been teaching me? The woman may be small, but it's like getting gut-punched by a bear. Nothing but flying tonight."

"Fine." Jeremy heaved a giant sigh. "If you insist."

"I do."

"All right, then we'll put this on you." Jeremy held up a headset that he'd gone into a smaller room to retrieve. "Fit that over your ears and cinch it down in the back so that it's snug. I'm going to put these on your forehead. They'll help you get the sensory part of the simulator." He held up a couple of vividly green suction cups.

"Fashionable," I said dryly.

He grinned. "They do the trick. Besides, I thought you liked green."

"Ha, ha." It was the wrong green. Blaze's uniform was a little darker. I stood still as he fixed the suction cups onto my forehead. "So . . . you don't mind it here, do you? Like really mind it?"

His hand stilled on the suction cups. "You're probably the last person I want to talk to about this, okay?"

I understood. It was my fault, indirectly, that he was here. So I nodded.

"Don't move your head, I'm still getting these on you."

"I'm sorry," I said.

He caught the subtext. This time, he sighed, a drawn-out noise. He stepped back to look at me. Not intensely. Just so that he could make eye contact. "Oh, well," he said. "It's not like it's your fault, really. Not like you were asking to become Hostage Girl, right?"

"Yeah, that was a gift I always wanted to return." And

now I was living and existing near said superhero and that was a little weird for me. I frowned when Jeremy pulled out his cell phone and aimed it at the suction cups on my head. "What are you doing?"

"Calibrating the interface." Something buzzed in the back of my head, and I frowned. It hurt a little, but the pain faded almost right away.

So instead I stared jealously at Jeremy's phone. "I wish I had one of those."

"A holographic interface?"

"No, stupid. A phone."

He lowered the phone. "Davenport didn't issue you one?"

I grumbled under my breath. "I'm in a media blackout. My TV doesn't even work, and they're not telling me anything, so I have *no* idea what happened to the guy who did this to me. It's really annoying."

"Is it? I'm feeling really disconnected from everything, but mostly I just want a phone so I can play games again." I wasn't the gamer that Jeremy was—he liked first-person shooters and role-play games, and I was content trying to get to new levels on Happy Pigs—but I bet with my new, isotope-given reflexes, I'd have some killer high scores. "You never really know how much you miss having a phone until you don't have one."

"Media blackout? That's weird, even for them." He pocketed the phone and adjusted something on my headset, and the buzzing in the back of my head started up again.

"How'd you lose the old one?"

"Not sure, but I'm going to guess Dr. Mobius trashed it."

Thinking about Dr. Mobius made me wonder again. My memories from the night he'd woken me up and drugged me were still patchy, but I distinctly remembered that he'd said "they're here," not "Blaze is here." Though maybe it was a good thing that my memory wasn't the greatest as I really didn't want to relive getting hit with a minivan in stark detail, honestly.

"Girl." Something touched my shoulder, and before I knew exactly what I was doing, I'd grabbed it and twisted it around. Jeremy yelped when I shoved his arm behind his back, expertly pinning him to the wall. "Uncle! I give! Let go!"

"Oh." I dropped him and stumbled back a step. "Sorry—sorry, reflex. I, ah. Just, sorry."

Jeremy wiggled his arm to bring circulation back and whistled. "Wow. I am *never* sneaking up on you. *Ever.* Damn." He hopped around, still shaking his shoulder and arm. "What were you even thinking about?"

"I, ah, I got distracted, sorry. I didn't mean to, just now, with you and the wall . . ."

"Either way." He sounded a bit strangled, and naturally so. His five-foot-tall ex had pinned him to the wall. Something in his eyes told me he hadn't really put it together that I was superhuman now. He kept a healthy distance from me. "I've connected the electrodes, and they've started their currents. How do you feel?"

"I think I'm okay." The buzz was growing a little, but I figured that was just part of the hologram program.

"Okay. I'm just going to be in the other room. If it gets to be too much, just shout, and I'll end the program." He grinned. "But yeah, let's see how you fly without a super-hero carrying you."

He left me alone, closing the door behind him. I didn't see any observation windows in the walls, but that didn't surprise me. There were cameras in the corners. After a second, I heard the tiny whine that preceded an announcement over a loudspeaker, and Jeremy's voice filled the room. "Activating the program now. Brace yourself, okay? It's a bit of a shock."

I nodded, since I figured he could see me, and settled into a resting stance.

"Three . . . two . . . one . . . Activating."

The lights in the room dimmed. My fingertips started to twitch inward, a tic I'd never noticed before. "Is, um, something supposed to be happening?"

"I'm not—actually, just wait for it, it's taking a minute to load . . ."

"Okay." My insides began to tingle, starting in my chest. I felt a bit short of breath as the twitch in my finger-tips grew bigger, moving from my palm, traveling up my wrists and into my elbows. My arms began to shake.

"Jeremy, I don't think this is such a good ide—" was all I got out before darkness crashed in, taking me away from the room and its eternity walls.

Chapter Fourteen

"Did I say it was okay for you to try the simulators?"

"No, Angélica."

"Did I in any way, shape, or form even *hint* that it was okay for you to go anywhere near the simulators?"

My back hurt. "No, Angélica."

"So what I want to know, in that case, is why you did, when you knew full well that you've got an isotope that has to be considered in every move you make?"

"Angélica." From where he sat, across the room, Guy looked up from his book. "Give it a rest. She had no idea what the simulators would do to her."

While I was grateful for Guy's support, I had to bite my tongue before I pointed out that I could fight my own battles. He had two years' worth of anecdotes to prove that wasn't actually the case. And besides, my battle at the moment was with a very irate Angélica, and I'd already learned trying to win against her was a long charge headfirst into futility. At least she'd stopped swearing at me in Portuguese.

"In my defense," I said, wanting to move my feet and knowing better, "I told Jeremy that I didn't think it was a good idea. I just realized it too late."

Angélica scowled and did another backflip. That was how she controlled her anger, I'd discovered. She'd been at it for hours while I worked on my standing strength. Oh, yes. Hours and hours. I knew that because we were rounding hour three. Guy's watch, on my wrist, said so.

I'd woken up in a strange room to find Kiki at my bedside. "You have visitors," she'd said once she'd checked that I was awake and cognizant. "Jeremy sent you flowers. I said that it wasn't a big deal, but he was pretty insistent. I kept them on the nightstand for you."

"Thanks," I said, and promptly tried to crack my jaw open with a wide yawn. "Where am I?"

"Medical. You've been out for twelve hours or so. Want me to let the visitors in?"

"Um, who are they?"

"Angélica and Guy."

Slowly, I sat up. For the first time in forever, I appeared to have woken up in a hospital room and nothing hurt. "Can I take a rain check on that? I need a hairbrush and a minute."

"No problem." As if by magic, Kiki produced one from her satchel.

"You must be psychic," I said as I tackled my curls.

"You're hilarious." She'd brought breakfast with her, and she sat with me, chatting about what had happened.

Apparently Jeremy had short-circuited me by accident. When I finished relating my take on the incident, Kiki gave me an assessing stare.

"And why didn't you try to stop Jeremy?" she asked.

I felt an invisible pressure against the front of my head, so I leaned back, away from her. "I thought it was part of the simulation."

She paused. "You felt that, just now?"

"Yeah, it was weird. What was it?"

"Your brain is a fascinating one, that's all," Kiki said.

"Was that *you*? Were you—were you trying to read my mind?"

She rose and brushed crumbs off of her pants. "I'm going to let Guy and Angélica in. Brace yourself. She's on the warpath."

"What for?" I asked. I hadn't done anything wrong. It hadn't been my fault that I'd blacked out.

Angélica hadn't seen it that way. Which was why, hours after sharing breakfast with Kiki, I was back in the training room, working on my standing strength with my trainer routinely doing backflips to control her temper and my own personal superhero sitting across the room with a book in his lap.

His reaction, by the way, had been the opposite of Angélica's ire. He'd come into my room that morning with her and laid his single rose on the bedside table by my empty breakfast plate. And had said in a mock-weary voice, "I go away to play guardian of the city for *one night*, and you manage to get yourself in trouble."

"Just proves I don't need you around to make trouble, that's all," I had said.

He'd laughed.

Now, six hours later, Angélica gave him a narrow-eyed look. "Why aren't you at a board meeting or whatever it is you spoiled rich boys pretend to do during the day?"

Guy looked absolutely relaxed in his khaki shorts and T-shirt. His feet were bare, just like mine. "I called in sick. I missed you and your sunny personality," he said, smiling sweetly at her.

"Hah," she said, but I felt her laugh. "You're just here for Girl."

"Too right I am," he said, and I felt a trill of excitement up my spine.

Angélica whipped around to glare at me. "Let's review," she said, and Guy shot me a sympathetic look that she ignored. "Are you allowed anywhere near the simulators?"

"No," I said, not bothering to sigh. She would only scold me for it. "And if I'm thinking about changing my diet, sleep schedule, workout schedule, if I want to have sex"—I did not look at Guy—"if I want to go on a three-day bender, if I want to visit Miami and dance naked on the beach. Any of that, I check with you first."

"Damn right you do," she said.

I noticed that Guy was staring rather intently at his book. He hadn't turned the page in a while. I wondered if he was thinking of the Negligee Fiasco. Great. And *I* was thinking about the Negligee Fiasco. And about just how well Guy filled out that T-shirt, and his skintight uniform and . . .

To make myself focus on my stance and back on matters at hand, I took a deep breath. "Why do superheroes wear such bright colors?" I asked without thinking. "I mean, you have to admit most of the outfits aren't the least bit fashionable. Look at Shark-Man."

"Sharkbait," Angélica said fondly, grinning.

Guy's intent look turned into a scowl.

"His outfit has to be the dumbest thing I've ever seen," I said, trying not to concentrate too much on the fact that Sharkbait was the one Guy had beaten up over my life-or-death odds chart. Whoops. "I mean, does the man just love the color gray or something?"

"Sharkbait's the odd man out," Guy said, closing a finger in his book to mark his place. He regarded me. "We wear bright colors so that people will see us coming."

"But won't the villains see you coming, too?"

"That doesn't matter." Guy shrugged at my dubious look. "Bright colors signify the hope we're bringing to the people we rescue."

I remembered how safe I'd always felt whenever I'd seen the flash of green streaking the horizon, knowing that Blaze had arrived at long last to pull me out of whatever stupid situation the villains had created. And I totally understood Guy's point.

Guy wasn't finished. He nodded at Angélica. "If you want to talk about bright costumes, ask this one here."

Her eyes narrowed dangerously. "Don't you dare."

"Bright, burns-your-corneas red," Guy said. "A one-piece with a little red sash and a red headband. Quite a fashion statement."

I turned my head to gawk at Angélica. "You were on active duty? How come you didn't tell me? And why are you in here training me when you're good enough to be out there saving the day?"

"One question at a time," she said, still glaring at Guy in a way that promised payback. "Yes, I was on the front lines, as you put it. I was happy there, but you have to follow your calling. My calling, Gail, is to help my fellow superheroes. Many of us come here without a clue of what we can do, how far we can push ourselves. If we know that, then we know what we can do to help. I like helping people discover that."

"By punching them in the face?" I asked.

"We do," Angélica said, "what we can do to help. And for that little bit of attitude, you can spread your feet wider."

I sighed and obeyed, though my thighs ached like nothing else.

"And you've never heard of me unless you're familiar with the Rio de Janeiro lineup of superheroes, so there's no need to bother you with my alias," Angélica said in a tone that signaled that this was all she was going to tell me about that.

I was dying of curiosity, but I nodded. Pushing Angélica to tell me something she didn't want to usually ended in bruises. "Red, huh? How bright was it?" I asked instead.

"My outfit was not as garish as Guy claims. I like color. I do not feel there is anything wrong with that." She batted at her ear so that the silver dangles with the bright yellow beads glittered and sparkled in the light. "And Guy had better stop giving away my secrets if he knows what's good for him."

Guy snickered. "She's probably right, but you know how it is, Gail. It's fun to bait her."

"If you say so," I said. "What about you, Guy? What's your calling?"

I didn't see him tense; I felt it. It was like the air currents between us electrified and jumped to life. I'd stumbled upon a touchy subject.

Angélica rescued me this time. "He likes to save the pretty girls," she said, and tapped my shoulder with the back of her hand. "Step your right foot forward more and stretch out your hips."

I asked the question that always seemed to be on my mind nowadays. "When's lunch?"

"Stretch your hips, kid." Angélica mock-scowled. "Now, for one more time, let's review. Somebody says, 'Hey, let's go play in the simulators,' and you say . . ."

I sighed. "No, Angélica."

"Good."

"But seriously. Lunch?"

AFTER LUNCH, ANGÉLICA declared herself tired of me, and headed back to talk to Cooper and Kiki about the effects of my stunt the night before.

"How do you feel?" Guy asked, as we left the cafeteria.

"Like I had a tiny, terrifying Brazilian woman glaring ferociously at me all morning."

He grinned at that. "She really likes you."

"If you say so. How long did you have to train with her before you went into the field?"

"Not long. I was . . . a special circumstance is probably the best way to put it. I was already seeking out villains to fight before Davenport discovered me."

"So was I, though I didn't actually seek anybody out," I said. "Davenport wouldn't have nabbed me if not for Chelsea. And if it hadn't been Chelsea, it would have been some other villain some other day. I'm foolhardy that way."

"Where are you getting that idea?"

"I don't know. Past experience, probably."

His frown deepened. "You don't think the villain attacks are your fault, do you?"

"I didn't always help things along," I said. "You remember what happened with Shock Value—"

"Let's not talk about Shock Value." He made a face.

"Yeah, his costume, talk about design flaws."

"No, I mean . . ." He broke off and cleared his throat. "Gail, do you know why you're a legend?"

I turned my head to give him a look, trying to figure out where he was going with this. I wasn't sure I liked being a legend within a secret society like this one. "Because there's a chart betting on whether I'll survive the next villain attack?"

"Who told you about that? Actually, never mind, I know who. You're a legend because you've survived things that not even a cockroach could."

I wrinkled my nose at that mental image. "Yuck."

"I mean it. If it had been anybody else in all of those hostage situations and train derailings and every other thing those bastards put you through . . ." For a moment, he looked to be in actual pain. I almost reached up to pat his arm or something, but pulled my hand back. We weren't on that level yet. "If it had been anybody else, they wouldn't have survived it."

"I don't know about that," I said.

Guy shook his head. "And you're selfless. After all you've been through, you'd think you would be the first one out through the doors when the bank's held up, or a madman takes over the mall. But you always insist on others going first. Every time."

"Whoa, whoa, wait a minute. You're giving me way too much credit."

"Am I?" Guy continued to stare at the floor. I wished he would look at me.

"You are," I said. "I made the others go first because I knew you would be there. Corny as it sounds, until you went to Miami, you had a perfect batting average of saving my life. Others might not have been so lucky. So it's not selfless if I know I'm going to be okay."

"What if you hadn't been okay?" Guy asked.

"I had faith that you were going to be there. And you were."

Guy finally looked up from the tiles to meet my eyes. "You really did," he said, tilting his head. "Didn't you?"

"I tend to be honest to the point of blunt," I said. Something fluttered low in my belly. Without the mask, his eyes looked different. Not as vibrant, and softer and friendlier. "I'm not that complex. If I like a person, I tend not to lie to them."

Slowly, he smiled. "So you like me, huh?"

"I mean, you're okay, I wouldn't get a big head or anyt—hey!" I laughed when he gave me a tiny shove to the shoulder. "So that's how it is, huh?"

Guy bit his lower lip, but he was smiling now instead of looking serious. "You asked about my place," he said. "Would you like to come see it?"

"Sure. It's not like I have anything else to do."

"I heard. I've got a fix for that."

And he led me in the opposite direction of my modest little suite.

"Wow. Just—just wow. All of this is *yours*?" In wide-eyed wonder, I did a slow rotation in the middle of Guy's loft, drinking in the sheer amount of space.

Guy shifted his feet, a bit embarrassed now that I was gawking like a tourist. "Not all mine. I share it with Sam."

"War Hammer," I said, and earned a surprised look. "Vicki had a date with him last night."

"Yeah, they're . . . a thing." He tilted his head, considering something I couldn't understand, and shrugged. "Vicki's a big girl. She can handle him."

I closed my lips over a lasciviously crude remark.

In a normal city, Guy's rent would have been through the roof. Not that he'd have a problem with that, seeing as he had probably come into an inheritance that would make even the most miserly of bankers goggle. His place would have been one of those artsy apartments, ones that seemed real only in movies where you wondered how two poor twentysomethings could afford such a space.

It was an open, two-story area. A sort of sitting room was shoved toward the back beside a wall of windows, but the dominant feature of the room was a large, olive green training mat. Nearby was a set of weights and barbells, and a punching bag. "Sam uses this space more than I do," Guy said.

"Aren't you and War Hammer supposed to be extremely strong?" I eyed the denominations on the barbells with interest.

"Davenport's got ways to make us normal if we want to work out like regular guys. You know, temporarily."

"Why would you want to do that?"

"Sometimes it feels good to just let loose and lift some weights." Guy shrugged. "Sam's got a lot of frustration. I have . . . no, had. I had my fair share of it, too."

I gave him a sage look. "You hated Angus as much as I did, didn't you?"

"He's such a jerk. Anyway, bedrooms are on the second level," Guy went on, leading me out of the training area and gesturing at the spiral staircase. He headed into a kitchen area, with a huge fridge, an indoor grill, and at least three sinks. They even had a prep sink.

"You cook?" I asked, surprised to see so many chef's tools on the counters. "I thought, being Bookmans, you guys would just have maids or cooks. You know, hired help."

"We did when we were kids." Guy smiled. "But I hate

having too many people around. When I first came into my powers, I was always hungry. Kind of like you now. Only I've always been a picky eater. So it was either hire a chef, battle it out at the cafeteria, or learn to cook."

"Let me get this straight." Surreptitiously, I ran a fingertip over the bread-dough mixer and checked it. No dust. "You can cook, you're built, you spend your spare time saving damsels in distress, pulling kittens out of trees, and helping little old ladies across the street. And you're telling me you're not secretly a robot? I don't think you exist."

He laughed. "I've never helped a little old lady across the street in my life. Geez."

"You didn't deny my robot accusation," I pointed out.

"Want a water?"

"Sure."

He opened the fridge, pulled two water bottles out, and tossed one to me. "Trust me, not a robot."

I narrowed my eyes at him over the water bottle. "Prove it."

With a shrug, he yanked up his sleeve, and I saw a three raised lines of scarred skin just under his shoulder. "Robots don't have these."

"Clever ones might. And by these, do you mean—" I reached out and poked him. "The muscles or the scars?"

His grin was surprise and delight rolled into one. It lit up his face. "If I have to be a robot, I'll be a clever one. There are worse things to be."

Like radioactive, I thought, but Angélica had assured me that that had worn off. So I grinned back at him and dropped my hand to my side. "I don't really think you're a robot."

"And I don't really think I'm all that clever." He ducked his head, still smiling. "But we all have our own battles to—"

Sensing something I couldn't even describe, I tensed. And less than a split second later, a voice called, "Hello?"

Guy gave me an odd look before he turned. "Hey, Sam. We're in the kitchen if you want to join us."

I looked up to see someone coming down the spiral stairs. When he came fully into view, one of my eyebrows shot up.

Sam Bookman was like a finished version of his brother. Where Guy was built along slender lines, Sam was brute *presence*. A Cubs T-shirt strained over a heavily muscled chest, showcasing arms as thick as tree trunks. While Guy's hair was burnished and coppery and sort of feathered around his head, Sam had a burnished blond buzz cut. They shared the same long, aquiline nose, though.

"Gail, this is my brother Sam. Sam, you remember Gail." Guy gestured at each of us in turn with his water bottle.

A corner of Sam's mouth tilted up. "I fished you out of a dumpster once."

"For which I will be forever grateful to you," I said immediately. "Especially if you never mention it again."

Sam gave me a full grin this time and headed toward the refrigerator. "She's cute," Sam told Guy, as if I weren't standing right there. Guy at least had the sense to shoot me an embarrassed look. "Any trouble on your patrol last night?"

"No, and I'll talk to you about it later. Want to see the upstairs?" The latter was directed at me.

"Sure." Though from where I was standing, there didn't look like there would be much to the upstairs. The apartment was totally . . . Guyville, I decided, as Guy led me up the stairs. Solid, muted colors without any frills dominated, and the weight-lifting setup definitely said that two bachelors lived there.

"And, here we are on the second level," Guy said. In the kitchen, Sam opened the newspaper and sat down with his orange juice, as though it were very early morning instead of the middle of the afternoon. "I won't bother you with Sam's room, he's a total slob. My room's this way."

I narrowed my eyes at his back as I followed him. "It's not going to be covered with stalker-type pictures of me, is it?"

He bit his lip again. "No, but that's because I'm awful with a zoom lens."

"Ha," I said. I hadn't known he could be funny, but I really, really liked it.

Guy inclined his head in a little bow and pushed open his bedroom door. Before I could see inside, though, he stopped in the middle of the doorway. He turned quickly, putting us face-to-face. "On second thought, never mind. Let's go out and do something. I can maybe see about getting you a topside pass for the evening."

I squinted up at him. "Must be bad."

He propped an elbow against the door and attempted an innocent look. "What must be bad?"

"Whatever it is you're hiding from me. Sam's not the only slob, is he?"

"I, er, it's not that, exactly." Guy scratched the back of his neck. Standing as close as we were, it was exhilarating to breathe in his comforting scent. Blaze's scent. "It's just that, well . . ."

With a shrug, he moved out of the way and let me get my first full look at his bedroom. Since I knew he was watching my face, I didn't let my jaw drop or anything. Really, I didn't need to worry. I'd seen worse messes. Just clothing—and he always wore such *nice* clothes—thrown this way and that on the floor, shirts over the back of his desk chair and the recliner in the corner, where I imagined he'd tossed them when he'd stripped. The bed was a rumpled pile of green sheets and a dark blue comforter.

"I haven't made the bed since . . ." Guy winced. "Ever, really."

He hurried into the room ahead of me and began to scoop things up, tossing them toward the corners. "If I'd known I'd be having company, I swear I would have cleaned."

"You saw my apartment when you came looking for me," I said, wanting to cringe when I remembered that I'd thrown at least three or four bras over my own desk chair. Oh well. The man had seen me in the tattered threads of a pink teddy. There had to be a line. "There's no need to clean on my behalf, Guy."

"Still." He dumped the pile in his arms into the corner and looked at me. "It's kind of a moment."

"Why is it . . . oh." I caught his meaning just a little too late. It was a big moment, having me here. Knowing who he was and somehow standing in his bedroom.

Guy cleared his throat. "Yeah, so . . . this is it, really. Your gift." With a snap of his fingers, he hurried across the room. The desk seemed to be the cleanest space in the room, which meant he either used it the most or the least. I couldn't tell. He picked up a small white box. "I almost forgot. Here."

When he held out the box, I tilted my head. That looked like . . . "A phone?"

"New line coming out next month. I got you one of the first ones. Jeremy mentioned you were going a little stir-crazy without any contact with the outside world, so I figured I'd help you out."

Before I could reach out and take the box, though, I drew my hand back. The Universe phone was one that had always been out of my price range by quite a bit. I'd known Guy came from a wealthy background—his father was probably worth more than the GNP of several third-world nations put together—but it really hadn't occurred to me until just that moment.

Guy's eyebrows drew together. "What's the matter?"

He had put a little green bow on top of the box, the same color as his uniform. It was such a silly little detail, and I stared at it. "It's kind of expensive," I said.

He gave the box in his hand a look, as if he was puzzled to still see it there. "I guess? I didn't really look at the price tag."

But I just shook my head.

He sighed and wiggled the box. "Remember the time with Dynamo-Lad?"

It took me a second to remember. The kidnappings had

begun to meld together into a montage of supervillains in bad costumes spraying spittle when they yelled in my face. "Was he the psychic who tried to hypnotize me?"

"With your phone, until I smashed it. Just . . . I don't know, consider this a replacement."

I remembered now. I'd been walking alone on a hazy night in June, and Blaze had swooped in from out of nowhere, snatched the phone out of my hand, and thrown it forcefully at a brick wall sixty feet away. It had shattered into bits of metal and plastic, and I'd come to realize that I was standing in the middle of the street in my polka-dot pajama pants with no memory of how I'd gotten there. Now, I fixed him with a look. "This phone is a lot fancier than the one you smashed."

"Consider it interest."

"Guy."

"Look." And he set the phone on the desk so he could cross his arms over his chest again. I was beginning to notice that he only did that when uncomfortable. He leaned against the desk, which put us on a more even height. "You don't owe me anything if you take the phone. It's not—you and me, I've never viewed us as a reciprocal thing. You've never been, and you never will be, in my debt."

"I don't know how you can say that to somebody whose life you've saved as many times as mine," I said. "I kind of feel like I'll always be in your debt. I wouldn't be here without you."

"And you wouldn't be here either if I'd been a little faster getting to that 'L' stop and had stopped Sykik myself."

I bit my tongue before I could tell him I'd relived that memory while on Dr. Mobius's operating table. Sykik, who'd had anemic look of a skinhead with a terrible mohawk, had been my first meeting with Blaze, and I suppose with Guy as well. I hadn't started at Mirror Reality until a month or two after that little near fiasco on the tracks. "You knew he was there? How do you always know?"

"Police scanner." Guy refolded his arms. "I have a system where—actually, it's not important. I wasn't fast enough that day, and Sykik fixated on you and sent your image to a bunch of local villains as retribution."

I rocked back on my heels. "So *that's* how it happened? I thought it was . . . something else."

"Like the media said, that I was in love with you?" Guy shook his head hard. "Not that—not that you're not great, you really are, you're—" He took a deep breath and I watched him actually count to five right there in front of me. His cheeks seemed a little pink. "It was just a vindictive little—little *pissant* trying to get back at an innocent citizen. You were in my territory, and you kind of became my responsibility, but Gail, you don't owe me anything. I don't want you to be in my debt."

I could feel my cheeks heating up a little, too, though I hoped I wasn't blushing. Inwardly, I had to marvel. I had become a supervillain target because of a thrown beer bottle. Not an epic superhero romance. I'd just pissed off the wrong dude, and he'd exacted a petty revenge that had disrupted over two years of my life.

"I think I need to sit down," I said.

In a blink, Guy was across the room, pulling me toward the bed. I sat down before my knees gave way; warily, he sat next to me.

"So it was all Sykik," I said. "Just . . . being a little bitch."

"You know villains. They're all secretly twelve," Guy said.

"That was it? This was all over a beer bottle?"

"Was that what you hit him with?" Guy surprised me by letting out a chuff of laughter. "I've wondered, but there wasn't, um, exactly a way I could ask. You've got amazing aim."

"I played softball back in high school, a million years ago." I rolled my right shoulder once, almost reflexively. A beer bottle, I thought again. It hadn't been a secret grand romance, which was honestly disappointing. It had been kind of an ego boost to think that maybe all of these situations were happening because I had a superhero secretly in love with me.

Vanity, thy name is Gail.

"Hey," I said, finally putting it all together. "Guy. When you said you didn't get there fast enough . . . have you been blaming yourself for this all this time?"

He was quiet for a long time. "You ended up in a lot of really bad situations."

"If they weren't my fault, they definitely weren't yours, either."

"Yeah. I know that," he said. "But I think it's kind of human to wish you'd been able to stop something bad before it could happen to somebody you like."

"You like me?" I asked before I really thought about it.

For a second, I saw his cheeks go even redder than they had been a minute before. Then I saw the same smile I must have sensed through the mask a hundred times before. "I mean, you're okay, I wouldn't get a big head or anything," he said, and it was my turn to give him a little shove on the shoulder. "But seriously, we've always had the connection. I didn't get noticed as one of the elite super-heroes until you started getting kidnapped, and nine times out of ten, I was the one coming to your rescue."

"All without saying a word to me," I said.

"Yeah, well." He ducked his head again, unfolding one arm from his chest to scratch the back of his neck. "I'm not all that great with words. But here." He was so tall that he was easily able to lean over and grab the phone from the desk. "Just please take it. No strings attached."

"You realize with my life, this will get smashed in a week, right?" I asked, but I finally took the box from him.

"I got the extended warranty on it," Guy said. "Gold package."

I made a noise that made him laugh.

"I can afford it," he said. "It won't put me out on the street or anything."

"You realize you're disobeying your old trainer, too," I said, admiring the phone as I pulled it free. It was lighter than I expected it to be, slightly curved, and the glass was smooth and unbroken. It was probably the nicest thing I'd ever owned. "Angélica says I'm not supposed to have anything like this."

"I won't tell if you won't. Jeremy helped me get all of your data on it—don't ask how."

"Okay, I won't. Thanks, Guy. I mean that. For the phone, for even thinking of it."

He took a deep breath and held out a hand. "Friends?"

I looked at his hand, shrugged, and gave him a kiss on the cheek instead. I had to hide my smile behind my hand at the way he went absolutely still. "Friends," I said, and hit the power button. "Though, I have to tell you, Guy, this is the most expensive way I have ever seen a guy go about getting my digits."

"I'm in a class all to myself," Guy said.

"Yes, you—" I broke off as I stared at my new phone screen.

"What is it?" Guy asked.

I held up the phone. "I have forty-seven missed calls."

"Uh-oh."

Chapter Fifteen

Rumors of my not being needed at Mirror Reality, Inc. had been greatly exaggerated, it appeared.

Most of the numbers for the missed calls on my phone, I didn't recognize. But the others, I did, and they surprised me.

"So, anyway," Portia's voice on the recording went on as I listened on speakerphone, "it's not like you can *blame* me for lying and saying we were fine without you. I was just so jealous, you know? You went away, and you came back with, like, a really hot bod, and okay, maybe promoting somebody from the mail room wasn't the greatest idea. Anyway, Angus wants you to call back ASAP, and he wants to know when you'll be back at work."

"This woman is your friend?" Guy asked. I'd moved over to sit at his desk, but he remained on the bed, cross-legged with his elbows on his knees. He rested his chin on his fists and frowned at me.

"Unfortunately," I said, deleting the voice mail.

"You need better friends."

"What, you don't find her charming and full of wit?" I asked as I pressed PLAY on the next message.

"Girl? Girl, this isn't funny! C'mon, pick up your phone." Portia's voice rose to a whine. "Don't you think you've punished me enough? Angus was just here and he's started giving me some of your work and I don't *understand* what's a pivot table and what's an expense report, and you need to come back to work right now. I'm sorry, okay? Just please come back."

I checked the time on that message. It was from this morning. There were two other missed calls from her between, but she hadn't left a message.

Feeling vengeful, I swiped my finger over the DELETE button.

"That explains about twelve of these calls," I said, frowning as I mass-deleted all of the texts from Portia. "But I don't recognize the missed number, and they didn't leave—oh, wait, he or she texted, I just didn't see it under the ten thousand frowny-face messages my charming BFF Portia sent."

"What's it say?" Guy twiddled his thumb against his chin.

The first message was simple: *r u dead???*

I showed it to Guy. "Somebody obviously doesn't believe in using full words in texts," he said, frowning. "Still no idea?"

"The number of people that would think to check on me and make sure I'm not dead is actually depressingly small," I said. "Jeremy uses full words, like I'm guessing you do, and Vicki doesn't have my number and wouldn't have any reason to—"

I broke off when a new text came through, from the same number. *girl if ur not dead, text me back. we have a problem. i think i know what chelsea was after.*

"Oh," I said, staring at the text. "It's Naomi—she's the one Chelsea attacked at the bank. I wasn't sure I wanted to hear from her again."

"Why?"

"She's trouble." I hovered over the REPLY button for a second. The last time I'd approached her, I'd been hit by a couple of energy blasts from a seriously deranged villain. But if she knew what Chelsea was after, that might help the others at Davenport track down Chelsea before she could hurt anyone again. So I texted her back: *Not dead, just complicated. Are you okay?*

"What kind of trouble?" Guy asked, and he sounded so serious that I looked up.

"That was a joke, sorry. Both times I've met with her, I've ended up unconscious because of a supervillain." I shook my head when he only looked more concerned. "I'm fine now. But Chelsea was at that bank because of Naomi. I don't know why. I've been a little busy dealing with superpowers and cancer to really figure it out, and Davenport doesn't seem to want to let me near electronics."

"Understandable," Guy said. "Can I see—"

The phone buzzed in my hand with an incoming call. Naomi Gunn was apparently somebody who was never far from her phone. I accepted the call. "Naomi?"

"Girl? You're alive. Oh, thank god, it wasn't a hoax."

"What hoax? You've called me, like, twenty times," I said. "Are you okay? Last time I saw you, you were kind of bleeding."

"And last time I saw you, frickin' Plain Jane was hauling you off over her shoulder. You took days to get back to me. What the hell happened?"

I looked around Guy's room, at the clothes piled on the floor and the man himself, sitting on his bed watching me. "I don't know if I can tell you."

"Why not?"

"I don't talk to journalists about my life, that's why. It never ends well."

"Only fair." She sounded stressed and a little out of breath, and I wondered just what the hell was going on. "Look, I don't have a lot of time. I'm kind of on the run for my life."

"From what?" I asked, giving Guy a puzzled look.

"It's more of a who. At any rate—" She broke off to swear vociferously, and I sat up straight.

A muffled sound of thumping came through the phone, and a hiss of static. I gripped the phone so hard I heard it start to creak. "Naomi? Naomi!"

There was no answer. Frantic, I checked the phone to make sure the call hadn't disconnected, but it was still live. Guy, across the room, was on his feet, a worried look on his face.

Abruptly, I heard Naomi curse again. "I'm fine, I'm okay," she said, but her voice was an octave higher than it had been a second ago. She also sounded like she was running. "Kind of being shot at, but I'm okay."

"What the hell? Naomi, where are you? My friend—he can come save you."

"No offense, but I'm safer if you don't know where I am. I've gotten away, for now, I think. I'm going to send you a picture of something, I want you to tell me if you recognize it."

"What, why? Naomi, do you need help?"

"I'll be fine." And she hung up.

I gave the phone a look, caught somewhere between bafflement and annoyance. "You know that feeling you get when you've missed something major?"

"I'm acquainted with it," Guy said. "What happened?"

"I have no idea. But Chelsea's got goons chasing Naomi. She got away, and she *sounds* okay, but . . ." I broke off to stare at the phone.

"I can trace the call and find out where she is," Guy said, taking the phone from me.

"I think she'll be gone by the time you get there. She's going to text me a picture. I have no idea why. But it has to be Chelsea after her, right? Is Davenport looking for her?"

"Naomi?"

"No, Chelsea."

"Well, the bank footage was damaged, and even with Vicki's description, it's a bit hard to track down a person like that if she's not actively using her powers."

"Gee," I said, "it really makes you appreciate the villains who stand on top of the Willis Tower and try to blast everybody with death rays."

"They lack finesse, but it does make some things easy."

Guy tapped a couple of buttons on the phone and handed it back to me. "I set up a trace. It shouldn't take long."

"Thanks for doing that. You don't have to."

"I hate mysteries. Wait here a second?"

Before I could ask him where he was going, he stepped into the closet and closed the door behind him. I was left alone in his room, but I didn't dare try to peek in the drawers or anything. So instead I stared at the missed calls on my phone and wondered what the hell was going on with Naomi and Chelsea.

Guy stepped out, wearing black and green, just as a text message alert buzzed on my phone. Naomi had sent me a slightly blurry picture of an open metal drawer. It took me a few seconds to recognize the inside of the safe-deposit vault where I'd fought Chelsea, but when I did, I frowned. Had she been at that bank for something other than Naomi? Inside the box was a piece of circuit board attached to a beige panel. "Do you recognize this?" I asked, holding my phone up.

He shook his head as he finger-combed his hair back. "What is it?"

"I don't know. It's from the bank, though, but she's not exactly being forthcoming with the facts."

"Jeremy's better with that stuff," he said, looking abashed. "Maybe you should ask him."

"Yeah, I'll do that while you're out." I looked his uniform up and down. He seemed so different while wearing it. The little flame on his chest had a couple of nicks and scrapes on it that I remembered well from our superhero-and-damsel days. "So this is an official thing."

"I'll walk you back first."

Back in my suite, I texted the photo to Jeremy and received an entirely unhelpful answer that it could be anything (and a question about if I was okay, which I answered in the affirmative and thanked him for the flowers). Naomi didn't answer when I texted her asking for more information, so I settled in with my new phone and started doing searches on Chelsea myself. Nothing came up. After a few dead ends (and a text from Guy that he'd found nothing at the coordinates and he was going on patrol now), I pushed all of that out of my mind and began a new search for Dr. Mobius.

Chelsea wasn't the only mystery in my life, after all.

ANGÉLICA GREETED ME a couple of days later with "You're in trouble," and I immediately started to panic. Did the woman have ninja spies everywhere? How had she discovered the cell phone? I'd hidden it away in the bottom of my new satchel during our sessions, powered down so it wouldn't ring in the middle of our lesson.

I swallowed hard. "What'd I do?"

"It's not what you did." Her grin seemed just a touch mean. "It's more what's about to happen."

I set my bag down in the corner, turning away to hide my relief. I really didn't want to lose my new cell phone. Naomi hadn't been in touch (though Portia had called twice), but Guy had put the most expensive data plan on it, and I'd been up late streaming *The Bird Also Sings*. I'd missed a lot in Chance's world since Dr. Mobius had kidnapped me. "It's going to be another day of beating the hell out of me, isn't it?" I asked.

"I packed plenty of crap-cakes."

"I knew you were going to say that."

"And you're going to need them."

"This day just keeps getting better and better."

"Lose the shoes."

As I crouched to untie the laces of my sneakers, I eyed Angélica. Today's stretch pants had a purple stripe across the knee; the muscle tee was a black tank top that showed off her upper arm definition scarily well. Those arms, I thought, would be pounding on me soon. She'd painted her toenails purple to match the stripe.

When I rose, my feet bare, Angélica smiled at me. "You really think that's what's going to happen, don't you? That I'm going to beat the hell out of you."

"Can't see why I would. It hasn't happened like a million times already or anything."

"What'd I tell you about sarcasm, kid?"

"That it's a valuable tool in our fight against—whoa!"

The first time Angélica had jumped at me, I hadn't seen it coming. Now, I saw the way she twisted her hips, and I easily sidestepped. She went breezing by, checked her charge, and swung back just as fluidly as I'd avoided her.

"You're learning," she said.

"I'm partial to keeping my skin."

"Heh. Your turn. Come at me."

Since arguing was useless, I stood still. Angélica had drilled it into my head that there wasn't a point in letting your opponent see your move until you were already coming at them, fists flying. It was similar to a philosophy I'd adopted in my many hostage situations—if you have an ace up your sleeve, keep it there until the chips are down.

So I waited, and I made my leap. Angélica dodged, as I anticipated, so I feinted, planted my foot, and swung into a roundhouse kick. The blade of my foot barely brushed her rib cage as she sprang back. She landed and immediately tried to sweep my feet out from under me, but I threw myself into a somersault to get away.

When I came up in a fight stance, she was grinning at me. "Definitely learning."

We traded off on attacking and defending. Sometimes I felt trapped in molasses while Angélica blurred right by me, somehow managing to be everywhere at once. No matter what I threw at her, she dodged or blocked. And she got in quite a few blows that I hadn't seen coming. By the time she declared a break, nearly an hour later, my ribs stung, and my cheek throbbed. I swiped at it, relieved to see no blood on my palm. It was probably a testament to the past few days that I understood I was going to have a spectacular bloom of a bruise on my cheek for a little while.

"You're sneaky," I told Angélica, as we reached for water. I took a deep drink and studied her over the bottle. "Fast. I don't get how you can be that fast. You don't *look* fast."

"You really haven't figured it out?" she asked between her own gulps.

"Nope. Maybe you're the devil and this is actually hell and that's why you're so fast and I have to eat this." I toasted her with the crap-cake.

"Try paying attention. Don't worry about dodging so much—I'll pull my punches." She grinned. "A little. But really watch me, study me. And let's see what you come up with. This is a valuable skill you'll need against any enemy, even if it's just your trainer."

"Is this an excuse to catch me off guard, so you can just beat on me harder?"

"Would I do that?"

"Yes," I said without hesitation. When she declared our break over, we stood in the same positions we'd taken earlier, and I waited for her to attack first, wondering what I was missing.

It took a few tries—and one good kick to the sternum—before I caught it: she was throwing her weight around. Not in the way that bullies did, either. Angélica was manipulating her mass to throw her faster one way or the other, like some kind of odd slingshot effect.

If I listened really closely, I heard a tiny *twang* every time she did it.

"You're part of the speed team!" I said.

She grinned and brushed sweat off her brow with her wrist. "Guilty as charged."

"How do you *do* that?"

"It's velocity-based. I can alter kinetic energy around me, basically changing gravity to make me faster or slower." As she talked, she stretched out her shoulder, then cracked her neck. "I've been able to do it all my life, but I never realized I was doing it until I was outrunning every boy in my hometown."

"In races?" I said. "Or were they chasing you?"

She smirked. "I run pretty fast, but I'm fastest in shorter, sharper movements. If I'm going long distances, I'd rather have a bike."

I nodded, and since we were taking a break anyway, reached for my water. Only to have it kicked out of my hand. "Hey!"

"You want your water?" Angélica asked. "Earn it. Come at me."

"Here we go again," I said, but I readied myself. Knowing what I did now about how Angélica's unique abilities worked, that time when I got a kick in, it wasn't because I was lucky.

I'd never seen a woman with a bloody nose look prouder.

Chapter Sixteen

WHEN I DRAGGED myself to my room, sore and more than a little tired after the session with Angélica, I found Guy leaning against my door, his hands in his pockets. He was in his regular clothing, dressed like a college student on spring break again, and I remembered that he kept a place in Miami. How he traveled between Florida and the Davenport complex so quickly, I had no idea, but I figured he probably had to dress "in character" all the time these days.

My heart leapt at seeing him. I was used to that reaction at seeing Blaze, but not Guy, even though I *knew* they were the same person, I nearly tripped over my own feet.

"Hey," Guy said, standing up so fast that I nearly suffered sympathetic whiplash. His wince, however, was all for me; he gestured at my cheek. "Ouch."

"You should see the other guy," I said.

"I have to ask: when you say the other guy, you do mean Angélica, right?"

"Yeah. Don't worry, I didn't run into any bad guys between here and the training rooms." I'd actually forgotten about my cheek. I imagined by this point, the bruise was probably in its ugliest stages. "I slipped a little. I don't think she actually meant to hit me that hard."

"Hey-a, Gail," said a new voice, and I turned to see Vicki strolling toward us.

"Hey, Vicki," I said. Since she lived down the hall, I was used to seeing her coming and going. If she was in a rush, it was always a bit like getting brushed with the very edge of a potent tornado. Today, she was kitted out in her superhero getup, dressed from head to foot in unrelenting black. Her matte white mask was hooked at her hip. "You two wanna come in?"

"I'd love to, but I don't have too much time if we're gonna hit up the Annals."

"The whats?" I asked.

Guy cleared his throat. "I had an idea for a way we might track down Mobius or Chelsea, and Vicki wanted to come along because I think she can help. If you're not too tired."

"Oh, neat. Let me just dump my bag." I'd showered at the training rooms, thankfully, so the reek of *eau de Gail* wasn't strong enough to repel nearby superheroes. "Give me two minutes."

"Take your time."

Inside, I dropped my bag and choked down a crapcake, washing it down with orange juice. There really wasn't time to do my hair, and I didn't have my makeup or anything cute to wear, which was really starting to get old. I sighed at the bruise on my cheek before I stepped outside.

"Ow. That looks really bad," Vicki said when I stepped back out into the hallway.

"It looks worse than it feels," I said. "Should heal soon. Just part of the whole get-hit-get-healed-by-the-thing-giving-me-and-saving-me-from-cancer cycle."

Vicki blinked at that one a couple of times. "I have to wonder—if you have cancer and you're, you know, healing yourself and only giving yourself cancer all over again, why's Angélica beating the hell out of you?"

"I think she's teaching me how to fight," I said. I was tired enough to ignore my tweaked pride. I might be learning to hold my own against Angélica, but I still ended up on the mat more often than not.

"But why?" Vicki asked. "That's what I'm talking about. You're exerting yourself with all of this healing all the time. I'm a little worried. Can't they just put you in Superheroes 101 instead?"

"In what? Is that a real thing?"

"Ray Goldstein teaches it," Guy said, as we entered the elevator together. "Everybody goes through it during their initial time at Davenport."

"It's totally boring. Like I care what some superheroes in the fifties were up to." Vicki's eye-roll was so impressive that I nearly asked her to mentor me in that instead. "But when I mentioned it to Angélica, she said you weren't going to take it, not for a while yet."

"Huh," I said. I'd had an average interest in superheroes before Davenport. Which was to say, I checked the

Domino site for gossip, paid attention when I heard my favorites mentioned on the news, and tried not to fall asleep in history class when my teacher sanitized the most interesting bits from the stories and the daring rescues of Kurt Davenport and the Feared Five. "Why's that, do you think?"

"She gave me that snooty look only Madame Angélica can do—"

"Vicki," Guy said, laughing.

"—and said it wasn't exactly any of my business even though that's a blatant lie because I am your superhero mentor." Vicki gave me an emphatic nod.

" 'None of your business' is Angélica's way of covering up the fact that she doesn't know something," I said, and both of my freakishly tall new superhero friends gave me surprised looks over that. "What? It is."

"You learn something new every day. At any rate, we figured since you weren't taking Superheroes 101," Guy said, "we'd go to the Annals instead. Luckily, there's a set here, so we don't have to 'port."

"We don't have to what?" I asked.

"Teleport," Vicki said. "You're not cleared for that."

"There aren't any superheroes with that power," I said, giving them both suspicious looks.

"And Davenport's just a regular company," Vicki said facetiously.

"Back the trolley up—you're telling me people can actually *teleport*, as in here one second, gone the next?"

"Oh, Girl," Vicki said, placing one hand on my shoulder and the other over her heart, like I was some sweet child she'd taken in off the street. "Are you in for a surprise."

As we walked to a part of the complex that I'd never visited before, they took turns explaining that teleportation did indeed exist, but it was such a rare power that there were less than two dozen people worldwide who could do it. In addition, the power had to be cultivated carefully—years of study, apparently—and Davenport had built special facilities to move between all of its different locations. The 'porters worked on a network, transferring people between these facilities.

This was, incidentally, how I discovered that I was not in Chicago anymore.

"This entire complex is in *New York City*?"

"We're really good at not telling you things," Vicki said.

I gave her a sour look. "You think? What's next, you're going to tell me we're secretly sisters who were separated at birth?"

"Maybe?" Vicki shrugged. "My mom took off, and Dad wasn't real big on sharing the family history. But we don't look that much alike so . . ." She trailed off, possibly at my horrified look, and grinned. The famous dimple appeared. "Girl, relax. I'm messing with you."

"She has eight siblings and is actually lying through her teeth, yes," Guy said.

"There are eight people in the world that potentially look like you?" I asked Vicki.

The grin only widened. "We're a menace to society."

"So that stuff you just told me about your mom and dad?" I asked.

Vicki made an "eh" noise and wiggled her hand. "Gotta keep the origin story interesting. Oh, look, we're here."

I looked over in surprise. Usually, going anywhere in Davenport meant half a mile of walking down long, identical hallways, past the indoor courtyards with the simulated sunlight, and into new parts of the complex. This had been a simple elevator ride though when I looked at the panel by the door, I noticed we were no longer in the sublevels like the ones that housed my apartment but actually aboveground.

"Davenport Tower," Guy said.

I swiveled on my heel to look at both of them, no longer shocked but accusing. "I've been living in the basement of Davenport Tower this entire time, and nobody thought to mention it to me?"

"Surprise?" Vicki asked.

"And here I've always wanted to see the top of Davenport Tower," I said. There had been so many movies—and so many dramatic saves—off the top of the tower. At one point, it had been the tallest building in the world, and it still drew quite a few tourists for its art deco style every year.

And the entire time, I had been living just below it.

"This part of the building's only open to Class Cs and above," Guy said, wincing a little as I turned my stare on him. "Technically, you're still in your adjustment period until Cooper says so, but we figured we'd, ah—"

"What your super straight-laced boyfriend here means to say is that we're breaking you out and breaking the rules, Baby Girl," Vicki said, propping an elbow up on my shoulder as we waited for the doors to open. They were taking an awfully long time to go about it, and my bones felt weird, like something was humming, so I suspected we were being scanned. Whatever these Annals were, they definitely felt important.

Guy made a choking noise. "You know that's just the media," he said to Vicki. "We're—we're not really dating. I'm not her boyfriend, I wouldn't force my attentions on her—"

"We understood you the first time," I said, and my voice came out surprisingly testy. I flinched.

"Right," Guy said, and the elevator doors opened. "Well, here we are."

A long hallway, lushly carpeted, stretched out in front of us. Along each wall, I could see portraits, hung at even intervals. "You brought me to a portrait gallery?"

"This is a memorial," Guy said. "Superheroes who make their mark are put in this gallery. Most of them gave their lives fighting the good fight."

"Most?"

"Not all of them are dead." Guy paused.

"And it's not exactly good luck to be in here," Vicki said, as the elevator doors closed behind us. "There's some dumb superstition that if you're in the Annals, maybe your life expectancy isn't the greatest."

"Neither of you are in here, right?" I asked, looking at the first portrait. Captain Fallout had died in the fifties, but he was famous for throwing himself over a bomb that would have destroyed a small mountainside town in California.

"Nope," Vicki said, drawing the word out. She flexed. "Not for lack of trying, though."

"Sam is," Guy said. "After he saved Chicago from Deathjab, they considered him worthy enough to be in the Annals. But anyway, I thought we could look around, see if anybody reminds you or Vicki of Chelsea."

"What?"

"Siblings and children of superheroes tend to become supervillains," Guy said.

"Like the Trouble Twins and the Snuggler?"

"Who were all really hot," Vicki said.

Guy and I stared at her.

"What? They were. So what if two of them were evil?"

"Anyway, to kick things off . . ." Guy gestured at the first portrait beyond Captain Fallout. The sober, hazel eyes of Kurt Davenport looked back at us. He looked to be in his prime at the time the portrait had been painted, a virile man in a dark suit. Apparently he hadn't wanted to be painted in the Raptor uniform, though the suit was as black as the cape he'd always worn.

"Just to double-check: Kurt Davenport *is* dead, right?" I asked. "I remember hearing that he died."

"Yeah, he passed away some time ago."

"But I still see stuff about the Raptor all over the Domino's website," I said. A thought occurred to me, and I remembered the smiling blue eyes of Eddie Davenport as he shook my hand, eons ago at the office. "Hold on—it's not *Eddie*, is it?"

"Nope," Vicki said. "Eddie's totally boring—"

"For a lawyer-turned-CEO who runs Davenport Industries," Guy said, his voice dry.

"—So the Raptor's actually Jessica Davenport."

"Raptor's a woman?" I tried to remember what the press had said about Jessica Davenport. They'd grown bored of her when she hadn't had a wild-child phase. Instead, by all reports, she lived a secluded, private life, as opposed to her brother's high-flying, talk-of-the-town ways. If she was skulking about the back alleys of New York City every night, though, that explained it.

Guy and Vicki both grinned, like they were in on some great joke. "Everybody's always surprised by that," Guy said. "Sorry. Didn't mean to make it seem like we were making fun of you or anything. Jessie's the Raptor now. And I imagine her son will take over for her when she decides to retire."

Jessie Davenport, though never married, had two kids with her ex. Harry and Lydia Rosemund, I remembered. They were occasionally on the covers of the tabloids, with other rich kids. "Isn't he fifteen?"

"Next month, and he can't wait to fill his grandfather's shoes." Guy shrugged. "He'll probably feel different when he realizes that the hero life isn't glamorous. But until then, he and Jessie have a deal—Harry goes to school full-time, finishes college, and she'll take him on as a sidekick. Probably the only way to keep him out of trouble."

"So the superheroing business really is a family thing, isn't it?" I asked.

"Right. And powers can sometimes be hereditary," Guy

said, pointing at the portrait next to Kurt's. The plaque proclaimed him to be Marcus Davenport, and I vaguely remembered hearing that Eddie and Jessie Davenport had had a younger sibling. He'd passed away about a decade before, as far as I remembered. The man in the portrait looked slim almost to the point of emaciated, his cheeks puffed out and his eyes—hazel, unlike his brother's—sunken in his face. "Marcus unfortunately inherited his mother's abilities, Villain Syndrome and all. It drove him mad. He's here because Kurt wanted it, but it's kind of controversial."

"Sad," I said.

Vicki cleared her throat, clearly uncomfortable with the somber mood, and slung a friendly arm across my shoulders to pull me forward. "C'mon, let's go see if we can find somebody who has Chelsea's chin or something."

They led me through the Annals together, sometimes talking over each other as they remembered various stories about the costumed superheroes on the walls. Vicki was quick on the draw, verbally, while Guy tended to take a moment to consider his answers. It felt completely different from all of the times he'd saved me, usually by charging forehead first into danger. As Blaze, he seemed resolute and he rarely hesitated. As Guy, the word I would have used to describe him was "careful."

"That kind of looks like Chelsea's nose, I think," Vicki said, stopping at a portrait of Major Quirk.

I tilted my head. "You were paying attention to her nose?"

"Photographers, darling. They always accentuate the

body parts rather than the whole." Vicki motioned in front of her face. "Hence the mask."

"That, and you don't want to get picked up on red light cameras when you fly too low," Guy said, tucking his hands in his back pockets and rocking back on his heels.

"Green boy here is scared to fly around traffic." Vicki jerked her thumb at him.

When I gave him a questioning look, he grimaced. "I hit a semi once."

"It was hilarious. I wish somebody had caught it on camera."

After that, we continued to stroll along, stopping at every few portraits to discuss the superheroes within, or to trade stories that we remembered from growing up. Vicki and Guy had the inside scoop—or "Scuttlebutt about the Supes," as Vicki termed it—so their stories differed from the ones I'd slept through in history class. None of them looked overmuch like Chelsea, either. But it was eerie, like walking in some sort of superhero cemetery. Most of the people whose pictures adorned these walls had died in the line of duty.

Like Guy, or Vicki, or Sam, or hell, even Angélica if she decided to take up fighting on the front lines again, might. Like I might if I decided to join the good fight.

Even though I'd stared death in the face more than fifty times, the thought made me uneasy.

"And here," Guy said, his fingers resting on my shoulder, "is the *pièce de résistance*. My brother, Samuel Lee Bookman."

"Samuel Lee?" I said.

"He got the normal name. By the time I came around, Dad didn't care enough to give me a proper name. Hence, Guy. Looks pretty serious, doesn't he?" Guy nodded at the portrait, and I took a minute to really study it. The familial similarities were more obvious here. I could see that Sam's eyes were the same shape as Guy's even if the color was different. They had the same chin.

But there would always be that odd sadness in Sam's face. Guy kept a clear-eyed view of the world.

"I think he's cuter than you," Vicki said. "No offense. I don't have a thing for gingers, unlike Girl here."

"I don't have a thing for gingers," I said.

Vicki turned and gave Guy a pitying look. "She just took your heart and stomped all over it, you poor thing."

"I'm sure I'll live," he said, his voice bone dry.

"What happened to you and Sam?" I asked, looking back at the portrait. "You seem frighteningly normal, all things considered, but he's . . ."

Guy opened his mouth, only to be cut off by a buzzing noise. Irritated, he yanked his cell phone out and read the view screen. His face immediately closed down. "I've, ah, I've got to take this. Excuse me."

And he flew away. It was the first time I'd seen him fly without the uniform, and it was just weird, like a cognitive disconnect in my brain.

"Ah, the hero phone," Vicki said. "I tried to change his ringtone for that once to the sound of a whip since he was always so busy rescuing you. This is, of course, before I knew you."

"Of course," I said. "How'd that go for you?"

"He rather meticulously replaced my entire mattress with bubble wrap and remade my bed around it. So when I tried to go to bed that night . . ." She made a noise like an explosion. "Scared the hell out of me *and* cost me my security deposit. Sneaky, sneaky."

I started to ask her about the security deposit, but then I remembered that in addition to the flight and super-strength, Plain Jane had the ability to shoot fire.

Whoops.

"He might take awhile," Vicki said, glancing over her shoulder at the way Guy had gone. "Let's just keep looking around."

We wandered the hallway while Vicki rambled on, keeping up with the narration. In the Annals, several of my favorite childhood heroes were finally given real faces. Songbird was a mousy woman with brown hair and black eyes. Surf Warrior had an overbite. Jester looked like a devilishly charming rogue, even out of his uniform.

"And here's where we take a turn for the bummer," Vicki said, as the hallway curved.

I carefully looked back at the entire hallway full of (mostly) dead superheroes behind us, then raised an eyebrow at her.

"Those people were heroes. It's expected of us, you know? But these ones?" She walked up to the nearest painting, which had a silver plaque below it as opposed to a gold one. I watched her run her hand down along the right side of the frame, where the wood was already worn. "These people were the ones we loved and lost."

Inside the portrait was a stunningly pretty woman with

sad eyes. She had no name, but the plaque read BELOVED WIFE OF INVISIBLE VICTOR.

"Oh," I said. "Um."

"Yeah," Vicki said, stepping back.

"Did you know her?"

"She and the other Feared Five were before my time. Gail Garson's boyfriend has a portrait down that way a little bit—we lost him at Honolulu in '72, I think— and everybody's here but Rita Detmer. Kurt Davenport wanted her in here."

"Even though she's Fearless?"

"Hey, love is love. She's not in here because she's still hanging out in Detmer. And also because I don't know if there's a portrait artist on this world talented enough to capture the amount of crazy that lives in those eyes. And no, before you ask, I haven't met her." Vicki rubbed her thumb along the edge of her mask. "You just hear stories. And here we have . . ."

I turned to look at the next portrait, and it jolted me back a step. The woman pictured had Guy's smile and Sam's eyes.

The plaque below didn't list her name, but it did proclaim her to be the BELOVED SISTER OF WAR HAMMER AND BLAZE. The date of death listed below was from over four years ago. She was beautiful, stunningly pretty in a way that even wealth couldn't buy, with corn-silk hair like Sam's. But her smile was crooked like Guy's. It was hard to tell from a portrait, but it seemed like a smile she used a lot.

So Guy had two siblings in the Annals. No wonder he'd looked worried.

"Guy had a sister?" I asked.

"Petra," Vicki said. "I met her a couple of times—models and rich people, you move in the same circles. She was Sam's twin."

"What happened to her?" I asked, but I remembered and shook my head. "Right, no sharing other people's origin stories. Sorry, I forgot."

"I'm sure Guy will tell you," Vicki said. "But let's keep going for now."

I sent one look over my shoulder back at Petra. Whoever had painted her portrait had done that trick where her eyes followed me all the way down the gallery.

We'd only made it a couple of portraits down when Guy returned. He wasn't flying this time, I saw with a surprising stab of disappointment. As weird as it was, I liked watching him fly.

"Sorry about that," he said immediately. "It's urgent. Vicki, I could use a sidekick."

"Sidekick, my ass. If anybody here's the sidekick, buddy, it's you."

"Yeah, yeah," Guy said, and turned to me with a pained look. "Can I get a rain check?"

"Sure. Is everything okay?"

"Yeah, it's probably nothing, but . . ." He shrugged. "No rest for the weary, right?"

"Right." I don't know what had me reaching out to touch his arm again. "If it's bad, whatever it is, feel free to come and find me later. I mean, you might have to wake me from the coma I fall into every night, but I'm always there to talk to."

He nodded once, tightly. "I might take you up on that."

"You two are sickening," Vicki said.

Guy ignored her. "You know how to get back?" he asked me.

It was a straight shot down a long hallway and a trip down the elevator, but it was oddly sweet of him to worry. So I gave him a smile. "If I don't remember, my body undoubtedly will. One of the perks of my very own pet isotope."

"Right. Bye, Gail."

"Knock 'em dead."

"Ha!" They took running leaps and flew off at the same time. Right before they turned a corner, she flipped onto her back and tossed me a little wave, and I grinned as I waved back. They were probably going to go grab his uniform first, I thought, and after that they were off to face the problems of the world, as they did most nights. No rest for the weary, indeed.

Chapter Seventeen

BACK IN MY suite, the first thing I did was check the cell phone I'd accidentally left in my gym bag to see if I could find where Guy and Vicki had gone. The Domino usually had up-to-date reporting on which heroes were engaged in battles and where, thanks to their street team, but there weren't any alerts yet. Wherever they'd been called, the battle was either too fresh, or it hadn't started yet.

I'd wondered how heroes knew to show up in certain places before, but now I was extra curious.

I pushed that curiosity aside since there were four missed calls from a number I didn't recognize. Evidently, Naomi had changed phones again. She hadn't left a voice mail, though, so I texted her back a "What's going on?" message.

Almost immediately, the phone rang. I swiped the TALK button.

"Oh my god!" The voice on the other end wasn't Naomi's,

but it was familiar. "You actually picked up for once. I was starting to wonder if you were *dead*."

"Portia," I said, closing my eyes and flopping back against my couch cushions. Why hadn't I checked the caller ID before accepting the call? "No, I'm not dead."

"Then why the hell haven't you been returning my calls?"

Mostly, I thought, because I had no desire to explain how a spreadsheet worked to somebody who had once spent an entire afternoon of work perfecting her duck-lips face. "I've been a bit busy," I said instead.

"You don't have a new job, do you?"

Technically, my job at the moment was to get through my transformation into a Class C alive. Davenport was supporting me. I wasn't actually cleared to leave the complex or anything, but they were providing clothes and a place for me to stay, and handling all of my outside bills, like maintaining my apartment. Angélica had pointed out that I could stay on at Davenport indefinitely, provided I contributed in some way after I'd adjusted to my new powers.

She seemed to think I had the guts to head for the front line. I wasn't so sure about that myself.

But this wasn't anything I could tell Portia about, so I said, "Sort of?"

She groaned, long and loud. "Angus will give you a raise, I know he will. You just have to come *back*, Girl. I am begging you. No, this is beyond begging, this is— what's beyond begging?"

"Groveling, I think."

"Then that. I am doing that. Please come back. Please, please."

"Portia, I can't actually think about this right now." The truth was, I didn't know if I wanted to keep living at Davenport. I mean, I'd actually kind of liked the freedom of the outside world. Right now I felt like I was being watched all the time by quite a few people: Vicki, Angélica, even Guy to an extent. They all hovered, which could get annoying. But when I'd lived in my tiny little apartment in Irving Park, I hadn't done much besides try not to be a target for villains, and work. My social life had been Jeremy, and that was it. No wonder I'd kind of reeled at having friends again when I'd come to Davenport.

But did I want to stay?

"Portia," I said, biting off the sigh before it could escape, "I need a couple of weeks before I decide anything."

It was like her whole demeanor changed. I could hear it through the phone: her straightening up, the breath she sucked in, all of it. And I wondered if I was just imagining things or if the isotope was improving my perception until she said, brightly, "Excellent!"

"What?"

"I'll just tell Angus you need some more vacation, and we'll see you again in a couple of weeks!"

"Wait, no, what—"

But before I could lodge the protest that I *hadn't* agreed to come back to work for Angus and Mirror Reality, Inc., she trilled a farewell at me and hung up.

I stared at the phone. "Somebody's in for a rude shock in two weeks," I said though I was alone. Angus and all of the others would just have to deal with the fact that I wasn't coming back. Probably. Assuming I wanted to stay at Davenport. It would not be long before the Mobium would take over all of my cells and reach its optimal balance in my bloodstream. Whether or not it would keep giving me and curing me of cancer had yet to be seen, but Kiki and Cooper seemed to think it was working to adapt my body.

Was that why they'd put me into such rigorous training instead of Superheroes 101?

I frowned and pushed the questions aside as I thumbed over to my missed-calls list. As fun as it wasn't to spiral into worry about the sickness in my blood that I couldn't actually feel, I couldn't forget the three missed calls. Though I figured I had very little chance of Naomi's answering if she hadn't responded to my text, she picked up on the second ring.

"Girl?" she asked.

"What's going on?" I asked. "Did you figure out what Chelsea was after?"

"That's not important."

"Not impor—how is that not important? You've been texting me for updates like crazy."

"Girl! Pay attention."

"To what?" I asked, and I heard the indicator beep that she'd switched over to a video call. Hastily, I pulled the phone away from my ear. Her face filled the screen. She'd somehow had time to get a nose ring in the past couple of days though I had no idea when. Wasn't she supposed to be running away from a Class B villain? "Uh, Naomi?"

"Shh," she said, and pressed a button on the screen. Instantly, the view changed from her face to a street. I could see cars parked along the sides of the road, some shops, and a street café off to the right. Most of the chairs and tables in the view had been knocked over—likely by the three super-powered beings fighting in the middle of the street. It was easy to make out Blaze and Plain Jane, but the third, dressed head to toe in white with a pink band over her chest and cowl, was unfamiliar to me. "Your boyfriend showed up," Naomi said needlessly, as I saw Guy swerve to avoid being hit by a flying chunk of concrete.

"He's not my boyfriend," I said.

I could *hear* Naomi roll her eyes.

"Who's the one in white?" I asked.

"Three guesses, and the first two don't count," Naomi said, just as the woman in white raised one of her hands. Yellow and green sparks streamed out, narrowly missing Vicki, who easily leapfrogged away and took off for the sky. The sight of those sparks made all of my limbs lock with a brief, harsh terror that stole my breath. "Yeah."

"Chelsea got a costume?" I asked.

"Guess she finally saw the value of not being recognized." Naomi's voice sounded grim.

"Where are you? What's going on?"

"Good help is so hard to find," Naomi said. "Especially when minions leave their wallets within easy reach of people with pickpocketing skills. Long story short: Chelsea hired some goons to find me, I figured out who they were, put a bug in some of their computer systems so I could break in and get phone records—"

"This is not a very short story," I said.

She sighed. "Fine. I tracked down Chelsea's cell phone and followed her. Better?"

"Where are you?" I asked, peering hard at the screen. Guy, who'd been trying to fly in and knock Chelsea out, took a full blast of the green stinging ray. He merely rolled out of the way and flew off, shaking his head.

"Another bank. I think she was trying to hit the safe-deposit boxes again. Whatever she's after, it's in a lot of pieces."

"Did you ever figure out who owned that first box?" I asked.

On the screen, Chelsea abruptly launched herself into the air—oh, great, she could fly, too, that was just *swell*—and Guy and Vicki took off in pursuit. The video call switched back to voice only. "Shell corporation," Naomi said. "Dead end. You get any luck identifying that piece?"

"None whatsoever." So Chelsea was definitely building something, and now she had a bright costume. I didn't understand any of it, so I focused on Naomi instead. "Are you okay?"

"I'm fine. I hid until your boy showed."

"He's not—" I seemed to be having that argument a lot today. Maybe it was better not to protest. "I'm glad you're okay."

"Why, Girl, I'm starting to think maybe you care about me a little."

"Don't be stupid, of course I don't want Chelsea to zap you." I didn't want Chelsea to zap *anybody*. "Can you give me any more information?"

There was a long pause on the other end of the line. "I'm not sure," Naomi said. "Not over the phone, at any rate. Can you meet?"

Could I? Angélica didn't want me wandering out in society and around people until they'd assessed all of my abilities and made sure there weren't any nasty surprises in store. But like it or not, I was involved in this Chelsea business because of Naomi, and she was obviously in danger.

Was this how Guy had felt about me?

"Girl?" Naomi prompted, since I hadn't answered.

"It might take me a little while," I said, making up my mind. What I could do, I had absolutely no idea. I wasn't a flyer or on the front lines like Guy or Vicki, but I had a feeling that Naomi wasn't going to come clean with anybody, possibly not even me. But she was in way over her head, and something was going on. "But I can do it."

"I'll let you know when and where," she said. "You're still in Chicago, at least?"

"Yes," I lied.

"I'm going to go talk to the bank manager and make a nuisance of myself, then," Naomi said. "I'll dump this phone and get in touch later."

"Okay," I said, and she hung up.

I immediately switched over to the Domino website, hoping for some kind of coverage. There wasn't video, but social-media updates were already flooding in, pursuing the fight across downtown Naperville and into less populated areas. They'd driven the battle away from people. Angélica had mentioned that she'd be teaching me tactics like that eventually, once we got past all the rudimentary core work.

Finally, after somebody mentioned seeing Blaze and Plain Jane fly away without the mystery woman in white, the updates stopped. I didn't bother to wait for the recap. Instead, I tabbed over to check some of the pages from my Hostage Girl days. Blaze had been my primary hero, so I'd always watched his tag on the Domino. In addition to that, I'd kept an eye on the Hostage Girl tag, and some of the heroes I thought were either dashing or just humorous. Not everybody believed in covering up with a mask or a cowl, but apparently a code of silence about Davenport Industries remained strong within the entire community. I'd been browsing sites like the Domino for years, and I'd never heard a word of it.

I made myself a few club sandwiches to nibble on while I browsed, thankful that Angélica had finally seen fit to bring me food from the commissary a few days before. I was fully absorbed in the latest gossip about some of the L.A. superheroes when I heard the footsteps approaching the door. Before Guy could knock, I called, "Come in."

His hair messy and stuck to his forehead with sweat, Guy poked his head in. "It's a little spooky when you do that," he said, as the door closed behind him.

I made a "What can you do about it?" motion with my hands. "It's life now. It's kind of useful though I don't imagine it would be if I decide to go back to Chicago. My neighbors were kind of loud before."

He stopped just inside the door. "You're thinking about leaving?"

"Maybe. Portia called, and apparently I'm on an extended vacation rather than fired. How are you? You look a bit . . ."

"Messed up?" Guy pushed irritably at his hair. I'd never seen him post-fight, either as Guy or Blaze, I realized. I'd seen him in the middle of battles with the enemy, in those lulls where he needed to catch a breath, but the aftermath, I'd never been privy to. He'd always flown off, usually leaving me at the hospital in Dr. Dimarco's capable hands. Right now, his Blaze uniform clinging to his chest and neck with sweat, I could see the exhaustion I'd never been allowed to see before. "Yeah. I'm sorry. I probably should have stopped home to shower and change first. But—really, Chicago?"

"What's wrong with Chicago?"

He frowned. "You just never seemed to like it that much, that's all. What's wrong with here?"

I looked around the suite. As nice as it was not to have to worry about rent, there was nothing personal in my apartment, and the lack of windows made it feel like a bunker. My clothing came from Davenport. My schedule came from Davenport. "It feels a little clinical," I said. "And now that I don't have to worry about keeping my job to hold on to the healthcare, I think things can change for the better. Maybe I'll pick up some hobbies again."

"Like what?" He accepted a sandwich when I nudged the plate at him and took a huge bite. "Knitting?" he asked once he'd swallowed.

"I don't knit."

"Drat. My ears get cold in the winter. I could use a new hat." He gave me a tired smile.

"You live in Miami," I said, and he shrugged as he took another big bite. "But yeah, hobbies. Maybe it'd be fun to join a softball team or something, provided I can regulate my strength to appear normal." I'd played in high school, but afterward, I'd been too busy working two jobs and saving up to escape my dead end of a hometown. And in Chicago, I'd been too busy getting kidnapped to do anything but work and recuperate. "I haven't really thought about it. It feels so weird to be in charge of my whole life again."

"Must be nice," Guy said, so quietly that I wouldn't have heard it without my enhanced hearing. When he saw my confused look, he shook his head. "Sorry. Ignore that."

"Okay," I said. I wouldn't have with Jeremy—if left alone with the things muttered under his breath, he tended to get passive aggressive—but with Guy, I didn't actually know him well enough to push. And frankly, I didn't really want to push him. I worried that our connection, which felt so natural because he was Blaze, and I was Hostage Girl, was a little more tenuous than I suspected. "Were you here to tell me you ran into Chelsea today?"

He fumbled the sandwich. "You know about that?"

"Naomi called, and she set it to video. I'm surprised Chelsea went with pink and white." I eyed him up and down, biting my tongue before I could ask him about the blast he'd sustained from Chelsea's stinging powers. Had it even hurt him? He looked tired and disheveled but not in pain.

"Were you expecting her to take up a costume?" Guy asked, giving me an odd look.

"Everybody does eventually, right? You have to stand out as a beacon. Part of the superhero-slash-villain way."

"You have a point. Are you going to finish that?" Guy asked, pointing at the fourth sandwich. I pushed it over to him. Apparently, I wasn't the only one who could burn through calories faster than a fire through dry brush. I got up to refill my glass, pouring one for Guy as well. He accepted it with a nod of thanks since his mouth was full. While he ate, I filled him in on the conversation with Naomi, including the bits of the fight I'd seen and the fact that she wanted to meet.

"Have you considered maybe they're working together?" Guy asked once I'd finished.

"What?"

"They might be trying to draw you out. Their goal might be you, Gail. The bank may have been an elaborate setup, and this might be the final piece of the trap."

I blinked at him. "But why? I'm not anybody special. Everybody who kidnapped or attacked me, they were always doing that just to get to you. I was their consolation prize."

"Or collateral damage," Guy said, looking grim. But he shook his head quickly, possibly to ward off dark thoughts. "Maybe it has something to do with Mobius? He did this to you"—he gestured at me, vaguely—"and then he disappeared, and nobody can find the bastard to get either a cure for you or an explanation. Maybe these two are connected. Didn't you say you met Naomi right before Mobius attacked you?"

"Yeah, but even if I did—connected, Guy? I don't know

if I can give Mobius that much credit. He seemed like he genuinely was trying to turn me into an addict rather than a Class C."

"The man was in Detmer for a reason, Gail. He's crazy, and he's dangerous."

"But it doesn't make sense," I said, shaking my head.

"By its very definition, crazy doesn't have to make sense."

"I was the one to seek out Naomi at that bank, not the other way around."

"Subliminal suggestions?" Guy said. "Or maybe you were convinced to do so in that time you don't remember. You said there's a lot of time that's just blank."

I thought back to the bank heist, and my conviction wavered. The timing *was* awfully convenient, given that I'd met up with Naomi twice and had ended up facing off against a villain shortly afterward each time. "I don't know," I finally said. "It doesn't feel like they're in cahoots."

He conceded with a nod. "All right. You're one of the best judges of character I know, so I'm inclined to go with your gut."

I gave him a weird look. "Guy, I worked with you every day for two years, and I had no idea you were the one scooping me off railroad tracks and buildings alike."

"So?"

"So I think maybe I'd have noticed if I'm such a great judge of character."

"You're allowed one fatal flaw. It's the hero way." He finished the last sandwich and gave me a tired grin. I shook my head at him, but, of course, I wanted to smile back. "What were you up to before I got here?"

"Just reading the Domino." I got up to rinse off the plate, talking over the sound of the faucet. "People think you've gotten boring now that Jeremy's become a recluse, by the way."

"They're not wrong," Guy said.

I stuck my tongue out at him for that. "Well, there aren't any worries that people are figuring out you're a redhead anytime soon, so there's that. Bolt's been accused of taking up-skirt shots again, and the Great Superb-O has officially come clean about who he is. I mean, we all knew who he was after those pictures of Kirstie Wentworth kissing him with the mask off came out, but it's nice that they've decided to go public now."

I'd meant to go on—Kirstie Wentworth was pretty famous, and the gossip about her was always interesting— but *something* made me stop though I wasn't sure what. I straightened like I could actually sense the change in the air. Curious, I turned around.

Guy had gone rigid.

"Is something wrong?" I asked.

He shook his head, but I could see the tension in his shoulders and jaw. "No," he said, and his voice was almost normal. I probably wouldn't have noticed the difference prior to my little run-in with my isotope-dosing supervillain, but now the unease was so obvious, it almost shouted at me. "No, I'm fine."

"Uh, okay. Did I cross a line or something? What's going on?"

"Nothing." Guy's jaw worked for a second. He wasn't glaring. In fact, he seemed to be struggling to keep a very pleasant look on his face. "I'm just a little tired after my fight, and I probably stink. I should have gone straight to my apartment instead of coming here and bothering you."

"I don't mind the company," I said, doing my best not to squint at him. "In fact, I'm glad you dropped by."

For a second, the tension eased a bit. His smile certainly seemed less forced. "I'm glad."

I opened my mouth to ask if he knew the Great Superb-O or something, if that was what was bothering him, but he cleared his throat. "I've taken up too much of your time tonight," he said. "I'm sure you want to get back to reading or whatever. Thanks for the food, and good night."

He didn't sprint for the door, but he didn't amble, either. Ten seconds later, I stood in my kitchen with a wet plate still in my hand, completely alone. I looked around for any clue that might explain it. "What the hell just happened?"

Chapter Eighteen

SOMETHING WAS UP with Guy.

Outside, the world was wondering at a new supervillain powerful enough to fight off both Blaze and Plain Jane. At Davenport, I wondered about Guy. He'd sent a text message the morning after our incident, a brief apology and a thanks for the sandwiches, with no explanation. I'd replied, only to receive silence in return. Vicki, who dropped by on her way out of town for a fashion shoot in Milan, had mentioned that he had some project at his father's company to handle, so he was probably busy.

Without Guy's company, I threw myself into training with Angélica. We were still working on the core basics, but we'd switched training rooms to an obstacle course. Rather than sparring, we raced across balance beams, low walls, and various pieces of furniture, trying to beat each other. I hadn't a hope of winning, not against a member of the speed team, but it was nice not to take a beating. It wasn't enough to distract me from Guy's weird distance, but I appreciated it nonetheless.

"How come I'm doing this?" I asked Angélica a couple of days into the obstacle course, as we were leapfrogging over the same wall.

She leapt straight up to grab the edge of a high wall, while I bounced off a corner and used my momentum to do the same. "Teaching you spatial reasoning," she said with a grunt.

"No, I got that part." We both sprinted down a balance beam, her two feet ahead of me. "I meant all of *this* in general. Why didn't I go to Superheroes 101 like everybody else who starts at Davenport?"

We catapulted off the building and into a block pit. Well, I catapulted. Angélica launched herself, seemed to flicker in the air for a second, and in a blink was standing at the edge of the pit. I had to crawl my way free. I clung to the side, panting, since we'd reached the end of the course.

"We talked about this," Angélica said, and I couldn't quite decipher the look on her face. "The adrenaline should be encouraging the Mobium to integrate faster."

"But if I'm constantly getting hurt and healing, doesn't it have other things to do? Wouldn't it have just been smarter to wait a little while and see what it does?"

"You said you wanted to be a hero. It seemed the most reasonable to let the isotope integrate with a taste of how you might live normally."

I gaped up at her and rolled to my feet. "When did I say that?"

"To Cooper? In Medical?" Angélica tilted her head. "You did say it, didn't you?"

"I said nothing of the sort. I said, 'I have cancer' and possibly some obscenities that I won't repeat here, then you showed up and started beating the crap out of me."

"Nobody asked you?" Her eyes narrowed.

I thought of Guy and his weird burst of moodiness before he'd vanished, of how I hadn't even realized I was in New York, and of the villains who'd spent years of my life gleefully abducting me. "Asking me things first isn't exactly common. Wait, are you telling me I could have said, 'I don't want to be a hero' and I could be sitting in a classroom right now? Because right now, that kind of sounds amazing."

She tossed me my water bottle. "You'll feel better after you hydrate."

"Yeah, yeah."

"Ray Goldstein doesn't have a class going on right now. So you're stuck with me, any way you look at it."

"Oh, joy," I said.

She nudged me with a none-too-gentle elbow to the rib cage. "Oh, c'mon, get some water in you, and let's try that course again. Maybe this time you'll beat me," she said, and just like that, the subject was dropped as we ran the course again.

A couple of days later, four days into Guy's silence, Naomi still hadn't sent me a meeting location, Mobius hadn't surfaced, and Chelsea was keeping equally mum. Frustrated, I did something I'd never done before on my own: I hit the gym.

Davenport had a gym for general use near the training rooms. I'd never actually gone though Angélica had mentioned I could make use of it whenever I wanted. She'd given me a hard look, which I'd taken to mean that if I didn't hydrate and keep my metabolism balanced properly, those privileges would be rescinded. In truth, I was usually too tired after my sessions with her to bother, but now I was positively brimming with anxious, frustrated energy.

The gym had a small indoor track surrounding a couple of basketball courts and some ping-pong tables. One entire room was dedicated to weight lifting, but I bypassed that in favor of some of the virtual-reality equipment. I wanted to run on a treadmill like the one Cooper and Kiki had made me use in Medical that first day.

"Well, lookie here," said a familiar voice, as I claimed one of the free machines, and I turned to see Jeremy grinning at me from the rowing-machine station behind me. Around him, screens depicted what looked like a crew race. "Haven't seen you down here before. Or in any gym ever, come to think of it."

"I know," I said, dumping my bag by the station. I stretched out my hamstring, which had bothered me the day before after a fall on the obstacle course. It was fine now, but my body healed faster than my mind remembered these days. "You always tried so hard to convince me, but alas. It took all of this to get me here. Not that I can say I'm surprised to find you here, though."

"Once a gym rat, always a gym rat." Sweat glistened on his skin, and he was breathing hard, but unlike me, he'd always liked that sort of thing. He propped his elbows on his knees, the biceps that I remembered well all but rippling. "How's your head?"

"It's fine." He'd asked me that every time he'd seen me since the disaster in the simulators. "Haven't felt that weird buzzing at all."

"That's good. What brings you down here?"

I bounced on the balls of my feet, loosening up. "Wanted to go for a run."

"*You?*"

"I run now. It's a thing." Hoping to deter him from mocking my anti-gym ways further, I turned and fiddled with the controls of the treadmill. I really wanted another desert run.

"So many changes," Jeremy said, his voice rueful. He shut down the rowing machine and strolled over to pick up the disinfectant spray so he could wipe it down. "You run now."

"Isotope," I said. "What are you doing?"

"Thought you could use some company," he said, looking up from the controls of the treadmill next to mine. When I narrowed my eyes at him, he grinned. "What, afraid you can't keep up?"

"I'm not the one that should be worried here."

He spread his arms wide, his grin broadening. "Big words for such a tiny person."

Forty minutes later, he lay on the ground, gasping like a landed fish. "I hate you."

"I told you not to try to match my pace," I said, switching my stride now that I wasn't holding back. Jeremy's face was bright red, and I could hear his pulse speeding, but other than that, he seemed fine. "Hydrate. You'll feel better."

He flopped dramatically on the ground. "I hate all of you classholes," he said between gasps. "Every single one of . . . you with . . . your stupid powers and your ability . . . to take a punch in the . . . face without even having the social grace to flinch."

"That sounds really specific." The hologram extended all the way around the treadmills, so it really looked like Jeremy was on the ground, being pulled along the desert roadside. Occasionally, the program glitched around him, pixilated lines of green and blue spreading over his skin like spiderwebs. They seemed to congregate around his hands.

"Yeah, well." Jeremy sat up and wheezed. "You don't need powers around here to have an adjustment period."

It still sounded way too specific, but I realized exactly whom he might have punched, and who wouldn't have flinched. "Jeremy, you hit Guy?"

"He deserved it."

"I'm not arguing that, but *why*?"

"Because he manipulated me into moving to Miami and I'd kind of been looking forward not to being mistaken for an idiot who wears skintight green and black." Jeremy guzzled from the water bottle and pushed himself back up, wincing as he climbed onto the treadmill and set it for a much slower pace. It messed with my mind a little since he was maintaining a limping walk and I was outright running, and the landscape moved forward at the same pace for both of us. "I didn't even hurt him. You should take more pity on me. I hurt my hand."

"I don't think I'm going to pity you, sorry."

"Worth a shot." He walked on, still struggling to breathe. "So you're mad at your boyfriend."

"No."

"Definitely mad."

"I'm not mad at Guy, Jer. And don't even start on the boyfriend thing. Everybody seems to think that, and it's just not true."

Jeremy snickered, and I glared at him. But instead of apologizing, he grinned. "It's nice to know somebody else can miss the mark with Miss Demanding over here."

I looked over and punched up the speed on the treadmill, easily adjusting my pace to match. He scowled.

"Yeah, yeah," he said. "You're special now. I got that after your trainer, that hot chick in Medical, your supermodel mentor—"

"The one you have a massive crush on—"

"—and the greenie all lit into me after you passed out on me. And now you go running."

I looked down at my feet, pounding into the treadmill belt below me. "I didn't ask for this. None of us asked for any of this."

"But you were lucky enough to get powers out of the deal."

I opened my mouth to point out that it wasn't exactly luck if my powers were also giving me cancer. But I was still watching my feet, mesmerized by the way my legs were moving easily, optimized for a long run. All of that had come naturally to me. I stood differently now. I noticed more and reacted quicker, and I moved with an economy that I'd seen Guy-as-Blaze exhibit. I stood differently. I ate differently. My sight, sense of smell, hearing, all of them had been heightened.

I felt powerful, a feeling I hadn't really experienced much since walking up to that 'L' platform as a brand-new Chicagoan. From the moment I'd picked up that beer bottle, I'd joined a game where every piece on the board had more strength and power than me. I wasn't their equal yet, and might never be, but I was no longer powerless.

"Yeah, I was lucky enough to get powers," I said.

"Exactly. So let me have this small victory where I crow over the fact that Blaze has screwed up."

"You're a very small, petty man," I said, but Jeremy grinned.

"Seriously, though, what's he done wrong? I need to know what I'm gloating about."

"Small," I repeated. "Petty."

Jeremy grinned and checked his watch, which was buzzing. "It's a little frightening how well they keep an eye on this place. You're wanted up in Medical. It's so nice to know that I don't have anything better to do with my day than be the Girl wrangler."

"You do look like you're kind of done with your workout, anyways," I said, since he'd sweated through his shirt and was still breathing hard.

"Now who's small and petty?"

We cut the cooldown short and because of it, I felt a bit weird when we stepped on the elevator together. The run had been nowhere near as satisfying as I'd been hoping for. Instead of allowing me to distract myself from moping about Guy, Jeremy had dug that topic right up and laid it on the treadmill at my feet.

Two floors up, the elevator stopped, and a woman stepped on. She was blond, stocky rather than lithe, and her eyes were infinitely familiar. From the way Jeremy tensed, he'd recognized her as well.

Jessie Davenport gave us both a nod. There was nothing of her twin brother's genial air about her though she wore a well-cut pantsuit that spoke of the same wealth. Jeremy, she dismissed easily, but her eyes lingered on me. My tongue abruptly tied itself into knots, and I was struck by the fact that I was now riding an elevator with *the* Raptor.

"You're the Godwin girl," she said. Her voice had a low sort of rasp to it, like she had been chain-smoking from birth.

"Yes, ma—yes, that's me. Gail." Foolishly, I stuck a hand out.

"Jessie," she said, shaking my hand. The minute she released her grip, she shifted, crossing her arms over the chest, and I recognized the stance as pure Raptor through and through. "You met my brother Eddie last year."

"I did. It was . . . memorable."

"Dunno why. He's rather boring, all told," Jessie Davenport said, turning back to face the front of the elevator.

I wasn't sure how to reply to that, so I just said, "He seemed nice."

"Then he's fooling you. But I can see why the Bookman kid would step in on your behalf." The elevator doors opened on her floor, and she paused, looking me up and down again. "Welcome to Davenport, Miss Godwin."

"Uh, thank you. Thank you very much."

The minute the doors had closed behind her, Jeremy and I both sagged against the back of the elevator. "Is she always that intense?" I asked.

He nodded emphatically. "That's the first time I've actually seen her *talk* to anybody. Usually, she just stands there and glowers."

"Okay, okay, drama queen."

The brief, mildly absurd encounter with Jessie Davenport had only made me feel stranger. My instincts had categorized her as a threat so quickly that the fight-or-flight reflex had kicked in, and I had some leftover adrenaline. I kind of wanted to go run an obstacle course or two with Angélica to calm myself down. But instead, we disembarked on the right floor for Medical and made our way through the winding hallways once again. By the time we reached the now-familiar door, I'd calmed somewhat. "You don't have to go in with me," I told Jeremy.

"Maybe I want a lollipop. The receptionists always keep some."

The woman working the front desk waved me back and didn't give Jeremy a second look, which meant they'd probably expected him to tag along. He reached the door before me and pushed through. "What's up?" he said by way of greeting.

About to scold him for not even bothering to knock, I hurried in after him and pulled up short. I'd been expecting Cooper and maybe Kiki, but they also had Angélica with them. Though they all turned right away with pleasant looks on their faces, I could read the body language as though it shouted at me. Angélica was incredibly displeased about something.

"What's going on?" I asked.

Cooper gave us a bright smile. "Integration Day," he said.

"What?" Jeremy asked.

"We think the Mobium has stabilized. Pull up a chair."

Because he was gesturing at a couple of white wheelie chairs, I pulled them over, giving Kiki a wide berth. She seemed friendly, but my gut made me want me to keep a nice distance between us. It seemed the isotope hadn't quite forgotten—or forgiven—her attempted mental intrusion after the episode on the simulators. Being farther away from her wouldn't actually protect me, I knew, but I felt better on the other side of the room.

She seemed to notice, for she gave me a sympathetic smile. I tried to give her an apologetic one in return.

"What does that mean?" I asked Cooper as I sat. "Integration? Like, I don't have cancer?"

"Sadly, no." He crossed to the computer bank against the wall. Instantly, the same charts I'd memorized from the handouts he'd given me at previous appointments appeared on the wall to my left. I raised my eyebrows. The numbers were significantly better across the board.

"Huh," Jeremy said, squinting.

"What?" I asked him.

He kind of waved at one corner of the screen. "Just kind of interesting to see it all broken down like that."

"Nerd," I said, smiling.

Before he could reply, Vicki strolled in, a little carry-on tote over her shoulder. "What'd I miss?"

Angélica narrowed her eyes at my mentor. "Did you come straight from the airport?"

"I got the text that it's Integration Day. I want to see Girl punch Cooper."

"I have to do that again?" I asked.

"We're testing everything we did at the beginning," Kiki said.

"Wait, where's Guy?" Vicki asked, lifting her sunglasses to her forehead as she looked around.

I folded my arms over my chest. "That's the million-dollar question, isn't it?"

"Oo-kay," Vicki said, drawing the word out. "I've missed some things. Got it. So what's up first?"

My friends waited around while Kiki and Cooper put me through my paces, testing my reflexes, strength, and endurance. Angélica remained silent, a stony look on her face, and I wondered exactly what she'd been discussing with Kiki and Cooper before I'd arrived. Mostly I was preoccupied by the empty chair in the corner, one that no doubt would have belonged to Guy had he come. He never showed.

But when it became time for me to punch Cooper in that goofy little apron, I nearly put him through a wall. He looked dazed for a second as he pushed himself to his feet.

"Happy Integration Day," he said.

Chapter Nineteen

EVEN THOUGH THE isotope and I had officially become one, I wasn't actually cleared to leave Davenport until Angélica had been assured that I knew how to take care of myself. "We think you'll kick the leukemia," she'd said on the way out of Medical, and my heart had thumped hard in hope. "But until you do, better safe than sorry."

Though I should have been happier about that—my strength and stamina were now permanent, which meant I wouldn't be helpless again—I felt an itch between my shoulder blades, like something was out of place. The feeling dogged my heels through dinner and more research on Chelsea and Mobius. As always, I slept like a stone, but my first thoughts in the morning when I woke up were of Guy.

Disquieted by that, I rolled out of bed early, grabbed a crap-cake instead of cooking myself breakfast, and started the hike across the complex to his apartment. He could have been at his Miami apartment for all I knew, or still out doing whatever it was he did all night, but I didn't mind the walk. If I'd said something to offend him, I wanted to know about it.

Sam answered the second time I knocked, squinting like daylight was a personal offense and not something that just happened. His hair had been brushed by wolverines. "Who're you?"

"Gail," I said. When he continued to stare, I added, "Godwin? Gail Godwin?"

For a minute, I thought he might have actually fallen asleep standing up. When he let out a massive yawn, I jumped. "Hostage Girl," he finally said, pointing at my face.

I gingerly pushed his finger aside. "Sure, okay, that's not weird at all. Is your brother here?"

"Upstairs." He shuffled to the side and, leaving the door open, flew back to the second floor.

Since the isotope hadn't seen fit to give me flight, I took the stairs. As I approached Guy's room, I could hear him moving about inside, so it looked like he didn't share his brother's apparent distaste for mornings. My hand wavered only a little as I raised it to knock.

I heard his footsteps approach. "Sam," he said, "it's not like you to kn—Gail."

Given the foot and a half height difference between his brother and me, it was actually a little comical to watch Guy abruptly lower his gaze. He kept his hands on his tie, which he'd apparently been in the process of tying.

"Good morning," I said, and it hit me too late: what if

Guy had had company the night before? What if I'd interrupted something?

Thankfully, Guy's smile bloomed, almost like he couldn't help himself. "Morning," he said, leaning against the doorjamb. "What's up?"

"I just thought I would drop by and see how you were doing. Haven't seen you in a while."

"Yeah." His heart rate picked up, I realized. It had spiked upon seeing me, but at my innocuous statement, I could hear his heart actually begin to pound. "I had a work thing, and then I was on patrol for a bit—Vicki should have passed that on?"

"Oh, she did. I just"—What, Gail? Thought you'd stalk him in the meantime?—"thought I'd see how that was going."

"Because you're really interested in the findings of the exploratory committee on the Bookman fiscal-earnings policy report?"

"Yeah, I thought it could use even more oversight, maybe some regulations or something," I said, my voice absolutely droll. Guy threw his head back and laughed, and I thought that was as good an opportunity as anything. At least he seemed like he was in a good mood. "Hey, Guy, I have to ask: did I say something to offend you?"

He abruptly stopped laughing.

"You left in kind of a rush the other day, and a lot of people have told me that I can be pretty direct. So I wanted to make sure everything was fine between us," I said.

"Direct," he repeated, giving me an odd look.

"They usually say 'blunt to the point of terrifying.' Did I do something?"

He crossed his arms over his chest, pulling them in close. "Everything's fine," he said. "You don't have anything to worry about."

That wasn't exactly an answer to my question, I realized, but I couldn't see a way to push the issue without fighting. So I just ducked my head. "Oh. Then I guess it might have been in my head after all. I'm sorry to bother you before work like this."

"You're never a bother." That, at least, sounded genuine. "If you've got some time, want to stick around? I am a master at breakfast."

"No, I already ate, and Angélica will get on my case if I'm late."

"Maybe later, then."

I nodded and gave him a little good-bye wave, but before I reached the stairs, I turned back around. "Sam's really not into the whole morning thing, is he?"

"Never met one he couldn't sleep through," Guy said.

"I figured. See you around, Guy."

"See you, Gail."

I wondered about it as I walked to the training rooms. Guy's heart rate, his casual evasion, all of that seemed to indicate I hadn't been paranoid at all. Something was going on. Either I'd done something, or someone else had, that night he'd come to visit me in his uniform. But whatever had happened, he didn't owe me an explanation. He'd saved my life a staggering number of times, and I really liked having him around, both as Guy and as Blaze. Ultimately, though, I wasn't in a position to ask him why he was so nervous and pretending not to be.

So, feeling as though I'd accomplished nothing, I headed toward the training room, where Angélica was waiting. At least hitting something might make me feel better.

HOURS LATER, I hit the mat with a grunt and an annoyed whine.

"You're coming along," Angélica said, bouncing to her feet. She beamed. "Kid."

"Please." I was panting and out of breath, but it was a good sort of winded. "I'm more than coming along. I'm kicking ass. And you can't be more than a couple of years older than I am, so calling me kid's just precocious."

"When you can consistently beat me, you get to decide what I call you, not before."

"I can think of a few things I'd like to call you."

"I've heard worse, *amiga*. Now, stop lazing around, I want to test a theory."

"What theory?"

"Not telling." Her grin spoke of pure mischief. "All you have to do is watch me and focus. Use that meditation technique I taught you."

I shifted my feet at that. Meditating was a skill I would probably never master, no matter how hard Angélica tried to make me sit and focus on my breathing. My thoughts always ping-ponged around my head, and I hated the quiet moments. Keeping busy kept worries and memories at bay, and meditation left me vulnerable to that sort of thing.

You don't face down dozens of supervillains without ending up with a few nightmares, as much as I tried to pretend that wasn't the case.

But now, I did as bade, closing my eyes so I could imagine an open door in the black space of my mind. I kept absolutely still until I could discern every detail, from the rectangle of golden light seeping through the cracks, to the texture and grain of the wood. Once I could make out the glint of gold on the doorknob, I reached forward in my mind and opened the door.

When I opened my eyes, the world jumped into sharp, almost painful focus. Colors brightened, the saturation deepening. Sounds became crystal clear. I could practically see Angélica's skin jumping at the pulse points and hear the way her body moved. Her heartbeat sounded like a symphony.

"Watch me," she said, and my ears itched. She rolled her shoulders and weaved her hands through the air in some kind of tai chi move I didn't recognize. When she brought her hand down against her thigh, the *smack* made me jolt.

"Theatrical," I said when she looked at me.

"Smartass. Turn around."

"Why?"

"Because I said to."

I turned and waited for the inevitable attack. "What now?"

"Just listen. Without looking at me, what am I doing?"

"Probably making face at my back," I said. She sighed. "Angélica, the isotope doesn't give me eyes in the back of my head. How am I supposed to know what you're doing if I can't see you?"

"Try listening. Tell me what I'm doing."

"I don't know what you're doing. I can't see you."

"I'm doing *something*. What is it?"

"Angélica, for the thousandth time—"

"What am I doing!"

"You're rolling your shoulders! It sounds really stupid, actually, and—how did I know that?" I spun on my heel as she placed her hands on her hips, looking smug. "Are you telling me my hearing's *that* good?"

"Yup. Has been for a while, but I don't think you've been picking up on it." She stretched out her hamstring, idly. "You've got the basic movements down, and you're comfortable with your body and how it moves thanks to the work we've been doing on the obstacle course. But now we need to work on your instincts, your awareness, and how you react to threats. You've been doing it subconsciously, but now we need to hone that skill."

"How do I use this to my advantage?"

"Ideally, you'd have time to get the measure of your opponent before the fighting starts, but in practical application, that technique tends to lead to you getting punched in the face. So you'll need to learn to multitask."

As with everything Angélica had taught me, it was easier said than done. I might have subconsciously been using my superior hearing, but consciously attempting to do so tripped me up. It was like trying to fight through molasses when I'd been sprinting through cotton candy for days, and Angélica didn't hold back. More times than

I wanted to count, I found myself on my back, staring up at a ceiling that I could see in remarkably clear detail. I wondered if all of Angélica's trainees were this hopeless. Every time I moved, a spark of color at the corner of my eye would flash, distracting me, or my ears would pick up some new and unfamiliar sound, and before I knew it, I was on my back again, counting little cartoon birdies.

Until it *clicked*.

Right before I took one on the chin, naturally.

Angélica leaned over me on the mat. "You okay?" she asked, looking a tiny bit concerned.

I was thinking too hard. About Guy, about Davenport, even about this new sensory talent. Sure, I had a new ability, but my body had done most of the rest of the work since Dr. Mobius had infected me. I was trying to lead with my brain, when really, I should be working the other way around.

I had powers now. I should trust them, not me.

"Kid?"

I snapped back to awareness. "Don't call me that."

"Good to see you're still with us. How's the chin?"

It hurt. "It's good. I'm ready to go again."

"That's what I'm talking about." She rushed at me the minute I was on my feet, but apparently I'd been expecting that, for I dodged nimbly.

Right away, I could sense the difference. Angélica seemed to agree, for she shot me a challenging look, and the fighting started in earnest. She sent me to the mat a few more times, but I persevered. And the first time I pinned her to the mat was sweet, sweet victory.

"Ha!" I had one of her arms twisted underneath her and was holding the other, my knees pushing her legs down. Realistically, she might have been able to muscle out of it, but I wasn't interested in letting that happen. "Points for Gail! Yah!"

She laughed. "All right, all right. Your match. Get off me."

I rolled off her and sprang to my feet. "And that, my friend, is how we do things in Gail-Town. Awesomely, that's how."

"Glad to see you're a modest winner."

"Hell no, I'm not. Your ass has been thoroughly kicked."

Her grin turned a little dangerous. I bounced onto my toes, anticipating a rematch even though I was burning through the last of my reserves. But she just shook her head. "Get some food in you."

"Sure you don't want to go another round?"

"Against you? Always. But you're starting to flag, and it stings my pride a little to admit that you still beat me. Eat your crap-cake." She tossed it at me; I caught it one-handed and shoved the entire thing down, gulping quickly to avoid tasting it. "Get out of here and go see that boyfriend of yours."

"Not my boyfriend, and I'm not sure he wants to see me right now. I think he's at work."

"Or he's standing outside the door."

When I turned, Guy waved at me through the little window in the door. I waved back. "How did you see that and I missed it?" I asked, rocking back onto my heels. Once she'd brought him to my attention, I could actually hear Guy outside the door.

"Because you've still got a ways to go." Angélica clapped me on the shoulder as she collected her duffel bag. "Catch you later, Gail-Town."

"Gail-Town? Kid is better than that."

"Too late. I'm off to the bike trails."

Before I picked up my bag and followed her, I took a second to pause and relax my senses. As cool as it was to sense everything around me, it could give me a headache if I kept it up for too long. Sometimes I felt better just being closer to the regular Gail.

"I saw the little victory dance," Guy said when I joined him outside. "Was that your first time beating her like that?"

"Sadly, yes. How was your day?"

"Inescapably boring. I'd much rather have sparred with Angélica for eight hours."

"Has it really been that long?" I grabbed Guy's wrist to look at his watch, and he put his hand over his face to cover a smile. I grimaced and let go; perhaps I'd spent a little too much time with Angélica if her lack of regard for personal space was rubbing off on me. "No wonder I ate so many crap-cakes today. She was teaching me about sensory awareness. Heady stuff. Exciting, too."

"Wanna go a few more rounds?"

I laughed before I could stop myself. "Uh, I'm flattered, but I've seen you punch through brick walls."

"I've got bracelets that would make us pretty evenly matched." But he jerked a shoulder, so we started walking away from the training rooms and back toward the residential part of the complex.

"How does that work?" I asked as I dug my water bottle out.

"I'm not sure. Davenport designed them, and I never questioned it. They wear off, and it's nice to be able to beat on a punching bag without having to worry about the structural integrity of the building."

"So it's not a secret compound from whatever caused your powers? I heard it was meteors."

"Where'd you hear about that?"

Another evasive answer, I thought. He wasn't confirming or denying. "I read it on the Domino. They had a whole series about perceived weaknesses in some of the big-name heroes. Yours was a compound that robbed you of your strength."

"Irresponsible journalism at its finest." Guy shoved his hands into his back pockets. "I'm not a fan of the Domino if you can't tell."

"But they love you," I said, drawing the word out like Vicki always did. Guy gave me a mock scowl for it. By the time we'd reached his apartment and he had dug out all of the ingredients for something French—Châteaubriand, whatever that was—he had managed to dismantle most of the Domino's theories from that article though he hadn't said anything more about his own origins.

"I can chop vegetables or something," I said, watching him prep the meat. He waved me off. "Territorial, huh?"

"One of my many flaws."

"Clearly, you have a lot of those. I mean, between holding down a full-time job, being an accomplished cook, and that superhero gig, you're just riddled with them."

"Hey, I have flaws." He finished dusting the cut of beef with spices and moved over to wash his hands. "Deep, awful flaws."

"Like what? And don't say being a redhead. I know some very nice redheads."

Guy wrinkled his nose at me. "That one's not on the list."

"Okay, so we're agreed. Redhead: not a flaw. What are the others?"

"Temper." Guy selected a knife and began to chop a carrot, julienne-style. "It's not usually bad, but it can be. I sometimes fall asleep in movie theaters. My ex told me that could be annoying."

"Okay, that's a little more understandable. But, really, isn't it the movies' fault for not being interesting enough?"

"My point exactly. And I'm not always the quickest on my feet, talking-wise. I get—I get tongue-tied."

I snitched a bit of carrot. "Tongue-tied, huh?"

"It's a problem. One I'm going to shut up about, ironically enough." He moved the cutting board away when I went to steal a second piece of carrot, and gave me a sly grin instead. "What would you say my flaws are, since you seem so knowledgeable?"

"You're too tall, for one thing," I said right away. "I have to crane my neck to look up at you."

"That one I can't help."

"Fine. Then you always lead with your left."

His head shot up. "I beg your pardon?"

"When you're punching villains. You always have. I thought once that maybe you wore a signet ring on your finger or something, so you could brand it into their cheeks, but with my new, sophisticated knowledge, I realized you're just lazy. I mean, if the villains pick up on that little quirk, you're screwed, too. I only know because of our long and storied history together."

Guy rocked back on his heels, closing his eyes. "Angélica is going to have such a field day with that."

I tilted my head at him. "That's if she finds out. What's my silence worth to you?"

"Dinner?"

"Sold. Are you sure you don't need any help? I feel kind of lazy sitting here, stinking up the place."

"No—and you don't stink. I mean, well, you kind of do, but it's okay." Guy shrugged sheepishly. He pulled out another carrot and diced it up quickly before he dared to look up at me. "Sorry for saying you stink."

"No, it's fairly obvious that I do. I can run back to my place real quick and grab a shower if it's bothering you."

"It's fine. My sense of smell is actually a little duller than most people's, so I can barely smell it." He pulled a bottle of ranch dressing out of the refrigerator and a plate from the cabinet.

"Really? So you're like the opposite of me in that way, then?"

One corner of his mouth curled up as he passed the carrot, ranch dressing, and plate over to me. "Right. So if one of us has to be the canary in the mineshaft . . ."

I dug in with vigor, happy to have food of any kind. "Your canary, reporting for duty. Hopefully minus the dying bit."

"Hopefully."

I looked from the vegetables to the rice simmering on the stovetop. It was the kind of meal that you would cook to impress someone, like a date, I realized. In fact, it almost felt like a date. There were appetizers—I wasn't allowed alcohol yet, so I'd stuck to water—good conversation, and hey, a really hot guy cooking for me.

Too bad I was in my workout clothes and probably looked really gross after hours of being thrown around the room by a speed-freak Brazilian woman with the most terrifying biceps I'd ever seen. Because I really, I discovered, wouldn't mind if it were an actual date.

I swirled a carrot stick through the ranch dressing. "I've noticed something weird about being here. People used to insist all the time that you were my boyfriend." Guy's head shot up. Interesting. "I mean, they were saying you were Jeremy, yeah, but it was still 'Blaze is Hostage Girl's boyfriend' all the time. And now, every single person I've talked to at Davenport has called you my boyfriend. As Guy, not Blaze and—whoa, holy hell!"

I rose halfway out of my stool in alarm when Guy brought the knife down on his hand. Visions of chopped-off fingers danced in my head, but he only shook out his hand and gave the knife—now horribly disfigured along its bladed edge—a disgusted look. "Third one I've ruined this month," he said.

"If I did that, I'd have lost half my hand. Are you okay?"

Guy held up his hand, which had a thin red mark spanning from his middle knuckle to the back of his thumb.

It hadn't even broken the skin. "S'fine," he said, looking down again.

"It's *fine* that you just tried to dismember yourself?"

"By accident. It happens. Benefits of being superhuman." When I just continued to stare, he raised his head again. "Gail, it's fine. Really."

I realized I was still half-out of my stool, and sat back down, willing my heart to slow down. "If you say so. Though I have to admit, that's the first time being falsely accused of dating me has made somebody try to lose body parts."

He glanced at me quickly, then back down at the drawer as he pulled out another knife, which he set to the side. "No, maybe they just lose their minds."

"Are you saying they'd have to be crazy to date me?"

"No!" Abruptly, he turned the same shade of red as his tie. He cleared his throat. "I mean, um, no. I was trying to say they'd just lose their minds over how cool you are. Not that they're crazy and—you're teasing me, aren't you?"

"Only a little." I felt bad enough to reach across the countertop and pat his hand. "You kind of left yourself wide open. I'm sorry."

He shook his head, his smile a touch rueful. "I'll forgive you this time."

"Much obliged."

He sighed and flexed his barely injured hand. Since I sensed it would be a bad time to interrupt or make a joke, I watched him and waited. He tapped the side of his thumb against the cutting board in clear agitation and finally cleared his throat.

"Look, I'm not good with words. Some of the others on the front line, they can banter with the villains and they're funny and insightful and they have the timing of comic geniuses, but I don't have that skill. I'm lucky if I can get two sentences out of my mouth in a row without sounding like a complete idiot."

I started to point out that he was doing a pretty good job at this point, but he gave me a look, so I bit my lip instead.

"So I guess I'll cut to the heart of the matter," he said. "Gail, are you being nice to me because I saved your life all those times as Blaze or because you like me? Guy Bookman, not Blaze."

That was the last thing I expected him to say. And whatever good feelings had been rising to the top, they abruptly fled. "I like Guy more than I like Blaze."

Guy stepped back in shock. "What?"

"You know what Blaze was to me?" I gave him a long look. This was something I had never shared with anybody, not even the therapist I'd gone to see for a few months, but he needed to know. "He was the one who came to save the day when once again, things were out of my control. He went through a lot of hell to get me out of some truly terrible situations, and I'm grateful for that, but you know what he wasn't?"

I leaned forward, and I put both hands on the counter-top. "He wasn't the guy," I said, "that *talked* to me."

"Gail—"

"You might not be good with words, but for two years, I got kidnapped by every villain strolling through Chicago and hounded by reporters for details about a super-hero who was all but a stranger to me. And it wasn't fun not having a single person believe me when I said I didn't know any more than they did. All I got from Blaze were long looks in the middle of the battle, the mistaken belief that maybe I had a secret admirer or was part of a tragic love story, and a rose with a little cartoon doodle when I wound up in the hospital yet again."

Guy shut his mouth.

"And then you left. You left, and Jeremy left, and I didn't know *anything*. Just—silence. The most I'd ever 'talked'"—and I used air quotes—"to Blaze was a walk we shared on some autumn night when I was working late, where you didn't say a word. So, yes, I like Guy a whole hell of a lot more than I like Blaze."

I took a deep breath, and it sounded like an explosion in the stillness that had come over the kitchen. My hands shook. I'd kept those feelings bottled up for so long, down so deep that even I hadn't realized I'd been storing them up. But once the words had started to flow, I hadn't been able to stop them. And I didn't regret them, either. My chest felt hollow, and my stomach had leapt up to my throat, but I didn't look away from Guy's face.

Red splotches had appeared on his throat above his loosened tie, but I couldn't tell if it was fury or humilia-tion, as an emotionless mask had settled over his face. But his eyes were the same eyes that had always stared at me from behind Blaze's mask.

The silence reigned for nearly a full minute before Guy finally spoke. "You must have hated me."

I ran a hand over my face. "No. Not even close. Never like that."

"I thought—" Agitated once more, he hooked his thumb under the knot in his tie and pulled it loose, yanking off the article of clothing like it had offended him. "I like you—it wasn't a love thing when I was saving you, but I've always liked you, and I respected you, how brave you always were. And then you were here out of the blue one night, and paying attention to me, and it was great. You don't know how much I always—that's not important right now." He scraped his fingers through his hair. "The thing is, I didn't think I could handle it if you just liked Blaze and tolerated me as Guy out of pity. But I see I misunderstood everything, and I didn't even consider that there might be other perspectives."

"Is that why you left the other day?" I asked, narrowing my eyes.

His nod was shamefaced. "You were talking about the Great Superb-O being an outed superhero, and I was . . . jealous. He had somebody that probably liked both sides of him. You knew I was lying, didn't you?"

"I can hear your heartbeat."

Guy balled up the tie and threw it toward the second floor. "Well, thank you for letting me have the dignity of my lie."

"Thank you for owning up to it."

"And I'm sorry." He looked beyond uncomfortable now. The red splotches had traveled up to his cheeks. "For all of the pain my need to keep my identity hidden put you through. I am sorry for that."

"Apology accepted," I said.

"Really? Just like that?"

"When you've faced as many villains as I have and been given supercancer as a result, you learn not to waste time dwelling." My hands were slowly ceasing to shake, thankfully, and I could feel my pulse calming. Now that that giant mess of emotion was off my chest, I felt lighter than I had in a long time. I hadn't realized I'd had that much darkness festering. "But maybe ask me next time rather than stewing about it. I'm direct, remember?"

"You are." Surprisingly, his grin flashed, and the tense line of his shoulders eased. "It's cute."

I wrinkled my nose. "I am many things, but cute is not one of them."

"Nope. Adorable." Guy leaned over and snatched up one of the carrot sticks, popping the whole thing in his mouth.

"If you were anything but nine feet tall and pure muscle, you'd understand why 'adorable' is not actually the compliment you think it is."

"So 'precious' is out of the question?"

"Put those bracelets on, let's go a few rounds. I bet I can kick your ass."

"And I bet it'll be darling."

"Okay," I said, finally laughing. "Now you're just pushing it. What's next? 'Dainty'?"

"I was going to go with . . ." He cocked his head as he gave the matter some thought.

"You've run out of options."

"No, I—yes, I've got nothing beyond using 'cute' again,

so I concede the field. Hopefully without you kicking my ass, as you've already done that once tonight." When I started to sink into my chair, he shook his head. "I deserved it. I'll wait until later to lick my wounds. Right now, I've got a dinner to serve."

Right on cue, my stomach growled. I covered my face with my hand even as Guy laughed.

"Hey, Gail?" he said when we finally sat down to the dinner he'd cooked (on his couch, since he and Sam apparently did not have a table).

"Yeah?"

"If I promise to never try and split myself into separate identities again, will you go out with me? I mean, we probably won't be able to date outside of Davenport because if people see you with a second tall guy with green eyes, they'll figure out I'm Blaze, but . . . I don't know, I like you."

"I'll think about it," I said, though his shy offer made me want to tap-dance. His face fell so quickly that I had to stifle my laugh. "I was kidding. Of course I'd love to go out with you. Though I hope you're prepared to deal with Vicki's telling us 'I told you so.'"

He looked at me over his plate, his eyes seeming even brighter than usual in the dimness of the TV screen. "I can deal."

"Good," I said, and I think we both pretended we weren't smiling through the incredibly good meal that followed.

Chapter Twenty

central city mall at 6:30 2nite, need to talk

THE TEXT FROM Naomi, the first solid communication I'd had from her in days, showed up on my phone ten minutes after Angélica let me out of training the next afternoon. At least the reporter had given me a four-hour window to somehow get to the mall. Given that I was in New York and not Chicago, though, I would need more than four hours unless I got help. Guy would be busy in Miami all day, as he needed to put in some face time as Blaze. Angélica would yell at me for having a cell phone, and Jeremy was as stuck at Davenport as I was, so that left only one option.

"Ah, my mentee!" Vicki said upon seeing me on her threshold. "Dropping by?"

"Bored and restless," I lied. I'd debated whether or not I should just be up front about the fact that I needed to get to Chicago. But if Naomi was indeed working with Chelsea, Vicki might feel the need to warn Angélica. So I'd just scope things out. "Feel up to entertaining me, mentor?"

"As long as I don't have to feed you." She stepped to the side to let me in. "Mostly because I don't have any food in here—I got hungry at three in the morning and went through, like, half the fridge. There's maybe a bag of chips if you're hungry, but watching you eat is exhausting."

"Yeah, so's actually eating everything I have to in order to survive," I said.

Vicki gave me a sardonic look and flopped, loose-limbed, on one of her black leather chairs. She was barefoot and wearing jeans and a simple white tank top. But even such a simple outfit gave me an opportunity.

"Jeans," I said, looking enviously at her while I folded one of my legs underneath me and sat on the couch. "I'd kill to have a pair of jeans right now, you have no idea. It feels like I've been wearing a school uniform for the past two weeks.

Vicki gave my outfit the critical eye. "I bet. Davenport uniforms are yawn-fests. You haven't cleaned out your apartment yet?"

"I haven't left Davenport at all. But even then, none of my clothes would fit. The day you pulled Chelsea off me, I was wearing my skinny jeans and my tightest belt." And I'd constantly had to pull up the waistline.

"Sounds like what you need, girlfriend, is a shopping trip."

And just like that, I had a way to get to Naomi.

"Actually," Vicki said, eyeing my shirt with its Davenport Industries logo, "let's raid my closet first. And then we'll go."

"I kind of want to go to the mall back near my place. I like one of the stores there."

"Chicago's fine with me."

"But what about the 'porters?"

"Leave that to me."

Vicki was nearly a foot taller than I was, so I borrowed a pair of shorts instead, but I could get away with one of her shirts, which showed off my minimal cleavage rather well (the one thing the isotope had stolen from me was an impressive bust line). "Normally, you'd go to Reception and get some money, since they haven't issued you a credit card yet," Vicki said, as we headed for the main part of the complex. "But what good is having an internationally recognized supermodel as a mentor if she can't make it rain a little?"

"You're the best," I said, absolutely meaning it. "But can I pay you back when I have money?"

"If you want. Whatever works." Vicki leaned over to press a button but quickly slapped her hand back over the door at the call of "Hold the elevator!" from the corridor.

Angélica rounded the corner and hopped aboard. It was the first time I'd seen her wearing anything but workout gear, or wearing makeup, and I immediately felt a stab of pure, annoying jealousy. Of course, she was a knockout. "Where are we going?" she asked, her voice pleasant.

I wanted to sink into the floor, but Vicki merely scoffed. "Girl needs new clothes. Honestly, it's the next best thing to slavery, keeping her in such Davenport outfits."

Angélica looked at me. "Didn't think to check with me first?"

"Kind of was hoping to sneak out. Does this mean we can't go?" I asked. Naomi was going to be annoyed if I stood her up.

"As it happens, I need a new pair of shoes myself."

"You're coming?" Vicki asked.

Angélica shrugged. "Girl trip. How could I resist?"

I eyed her. "How'd you know we were going shopping?"

"Girl, what can I say? You're my life. I make it my business to know everything about you."

"Stalker."

She grinned. "Also, I need new shoes. So where are we going?"

"Girl wants to go to her old haunt, and I thought it would be fun. You know I adore finding a new mall. The 'porter should be able to take three of us in one trip, too."

"Sounds good," Angélica said.

We disembarked, heading down a long, carpeted hallway similar to the Annals. I wondered at these 'porters that Guy and Vicki had told me about. I'd seen a variety of powers before, but teleporting had always seemed like something out of a Saturday morning cartoon. If villains were able to just hop from one place to another spontaneously, that changed the battlefield. What would stop one from simply plucking up a hero without the ability to fly, teleporting somewhere very high, and dropping the hero?

And what did it feel like to teleport?

Vicki pushed through an unmarked door. I expected some kind of futuristic room full of fancy equipment and retro lighting, but instead it was a reception area for an office. The receptionist behind the desk gave her an expectant look.

"Three for Chicago," Vicki said.

The receptionist pushed a yellow binder across the desk. "Sign the log. Full names, please."

One by one, we signed on the next line of the little spreadsheet, and I goggled that such a fantastical thing could be surrounded by the mundane. Once Angélica, who'd taken the pen last, had scrawled her signature, the receptionist cleared her throat. "Gregory is available in Room Two."

Vicki led the way down a little hallway that smelled like coffee and printer ink. All of the doors were labeled like offices, with room numbers and names, so when Vicki pushed open the door to Room Two, I expected a cramped little office with a motivational poster of a cat dangling off a tree branch. Instead, we found a slightly overweight man in his forties sitting cross-legged in the middle of the room, playing solitaire with a deck of cards. He wore a short-sleeved button-up shirt and a tie.

"Gregory," Vicki said, throwing her arms wide. "My man."

He looked up at her and kind of smiled. "Ah, good, I was looking forward to Miami. Been wanting a smoothie."

"Sorry, Chicago this time."

"Deep-dish pizza instead, got it." Gregory gave me a once-over. "First-timer?"

"We're initiating her."

"It's not going to hurt, is it?" I asked, giving the empty office a wary look.

"Tingles a little." Greg stacked the cards and pushed them into his pocket. " 'Bout a split second, put together. Some people get headaches. You going to be one of those people?"

"I hope not."

"It'll be okay," Angélica said.

I watched as Gregory pulled a piece of cord out of his pocket. The other two seemed to know what to do; Vicki immediately stepped to Gregory's right, and Angélica nudged me forward. Greg wrapped the cord around all three of us and instructed us to hold on to one of his arms. Angélica did so by putting her arms on either side of me, which only served to make me nervous. "Ready?" Gregory said.

"Rea—" Vicki started to say before Gregory turned blue like an activated bug zapper, and my world exploded into noise.

It was like being battered straight to the skull with a jackhammer. Instinct had me clapping my hands over my ears and dropping as unrelenting, loud, sheer walls of noise pounded at me, a cacophony of torture. It drilled into my head, splitting it into two equal halves of sheer agony.

"Gail? Gail!" The voice, a low contralto, pushed around, pushed *through* the wall until I heard Angélica in my head, above the breathing, above the car engines, above the roaring. "Gail! Listen to my voice. It's all in your head, got it? It's all in your head."

I curled up tighter, only partially aware that there were arms around me. My head hurt so much, so, so much—and something pinched my shoulder.

Instantly, it was like somebody turned the volume down. "Ow! Cut that out."

Something pinched my other shoulder, and the noise faded away entirely. I opened my eyes to see Gregory, Vicki, and Angélica staring back at me. "What the hell just happened?" I asked.

"We just 'ported," Vicki said.

I looked around. We were in the same room with the circle on the floor. "No we didn't."

The other three laughed, which I felt was a little unfair. "Apparently you're one of the ones that have an adverse reaction. It'll wear off within fifteen minutes," Gregory said. "I'll see you ladies when you get back."

My head felt as though somebody had stuffed it full of cotton batting. "You're all nuts. This is some kind of sadistic trick, isn't it, to warn me about what happens when I don't follow the rules?"

Angélica pulled on my shoulder, forcing me to climb to my feet. "C'mon," she said, marching me out the door and back down the little hallway.

It wasn't until we moved into the reception area and I got a look at the receptionist that I realized anything had changed. Instead of a kind grandmotherly type manning the desk, there was a gigantic black man who was hunting and pecking at the keyboard with two fingers. "Welcome to Chicago," he said, and then squinted at my face. "First time?"

"It's that obvious?" I asked.

He gave me a polite smile. "They always look a little dazed."

THE NEW YORK CITY 'porting station was in Davenport Tower, which made sense, but I was surprised to find myself exiting the Willis Tower in Chicago. The instant I stepped outside, everything felt *familiar*. This, I thought with a happy inward sigh, was my stomping ground. This was where I belonged.

"Feels like home?" Angélica asked, reading my thoughts perfectly. "You were always picking up the air currents, the smells, the sounds, even the feel of this place without being aware of it. Now that your senses are heightened, you notice it more. Feels great, right?"

"Feels awesome."

We caught the train across town to the Central City Mall, which I suspected Naomi had chosen because it was close to all kinds of public transit. Even the train, which I'd always thought stank of rotting humanity, seemed welcoming to me. "You really do love this town, don't you?" Angélica asked, as a couple of people down the train sneaked furtive looks at Vicki.

"I started saving up to move here when I was fifteen," I said. Granted, I'd run afoul of the supervillains almost right away when I'd finally moved here, but that didn't diminish Chicago's luster for me. "It's the first place that felt like home."

"Home," she said, a sigh in her voice. For her, home was Rio, thousands of miles and an entire climate change away. I wondered again why she'd left. "Must be nice."

"Aw, cheer up. Maybe I'll buy you a hot dog," I said, and the look of sheer disgust on her face made me laugh.

A COUPLE OF hours later, I wasn't laughing. "All right," I called through the curtain. "You can stop anytime."

"I can't. I really can't," Vicki said, and continued, as she had been for the past fifteen minutes, snickering. "The *look* on the woman's face when you didn't even know your own size! I mean, I haven't seen anybody that surprised since I attacked Near Death Man while he was in the shower."

Even though I wasn't wearing a shirt, I whipped aside the curtain to my dressing room to gape at Vicki, who stood in front of the three-way mirror, twisting this way and that to check the cut of a blouse. "You took down Near Death Man? I thought that was War Hammer."

We were on hour two of shopping, which meant that we'd moved on to the frivolities, as Vicki had called them. She had deemed hour one time for picking up necessities, which to me meant pretty much everything. To Vicki, however, necessities had meant heading to her namesake's store.

"Lingerie, darling," she'd said, while I'd insisted that I only needed the basics. "If the sexual sparks that fly whenever you and Guy are around are any indication, you need plenty of it. And right away. I mean, now that you know who he is, what's to stop you two from going at it like rabbits?"

Though I'd thanked her not to mention animals in the same sentence as my sexual habits, she'd merely laughed and insisted that I get lingerie—and plenty of it—on top of the more practical underwear. And truth be told, she had a point. I hadn't even so much as kissed Guy, and sex was off the table until I'd been cleared, but maybe it would be nice to think ahead.

We'd moved on to everything else. We had the dressing rooms to ourselves, as the mall was mostly empty. Angélica sat in the spare chair, legs pulled underneath her, while Vicki and I tried on clothes.

"I got the first takedown," Vicki said, referring to Near Death Man. "War Hammer got the final one. The one that stuck, if you will. So he gets the cred. But I caught Near Death Man first, it should be known."

"While he was in the shower?" I asked, crossing my arms. As Vicki and Angélica cared not a whit about modesty, I'd decided to ignore it as well. I wore only one of my new bras and a pair of jeans. They fit like a dream, which made me want to dance at the thought of having nice-fitting clothes that actually looked good. But I'd learned the hard way that dancing in the stores made the sales staff give you odd looks. As they were already looking at me strangely because I hadn't known my size, I decided that maybe it wasn't wise to push the matter.

"I was going to let him dry off and put on a towel." Vicki twisted to look over her shoulder at me. "Honestly, I was, but he threw the soap at me. What else could I do? And just so you know, catching a naked, slippery man is a lot harder than it looks."

"Hasn't stopped you before," Angélica said.

Vicki very maturely stuck her tongue out at her and went back to checking out the blouse.

"Speaking of men," Angélica said, pinning that gaze on me, "I happened to run into the younger Bookman this afternoon. He had a spring in his step."

"I don't see why. I didn't sleep with him, if that's what you're getting at."

"And you'd best keep it that way until you're cleared." Angélica gave me the hairy eyeball.

"At least let me do the crime before you make me do the time, woman."

"Do the time, or do the Guy?" Vicki asked.

"That was terrible, and you should be ashamed of yourself."

"And yet," Vicki said, spinning in place even faster. She seemed to be checking out the structural engineering of the top at this point. I figured that was probably a necessity, given that she'd been known to break the sound barrier. "So why *was* Mr. Bookman so happy, Angélica? He's been rather grouchy the past few days."

"Your guess is as good as mine." And they both turned expectant looks on me.

I hunched down and pulled on the next shirt to try it on. It, like the others, bagged around the bustline. "Maybe I agreed to go out with him last night. But you didn't hear it from me."

I'd never heard a supermodel squeal that loud.

"I mean, it kind of makes sense. We knew each other from work, we had that whole Blaze-and-Hostage-Girl thing, he's really cute, and smart . . ."

"Sure," Vicki said, drawing the word out as if she didn't quite believe me. She crossed her arms over her chest and grinned, wide and sarcastic. "And the fact that both of you are superheroes and incredibly hot for each other had *nothing* to do with it, right?"

I sighed and whipped the curtain between us closed.

Chapter Twenty-One

"Ooh. Now THESE, these are nice!"

Angélica hadn't been bluffing, I discovered when she finally dragged Vicki and me away from the clothing and into the shoe department. If anything, she'd been playing her interests down. Angélica Rocha didn't merely need a new pair of shoes.

By my last count, she appeared to need at least seven.

I eyed the latest pair in an unending parade. "How are these different from the last ones, again?"

Angélica, grinning without any sign of remorse, leaned down to tap the straps that crisscrossed her ankles. "There's silver here."

"I think you're lying." I squinted at the shoes. Truthfully, shoes had never been my thing. I'd worn flats or pumps around the office, but whenever I could get away with it, I usually left my commuting sneakers on. Angélica, evidently, belonged to a different school of belief.

She'd already explained to me that for her, the shoes dictated the outfit. And if she had anywhere near as many shoes as she claimed to have, her closet must have been the size of an industrial bunker.

"So," Angélica said, turning to Vicki, who'd become her comrade. "You like?"

"Twirl." Vicki pursed her lips as Angélica did so. "The silver looks good against your skin, but . . ."

"You're right." Angélica nodded. "Absolutely right. Definitely a 'but . . .' pair." She dropped down onto the little bench and eyed my shopping bags piteously. "You're sure you don't need any other shoes?"

I wiggled my toes in my new canvas sneakers. "I'm sure."

"There's a really cute pair of red heels back there that I think will look really good on you."

"What am I going to do with red shoes?"

"What aren't you going to do with red shoes is a more appropriate question," Vicki said.

"Yeah, sure, uh-huh," I said. Though I wanted to check my phone and see what time it was, I didn't dare with Angélica around. I still had over an hour until I needed to slip away and meet Naomi—how I was going to do that, I hadn't figured out yet—but just waiting around and wondering what her game was made me feel restless. I bounced on the balls of my feet.

Angélica caught the movement and frowned. "When's the last time you ate?"

"That really greasy pizza in the food court before the Great Shoe Hunt began."

Angélica nodded, calculating. "There's a pretzel stand right outside," she said.

A hot-from-the-oven soft pretzel sounded heavenly and it would give me a chance to text Naomi that I had arrived. I pushed myself to my feet. "Want one?" I asked, including both Vicki and Angélica in the offer.

"Oh, simply can't, darling," Vicki said immediately. "Fashion week's coming up, and those horrendous cameras pick up every bite."

"Right, sure, like you're any less of a human garbage disposal than I am. Angélica?"

"No, I'm good."

The guy at the stand had a little TV hooked up in the back of the booth. He misinterpreted my glance at it and ducked his head, looking defensive. "Boss doesn't mind. Your pretzel."

"Thanks." I took a huge bite while he ran Vicki's credit card. "You get HBO on that thing?"

He laughed. "I wish. Just local channels."

"Alas." The TV cut off mid-commercial to a Special News Bulletin. I recognized one of the news anchors who always sat on the superhero desk.

"Your credit card," Pretzel Guy said, holding it out.

I took it without looking at him. On the screen, the news had switched to the helicopter cam. They were apparently following somebody they believed to be a villain though he or she was little more than a white blur in the distance against the skyline. "Something's going on," I said.

Pretzel Guy glanced over his shoulder at the TV. "Of course it is."

The helicopter was apparently gaining on the blur. I stuffed the card in my pocket. "You mind if I hang around for a minute?"

Given that it was a Wednesday evening and the mall seemed pretty dead, Pretzel Guy shrugged. "Help yourself."

"Thank y—"

"Wait a minute." Pretzel Guy leaned closer to the TV, too. "That's—that's right outside the mall—"

Right as he spoke, the camera finally stabilized long enough for a clear shot. The blur became a reality, a familiar white and pink mask filling the screen for one angry moment.

"Oh, crap," I said. I dropped the pretzel and sprinted back to my friends. Angélica saw me coming first; she sprang to her feet (one was still bare). "What is it?"

"Chelsea. Incoming and coming fast."

Vicki immediately crouched to lace up her boots. "You think it's the museum?" she asked Angélica.

Angélica nodded. "Has to be."

That wasn't quite true, I realized. Naomi had set up the meet. Even if I didn't think she was in cahoots with Chelsea, it was still too big a coincidence to ignore.

Vicki looked at me, but she still spoke to Angélica. "Stay or go?"

"Get your mask on. We'll meet you upstairs."

Vicki nodded and, boots laced, took off.

I immediately rounded on Angélica. "Museum?"

"There's one on the third floor with some old artifacts. Mostly useless, but you never know with villains. Either that, or she's here for you, and there's no reason she would know you're here." Angélica paused in the middle of doing up her laces and gave me a careful look. My stomach immediately sank. "Or is there?"

"Um, so don't get mad, but I promised a friend I would meet her here at six thirty," I said. "My friend from the bank. It's possible Chelsea knows she's here."

"You were going to tell me this when?"

"Uh," I said, and Angélica glared. "Sorry?"

"It changes things. Do you know where your friend is?"

"No, but she's nuts about superheroes, so actually, the museum's a good guess." I followed Angélica out of the shoe department and to the clearance section behind the menswear, where she grabbed a couple of ski masks off the shelf. She tossed one to me. "You're not cleared for field duty yet, but it's an emergency. Keep your identity hidden."

"I'd rather not let the villain with the angry zapping powers know she didn't kill me dead enough the first time, yeah," I said as I yanked the balaclava over my face. It mussed up my hair when I lined up the eyeholes, but that was something I'd have to worry about later. "I'm not supposed to meet Naomi for another hour. Why would Chelsea be here already?"

"Don't ask me to ever understand villain logic."

I tried to call Naomi as we rushed out of the store looking like tiny muggers in our mall clothes and our ski masks. "She's not picking up. Typical."

"Just who is this friend, again?"

"She's a reporter—" I broke off when Angélica let out a ripe curse. "What? Is that bad?"

"Reporters are a collective pain in the ass for those on the front line. It just figures you befriended one."

"It's brought me more trouble than it's worth, trust me."

Even though it had seemed empty earlier, the mall was now full of people crowding the stairs and the escalators as they ran for the exits. Angélica glanced around once and turned her back to me. "Hop on," she said.

"What?" Feeling foolish, I clambered onto her back—and swore, clamping on when Angélica went from a running leap to a thirty-foot vertical jump, leaving my stomach behind. She caught the railing on the third-floor promenade and hauled both of us over. "A little warning next time!"

But she wasn't listening. "Get downstairs," she said to the nearest people as I jumped free. "Calmly. Don't trample anybody. It's going to be—"

Over our heads, something crashed. I yelped and dodged out of the way of falling glass, wincing as people began to scream. "Go!" Angélica shouted at the civilians, and Chelsea descended from the ceiling.

She stopped in midair above the pile of broken glass, tall and erect. A little cape lined with pink silk wafted in the mall air-conditioning behind her. My palms went cold.

Even worse, she hadn't come alone. A group of armed men hustled up. I recognized the two henchmen from the bank by the way they walked, but there were six others dressed in the same unbroken black. A pale kid with the worst hipster haircut I'd ever seen trailed behind the group. He gave the impression of being lost and quite unsure how he'd gotten there in the first place, unlike the spindly blonde woman walking next to him. She, I was positive, had never met a fight she'd backed down from.

"Oh, great," Chelsea said when she saw Angélica and me. "This is all the security this place has? A couple of midgets with ski masks?"

I opened my mouth, but Angélica's look promised pain if I spoke. I closed my mouth.

"Seriously, though," Chelsea went on when neither Angélica nor I said anything. She lowered herself to the ground, where she still towered over both of us. "You're it?"

"No, they're not," Vicki said from beside me. She hovered, bobbing slightly, in the air over the railing about three feet away from me. The Plain Jane mask looked oddly plastic in the mall lighting. "And more backup's on the way. This an even enough match for you?"

Chelsea sniffed. "Certainly. Now we might even break a sweat when we destroy you."

Vicki stepped daintily onto the top of the railing and hopped down, standing between Angélica and me. I kept my eyes on the spindly woman and the kid, somehow sensing that even though Chelsea's henchmen had guns, these two were far more dangerous.

"I'm not letting you get into the museum, Chelsea," Vicki said, "so you might as well just turn around and go home."

Supervillain banter, I thought, rolling my shoulders. I'd sat through attempts at it so many times, I kind of wished they'd get to the carnage already.

"Your sidekick looks a little bored," Chelsea said, nodding at me. She gave me an assessing look. I stared back at her coolly, hoping that she couldn't tell my hands were trembling.

Vicki laughed. "She was looking forward to a real fight, but I said it was just going to be you and your goons." She smirked at the kid with the bad haircut. "Hello again, Konrad. I see I left a nasty little scar the last time we ran into each other. Whoopsie. That was clumsy of me."

Konrad bared his teeth, suddenly looking a great deal less lost. Now that Vicki had brought it up, I could see a scar running from his hairline to the tip of his chin.

I had to hand it to Chelsea: she certainly had the element of surprise down. Even with my reflexes, I barely saw it coming. Her arm came up, ready to spew bee-stinging pain on everybody, and I reacted. I slide-tackled Vicki, sending her backward and into Angélica so that the green-and-yellow beam shot harmlessly over our heads.

All three of us bounced to our feet as Chelsea's henchmen raced forward, surging around her to get to us. Angélica took two running steps and blurred out of existence for a second, appearing right above the first of the goons and dropping down. He hit the tiles, already unconscious. I knocked the second man's feet out from under him and brought my elbow down on his cheekbone. When he tried to grab me around my middle, I hit him again. He stayed down this time.

"Wanna tango, Konrad?" Vicki asked, her laughter floating on the air as I ducked a blow from the butt of a rifle. When I spun around to throw the same mercenary over my shoulder, I saw her flying away, Konrad dashing after her.

I knocked out a third henchman, spun, and that was when I spotted Naomi.

She stood in the front window of the superhero museum, eyes wide as she gaped at the fight happening on the main concourse. I waved at her to get away, to get to cover, and someone grabbed me from behind.

For a second, the old panic set in. I was being taken, kidnapped yet again, helpless to stop it and—wait a second, I had muscles. I threw myself forward, using my body like a fulcrum so that both of us flipped the same way. I heard a *crunch* as we landed, but I was already rolling to my feet, looking to neutralize the threat.

The henchman who'd grabbed me lay still, eyes closed, so I looked around for Angélica instead.

She'd apparently made short work of the rest of the thugs. Now, she fought the skinny woman I'd noticed earlier. The woman was a lot spindlier than she had been, though, for as I watched, rooted to the spot, she stretched out her limbs like she was made of some kind of rubber, and tried to choke Angélica. My trainer wasn't having any of that; she blurred out of the way, bounced forward, and socked the woman in the gut. I had the very absurd experience of watching the woman's entire body ripple as if she were a bag full of liquid.

"Weird," I said.

Angélica took a bad kick to the thigh, grunted, and launched herself to safety. "Gail!" she said, pointing over my shoulder.

I whipped around and realized that Chelsea had slipped into the museum, heading right for Naomi. I scrambled for the door, tripping over the guy I'd knocked out. Facing Chelsea by myself wasn't exactly something I *wanted* to do, but it wasn't like I had much of a choice.

The museum lobby was an open space laid out with very nice marble floors. A floor-to-ceiling tribute to the earliest days of the fighting superheroes covered the walls, done in that newspaper-retro look. Glass cases along the wall held old uniforms. Just inside the doors, a service desk kept a lonely and dusty ficus tree company.

I didn't see any sign of Chelsea or Naomi, so I paused and listened, drowning out the sound of the fights from outside. After a second, I pinpointed the sound of two sets of running footsteps, and took off in that direction. It reminded me of the bank, listening to Naomi's screams as I'd sprinted down those hallways. Here we were again.

Meeting up with Naomi Gunn was indeed very bad for my health.

After the lobby, the museum was a warren, probably not meant to accommodate groups larger than five or ten at a time. Narrow corridors twisted and wound through exhibits that were mostly dark, save for spotlights on the costumes and knickknacks that belonged in old-time superhero lore. It felt like a gimmicky tourist attraction, which was why I'd never been there. They seemed to pride themselves on having real superhero artifacts, though knowing what I did about Davenport Industries, I figured they hadn't gotten anything close to the full story.

I raced past Gail Garson's first uniform, its garish reds

and pinks dulled by age, and nearly tripped onto Hatchiko's motorcycle. Couldn't Chelsea and Naomi have picked a nice, open space that lacked valuable obstacles?

Up ahead, I heard voices, but I wasn't close enough to discern words. Still, it was a toss-up as to who was more surprised when I rounded the corner and stumbled into the 1950s exhibit on the Superhuman Registration Act: Chelsea, Naomi, or me. Chelsea had lifted Naomi over her head by the lapels of her jacket, and Naomi looked more than a touch worried.

"What the hell?" I asked. I charged forward.

Chelsea switched to a one-handed grip, freeing her other hand. Sparks tickled at the edge of her palm, inches away from Naomi's face. "Ah-ah-ah, don't take another step."

Naomi wouldn't survive a close blast like that. "Let her go," I said again.

"Or you'll what? Ski mask tells me you're not exactly super-powered, little girl, so why should I listen to you again?"

"Maybe it's part of my look," I said.

"It's a bad look."

"When I care about what villains think, I'll ask a better one than you. Put her down."

"When she tells me where she hid her research, I will."

I froze. Naomi slid a single, guilty glance toward me, which was all I needed. "Research?" I asked, ripping off my face mask. "You told me this was over a story she didn't like."

"Ah, Hostage Girl." Chelsea rolled her eyes behind the mask. "I should have known."

"Technically, I wasn't lying. She *isn't* happy about a story I wrote about her." Naomi's feet were still kicking a couple of feet off the ground, and she wasn't that short. "So I didn't actually lie to you, but I . . ."

Chelsea evidently tired of the pleasantries. "Where is it?" she said, shaking Naomi like a dog.

The reporter's teeth clicked together. "I destroyed it," she said. I used their distraction to ease back a step, resting my hand on baseball from the 1957 World Series, which had famously socked good old Invisible Victor in the gut while he'd been trying to sneak a close-up look from behind second base.

"Lies. You journalists always back up your work. Tell me where it is!"

I had to hand it to Naomi: she might be a lying pain in the butt, but she had a backbone. She glared at Chelsea, who had the swirling, stinging ray of death inches from her face, and shook her head. "I won't help you," she said. "The research is gone."

"Liar!" Chelsea started to move her hand. My grip tightened on the baseball.

And everything erupted into chaos as the floor underneath us started to shake.

Exhibits toppled like dominos, alarms shrilled, and Chelsea dropped Naomi in surprise. The reporter hit the ground and immediately threw herself off to the side so that Chelsea's stinging ray bounced uselessly off a placard.

I shoved away from the wall with my free hand, ducking out of the way as a second ray caught the outer edge of my arm. It sent a burst of agony straight to my brain.

Naomi scrambled to her feet and took off running. Swearing, I ran across the heaving ground after her. Chunks of plaster began to rain around us. I saw Chelsea duck under a doorway as I stumbled on.

Hands grabbed me when I rounded the corner, pulling me to safety under an overhang. "What the hell is going on? Shakin' Dave is dead!" Naomi said.

The earthquake villain who'd terrorized Chicago for nearly two months had been taken out by War Hammer, and Chicago wasn't exactly a hotbed for natural earthquakes. So I thought back to the confrontation with Chelsea and her minions. There must have been a reason that Vicki had singled out one of them, and I suspected we were being treated to it right now. "If I had to guess, I'm going to say a guy named Konrad is doing this," I said. "We need to get out of here before Chelsea comes and finds us."

"Or the building takes us down with it." Naomi crouched, her knuckles bright against her dark skin as she grabbed the corner to keep from being knocked over. I had to balance without any help. "Girl, she's trying to kill War Hammer and Blaze."

"*What*?" I whipped around to look at her. "Why?"

"I don't know! She paid me to research them, and I took the money because I thought it was for a paper or something. That was why I first approached you last month."

At that point, I didn't much care why she'd done it. If somebody was trying to kill Sam and Guy, specifically, that was definitely a bigger concern. "Did you find out how to do it?"

Naomi nodded, and I cursed roundly. "She doesn't know right now, right?" I asked.

"No. Why?"

"Because I'm 95 percent sure Blaze is on his way, and I don't want my—I don't want him flying into a trap." The shaking abruptly stopped. All around us, things groaned ominously, and I could already smell smoke. Great. This was just getting better and better. "We have to go. We have to go now."

"Good id—"

Naomi broke off midsentence as Chelsea rounded the corner and let loose. I shoved Naomi out of the way so that the full force of the blast hit me, knocking me back. My entire world sucked itself into one searing point on my chest, and I was consumed by thousands of invisible bees, all of them biting and tearing away at my skin. I let out a scream, falling to the ground.

And then I heard a *thwack*.

The stinging halted abruptly. Freed, I rolled away. Chelsea staggered, holding her forehead while the baseball I'd dropped during the earthquake bounced to the ground at Chelsea's feet.

My nemesis looked at Naomi, who stood her ground and glared her back. "You're going to regret that," she said, and raised her palm.

"No!" I shouted, already running forward.

The blast struck Naomi on the forehead, and she collapsed. I made a running leap and catapulted off some rubble, intending to finish Chelsea with one punch. Her palm came up in slow motion, aiming right for me. A green blur to my left was the only warning either of us had.

Blaze hit Chelsea like a very annoyed freight train.

The two superhumans plowed through the Commodore of Corruption's old penny-farthing bicycle and into a wall, and the fighting truly began. Since neither really had to worry about healing, and they were both super-strong, it was like watching two gladiators go at each other, all deadly grace and brutality. I gawked for a second, transfixed, before I came to my senses and started running for Naomi.

Two steps later, the shaking started again, this time much harder. I flew back, tossed like a rag doll against a glass case. The support structure of the building let out an almighty groan. Whoever this Konrad was, he was about to bring the place down around our ears. I heard a *crunch* above me and rolled out of the way of a falling piece of cement just in time.

"Naomi!" She was in even more danger out there in the open like that. I couldn't get to her, not with the ground heaving. "G—Blaze! Naomi!"

He and Chelsea fought on without hearing me.

"Crap," I said. When I tried to soldier forward, the floor *opened up around me* like the pits of hell, provided hell could be found in the Baby Gap two floors below. I stared at the gaping hole and the cute baby clothing below in horror. "Oh, this is not good. This is so not good."

Well, if I was going to die in a baby-clothing store, at least it would probably still be considered a noble death. The second the quaking died down to tremors, I backed up as far as I could amid the debris, took a deep breath, and made a running start.

Something snatched me out of the air.

"What are you *doing*?" Guy set me back on my feet. Evidently, Chelsea had been vanquished, or at least knocked out, because I could see her lying facedown about twenty feet away. "That would have killed you!"

"Naomi!" I pointed around him.

"I'll get her. You stay here and try not to fall to your death."

"Fine. You save her," I said, "but I have to go. Angélica might need me."

I could see that he really didn't like the idea, even with the mask hiding his face. "You have to save the hostage," I said. "That's what you do. If there's anybody that knows that, it's me. I can take care of myself."

"You always could," he said, and before I could so much as blink, he'd whipped the mask up and kissed me fiercely. He yanked the mask back down. "I have wanted to do that for a long time. Stay safe."

"You, too!" I somehow managed to stammer that out though I had no idea how. We were definitely, I thought, going to explore that one again later when the building wasn't falling down around our ears. For now, I cast an uncertain look at Chelsea—was it right to just leave her like that?—and decided helping Angélica was my bigger concern.

I had to double back to find a way out of the museum. Tremors continued to rock the floor as I ran on, clearing priceless artifacts like they were hurdles. Alarms wailed left and right, making my ears hurt, and the power flickered, giving the entire place an air of some forgotten, post-apocalyptic society.

Chelsea had gone a long way just to get to one reporter.

I made it back onto the third-floor concourse right as Angélica delivered the final punch to take out the spindly woman. She raced to me, looking panicked. "Oh, thank god, you're okay," she said, grabbing me for a quick hug. "*Are* you okay? Where's Chelsea?"

"She got me a bit, but I'm fine. Guy showed. I left her back th—"

Angélica grabbed the front of my shirt and threw me to the side. I hit the ground, sliding toward the railing, as she was briefly enveloped in a cloud of green and yellow.

"*No!*"

A scream of pain wrenched out of Angélica as Chelsea zapped her. She'd come out of nowhere. I lunged to my feet, but one of Chelsea's thugs was suddenly in front of me. I didn't see the fist until it was too late.

His punch drove me back and over the railing. Though my heart dropped to my stomach, I grabbed a support beam and hauled myself up. I leapt back over the railing, twisting in midair to smash his nose with my elbow and his balls with my knee.

Angélica's scream cut off. She hit the ground the same time my opponent did.

"No!" I said again, already racing for her.

Chelsea shot a blast at my feet, making me trip to the side. "That was a stupid thing your friend did," she said, as I rose in a crouch, breathing hard. Her smirk deepened. "Think you can take me, little girl? You survived it before."

"Shut up," I said.

"She had to play the martyr, didn't she? Too bad I pumped her so full her heart stopped."

I'd seen Angélica heal from a broken nose, right in front of my eyes.

"Not likely it'll get started again, either." Chelsea looked down at where Angélica sprawled, pale and still. "Not with the voltage I hit her with. Pity."

The sound that ripped itself from my throat wasn't human, wasn't even of this world. It was indefinable, it was eerie, and it was somehow coming out of me. I charged forward, kicking out.

Chelsea and Guy had been pretty evenly matched. But neither of them had had the rage, the all-consuming, driving force of it, pushing them forward. I set in on Chelsea like a rabid dog, kicking and punching and using everything Angélica had taught me without abandon. My instincts took over. Every time Chelsea raised her palm to unleash her power, I slapped it away. Every time she got back up, I knocked her down.

If this had been a boxing match, I had her on the damn ropes.

Or so I thought.

When I moved in for a right cross to finish the job, Chelsea pretended to fall, feinted, and twisted. She shoved both hands into my midsection and let loose.

The first time she'd hit me, it had been like bees crawling around my skull, stinging away at every inch of flesh.

Now the bees were biting and tearing at me, and there were thousands more, consuming me whole. I screamed and writhed, Chelsea's laughter burning my ears as the pain went on and on for an eternity.

And *finally*, it stopped. My vision had tunneled to the point where all I could see was her gleeful face behind her mask, her eyes promising death and pain. Something closed over my windpipe and I was hauled up, to my feet, off my feet, dangling in the air.

Every system in my body went haywire. I couldn't breathe. I couldn't *breathe*! I clawed and scrabbled with my fingernails, trying to kick, trying to do anything to get away, but Chelsea had a grip like iron. The stinging torture had sapped all of my energy, so the best I could do was slap feebly at her.

Chelsea laughed. "Not so tough now, are you?"

"Let. Me. Go," I managed to wheeze.

"Sure. No problem."

Bad wording, I saw right away. Chelsea wasn't just dangling me in the air. She was dangling me over the ledge, right above the mall fountain.

Oh, damn, was all I had time to think when she released her grip. I hadn't kept my promise to Guy not to fall to my death.

Chapter Twenty-Two

I WOKE UP on a stretcher. While it wasn't a first for me, it was unusual enough to make me pause. Blaze usually flew me straight to the hospital since he was faster than any ambulance.

Then everything *hurt*, and I stopped thinking about Blaze. Sirens wailed in my ears, and the early-evening sky arched over everything, just beginning to turn pink around the edges. I could see the underside of a paramedic's chin, and she definitely didn't look familiar.

All at once, it rushed back to me: Naomi. Guy. Chelsea. Angélica. I tried to sit up. Angélica. Where was Angélica? She needed my help—she couldn't be dead, she couldn't be.

"Easy there," the paramedic said. "You're at the Central City Mall. There was an accident, but we've got you, you're going to be okay. Can you tell me your name?"

"My friend," I tried to say, though my throat screamed with fire and refused to cooperate.

"I need you to tell me your name."

"It's Gail, and I need to know—my friend Angélica. Angélica Rocha, she was hurt, she needs help, is she okay?"

"I'll find out in a minute, but my priority is you right now. Can you tell me if you're hurt anywhere?"

Before I could reply to that, I heard somebody running up to the stretcher. "She's one of mine," said a voice I recognized.

The paramedic gave me a wide-eyed look. "*Oh*," she said. "I didn't realize. She looks so normal."

"It's fine. Your discretion is appreciated." Just like that, the paramedic vanished, and Kiki took her place. She wore a polo shirt and had her hair tucked into a green ball cap that said DALLOWAY INTERNATIONAL on the front. Her assessing gaze was critical as it swept over me. "You okay?"

"Not really." I gritted my teeth when she helped me sit up. My rib cage felt like it was on fire. I kept my breaths shallow to avoid feeling like I'd swallowed hot coals. "I think I got thrown into a fountain. My ribs hurt some."

"That would explain why you smell like a swimming pool. Can you walk? I don't have room for a second stretcher."

"Yeah, but not well. I—I'm running on empty. Angélica? Vicki? Guy?"

Kiki handed me a crap-cake, but my hands shook too badly for me to unwrap it, so she did that for me. We were in some sort of emergency-services site that had been set up outside the mall. "Vicki's fine," she said as she hustled me through the parking lot, among the emergency teams. "I sent her back to headquarters, and Guy's dropping off your pet reporter. He's okay, too."

"Angélica?" I asked with a horrible sense of dread.

Kiki paused, and my world threatened to collapse. "She's not good," she said. "Eat that. You're trying to heal on no reserves, you'll only make yourself worse."

But all I could do was wonder exactly what *not good* meant. "Is she going to die?"

"I don't know, Gail. Eat."

It hurt my jaw to chew, but I managed to swallow the crap-cake by the time Kiki had pulled me to an ambulance with the same Dalloway International logo on the side. When she opened the back door, my breath clogged up in my lungs. Angélica lay on the stretcher, strapped in. Never very big to begin with, she seemed impossibly little and frail. Just the day before, I'd driven the blade of my foot into her chin. She'd laughed (and returned the favor). Now it looked like if I so much as pressed a fingertip to that glassy skin, she might crumble into a thousand pieces.

But she was breathing. Her chest was moving, slightly. She was alive.

"I can tell you more once we get back to headquarters. Put these on." Kiki handed me a bag of clothes. I fumbled, my hands unsteady, but I managed to get the shirt on. My ribs sang with pain. And when I bent to get the pants, they let out one short scream that had me doubling forward and swearing.

"Uh, Kiki?" I asked, my voice a hoarse whisper as I tried to breathe past the agony. "The pants. I can't—my ribs—"

"Someday we're going to have a talk about your definition of 'my ribs hurt some,'" Kiki said, her voice gentle as she helped me out of my pants and into the new ones. My clothes now matched hers, a Dalloway International paramedic's uniform. "Hold still, and try not to scream."

"Why? What are you—oh—sh—" My eyes rolled back into my head as Kiki's fingers probed my rib cage, but somehow, somehow I fought off the gray that descended over my vision.

"Two broken, two cracked," she said. "Sorry about that."

"I hate you," I said, gripping the side of the ambulance to stay upright.

"Sorry," Kiki said again, and directed me to get in the passenger seat. "Buckle up." With an ease that said she'd done this before, she flipped on the siren, and we roared out of the parking lot. I stayed braced in my seat and breathed shallowly, praying that the pain would stop. When Kiki held out another crap-cake, I only moaned.

"It'll make the pain go away faster," she said, and I took the unwrapped crap-cake, chewing despite the awful flavor. "How do you feel? Honest assessment."

"Like Chelsea grabbed me by the throat and threw me into a mall fountain. Did she get away?"

"I think so."

"I hate her more than I hate you at the moment."

"Noted. Any other pain besides your ribs?"

"Throat, knee, head, all over, but not as bad as the ribs. I'll survive it. Worst is the fact that I'm clammy from the damn fountain water, and who the hell knows what's in that?"

"Hopefully, a lot of chlorine." Kiki muscled her way between two sedans with a thin coat of paint to spare.

"What happened to Naomi?"

"Guy's bringing her to the hospital in New York. Davenport's dealing with her now."

I groaned. "Hopefully she has a better time of it than Jeremy is."

Kiki didn't have a reply to that. When we finally pulled into Dalloway, she cut the sirens and hustled into the back to pull Angélica's stretcher free. I followed more slowly since moving too fast meant my entire field of vision started to go dark. Though two men in scrubs rushed up to help, Kiki flashed some sort of badge at them that had them scurrying away. She posted herself at the end of the stretcher and nudged me up to the guiding spot, gesturing that I should just keep up. Once we were out of earshot of the others, she said to me, "Keep your head down."

Abruptly, the smell of disinfectant made me want to throw up. I started to bend over to gather my breath, but that only made everything hurt more.

"Gail? Gail, focus on my voice. Shut down whatever open senses you've got going on. I know Angélica taught you how to do that."

It took every bit of strength I had left, and I rankled at Kiki's businesslike voice, but I managed to close out the overwhelming smell by breathing shallowly through my mouth. "You okay?" she asked again.

"I need morphine and a nap," I said, as we climbed into an elevator.

"Oh, you poor thing!"

I reared back, ready for an attack, but only felt sheepish when I met the gaze of an on-duty nurse in the elevator with us. She was eyeing my neck, which must have been bright red and bruised from Chelsea's grip. "It's fine," I said, looking down and away. "Barely hurts."

"We had a bad run yesterday," Kiki said. "The guy came out of nowhere, but Kristy's tough. She handled it."

Kristy? I looked like a Kristy?

"Has somebody checked that out? That looks painful, honey," the nurse said.

Since the ache in my neck was now nothing compared to the cesspool of pain that my rib cage had become, I said nothing.

"Last night," Kiki said. "I sat with her the whole time. She'll be fine. If you'll excuse us?"

As she started to push the stretcher forward, the nurse narrowed her eyes. "I think you're going the wrong way, ladies."

Kiki sighed and lifted her shirt, just a little, to show off the ID badge clipped to her waist.

I watched the nurse's eyes widen, cut from Kiki to Angélica on the stretcher. "Oh," she said. "I had heard about this, but . . ."

"Nothing to see here, I promise."

But that clearly wasn't the case. Whatever the badge meant—and I had my suspicions—it definitely doubled the nurse's interest in me. I felt her eyes studying me with renewed interest. When I looked up, she glanced away quickly, and I wondered if somebody was going to have a superhero-sighting story to tell over dinner when she got home.

It made me feel kind of sick and dizzy. Actually, I was

beginning to realize that the two crap-cakes I'd swallowed were making me feel sick and dizzy.

"You've gone white," Kiki said, when the nurse found other things to do, and we were on our way again.

I swallowed, a gargantuan effort. "I'm okay."

Though I clearly wasn't. White began to sparkle at the very corners of my vision. I battled it back, and I had to grip the sides of the gurney when the world wavered in and out. Even that didn't prove to be enough, though. I stepped on the outside of my foot, my ankle twisting, and hit the floor with a groan of pain.

Instantly, Kiki was next to me, looking worried. She felt my forehead with her palm, and I nearly threw up when that only exacerbated the agony singing up my rib cage and spine. Dizziness made the world tilt on its axis. "Gail," she said, and I blinked away afterimages of the lights overhead. "There's a room not far ahead. We can rest there. Do you think you can make it? Can you do that for me?"

Clammy sweat sprouted on my forehead underneath the cap. "I—don't know—"

Kiki grabbed my chin, turned me to face her. "Gail. You can do this."

"If you say so."

It took me a good solid minute of breathing hard before I could push myself back to my feet. Kiki helped, guiding me so that I was gripping the bar alongside the stretcher. "Hold on tight. Don't let go. Just hold on." She released me and moved to the back of the stretcher.

My legs jerked forward of their own volition, propelling me onward. I staggered like a drunk, but I moved. "Good," Kiki said in a low and soothing voice. "Just keep walking. One foot in front of the other, right?"

My fingers spasmed on the rails. "How far?"

"Keep walking."

Every breath drowned me deeper into an angry sea of red heat. Every step siphoned oxygen out of my lungs, drained the blood out of my head. I pushed forward, head down, vision closing in like a narrowing tunnel, until: "We're here," Kiki said.

Something beeped like one of the panels at the Davenport complex, and Kiki took me by the elbow, pulling me forward. I looked around hazily, long enough to realize we were now in a room indistinguishable from the rest of the hospital except that there was a heavy-duty lock on the door and far too much fancy equipment crowded inside.

"What is this place?" I asked, tilting a little.

Kiki moved around the stretcher to take me by the elbows again. I whimpered as she leaned me up against the wall. "I need to put Angélica in the bed," she said, "and then you can lie down on the stretcher. Okay?"

"Just be quick."

Even though I knew she hurried, transferring Angélica's limp body to the bed with ease, it still felt like hours before Kiki helped me climb onto the stretcher. I sagged against it even though the movement sent little aftershocks of agony all through my torso and neck.

"What happens now?" I asked.

"We wait for backup," Kiki said. "I can't transport both stretchers at once."

"And Angélica? She's going to be okay," I said. "Right?"

Kiki fitted an oxygen mask over my trainer's face. "She's faced longer odds, and she's tough. I wouldn't count her out just yet."

"She's going to be okay," I said, and this time I made sure it wasn't a question.

Kiki moved between the stretcher and the bed, stepping deliberately into my line of view. "I'm going to give you some morphine," she said.

"You can't knock me out. What if she—I mean, I need to—"

"Just to ease the pain, I promise." She removed a wicked-looking needle from the cabinet. When I offered her the crook of my elbow, she shook her head and moved my shirtsleeve up farther, running a cold wipe on the outside of my arm. "Hold still."

I did my best not to flinch, though it didn't hurt that much. When she drew the needle out, she gave me an assessing look and dug her phone out of her pocket.

"Backup?" I asked.

"In a way." She hit a number in her contacts and handed me the phone. "It's Guy. Why don't you talk to him while I see if I can help Angélica?"

It was a classic distraction technique before the morphine set in, I knew, but I didn't care because Guy's voice was asking, "Kiki? Is something wrong? Is it Gail?"

"Hi," I said.

I heard him exhale in relief. "Gail. You're all right."

I looked down at the paramedic's uniform and my screaming rib cage. "I'm . . . in one piece."

He paused. "How bad?"

For a second, I was tempted to lie and downplay it. "Chelsea threw me into the fountain," I said. "Don't laugh."

"I wasn't going to. Where are you?"

"Where else? The hospital, though Kiki says we're just waiting for backup. My ribs are a little messed up." My hand was shaking, which made it difficult to hold the phone steady, and I could feel my gorge rising once more. It appeared my body wasn't really holding down the crap-cakes too well. I bit down on the inside of my cheek. "Kind of surprised you weren't waiting here with my rose, actually."

"Sorry. I'm in New York with Naomi. She's not awake yet." He sounded frustrated. "But I will get you that rose ASAP, I mean it."

"Good. It's not a real hospital trip without it." Was I making any sense? I doubted it. Everything felt weird and disconnected. I stared at Angélica, and at Kiki, who was inserting an IV into Angélica's wrist. "Guy, something happened. Angélica, she got hit bad."

"Is she going to be okay?"

"I . . . don't know," I said, and the words stuck in my throat a little. Angélica might not be okay. This wasn't like one of the hundreds of times Blaze had rescued Hostage Girl. Somebody might actually die, and that somebody might be my friend. "I'm worried."

"She's a fighter," he said right away. There wasn't any

hesitation in his voice; he sincerely believed that Angélica wasn't in any danger. "Trust me, she'll be back to mopping the floor with you in no time."

"Hey," I said weakly. "I'm starting to hold my own."

"I know you are, and—Gail, hold on a minute, something's happening." I heard him cover the phone with his palm, but his voice still leaked through. "I don't recognize you—where's your ID? You don't have the clearance for this floor."

I didn't hear the reply. In the room with me, Kiki looked at the monitor, eyebrows low over her eyes. Her frown deepened.

"Gail?" Guy asked. "I have to go. I'll see you soon, okay?"

"See you soon," I said.

He hung up just as every monitor in the room started shrilling. Angélica's body began to shake and seize, her limbs jerking while her head lolled. Kiki cursed and slapped a red button on the wall.

"What the hell?" I asked, starting to scramble off of the stretcher. The morphine hadn't kicked in yet, so moving that abruptly made the world go temporarily dark. I clutched the edge of the stretcher and tried not to be sick everywhere. "What's going on?"

"She's seizing," Kiki said, rolling Angélica onto her side. "People are on their way—stay there."

Terror made me want to disobey. Angélica twitched violently as Kiki threw blankets over the railing on the bed. I'd seen seizures before, thanks to some truly noxious gas that Demon X had used once, but this seemed more severe. Angélica's eyes rolled in her head, and it was *wrong*.

And then the frantic beeping turned into one long note, and I looked at the monitor to see a flat line.

My stomach dropped.

The door flew open, and nurses raced in, bringing both a sense of order and chaos with them. Kiki went from a worried friend to the doctor in charge, issuing orders with an urgent calmness. I couldn't take my eyes off Angélica's face, now slack and empty.

Kiki's voice faded in and out like I was listening to her underwater. "—Asystole—prep for intubation—" Nurses in their identical scrubs moved in some kind of choreographed dance I didn't understand, wheeling machines around the bed.

The EKG monitor continued to let out that low tone, never pausing, never ending. "No!" I shouted. "Angélica—no—"

"Somebody get her into the hallway," Kiki said, not looking at me.

I tried again to get off the stretcher—why had her heart stopped? Why wasn't she healing?—but again, the world spun and flickered. Nausea forced me back against the stretcher with a moan, so all I could do was lie there as a nurse wheeled me out into the hallway.

The last glimpse I had of Angélica was her deathly pale face as Kiki and the nurses gathered around, trying to save her life.

"You have to let me back in there," I told the nurse. "That's Angélica—she's my friend. She can't die. She *can't*."

The nurse just shook her head. "I'm sorry. They're doing everything they can."

I wanted to break down and cry. I'd never been much of a crier, not even when I'd faced down villains, but everything hurt so much, and Angélica was in there dying. She was my friend. She was supposed to meet me in the mornings and beat the crap out of me and give out real hugs and condescending nicknames. She wasn't supposed to be having seizures because she'd taken a hit that was meant for me.

"What's your name?" the nurse asked.

"Gail."

"Gail, I'm Jenna. I'm going to wait with you while they work on your friend, okay? Tell me, are you in any pain?"

"Kiki—she gave me morphine, but it's, I mean, I don't know how it affects me now that I'm—" I broke off and swiped my hand under my nose, which had started to drip snot everywhere from the unshed tears. The hospital room must have been soundproofed because I couldn't hear anything through the wall. I had no idea if Angélica's heart had started beating again.

"Okay. We'll get it squared away, no matter what it is," Jenna said. "Where does it hurt?"

I opened my mouth to tell her, but something else entirely came up. I leaned forward and spewed without warning, right there on Jenna's shoes. Mortification skyrocketed. I moaned and tried to babble an apology, but she only shook her head and helped me clean my face. "I've had worse."

"Your shoes," I said.

She barely spared them a glance. "Happens all the time. I've got another pair in my locker."

I nodded miserably. "Angélica wanted new shoes. S'why she came, and now she's—"

"Shh. It's okay. I'm going to call and get this cleaned up, no worries."

She moved the stretcher a little way down the hall and set up a little CAUTION! WET FLOOR! triangle next to the pile of sick. Too dizzy to move, I watched the door, waiting for Kiki to come out and announce that everything was fine, that it had all been a bad fever dream from the morphine.

When the door opened, though, Kiki's face looked absolutely grim.

"No," I said. "No, no, no."

But Kiki just looked tired, her face drawn and pale. "Gail . . ."

"No, don't say it. Don't tell me she's dead, don't you *dare*. She's fine, she's going to be fine, she heals like *that*."

Kiki opened her mouth, but before she could say anything, we all heard a throat clear.

A voice said, "Gail Godwin?"

Jenna, Kiki, and I all turned as one. The morphine had finally begun to make me feel floaty and disconnected, but I was still cognizant of the fact that there were several men standing in the hospital corridor. And they were bad news, even if I recognized the one in the middle, wearing the well-tailored Italian suit.

The first time I'd met him, Eddie Davenport had smiled at me. He wasn't smiling now. His face was like something carved from stone—cold, immobile, hard. And he was frowning at me, somberly, his hands folded together in front of him.

"What?" I asked, my tongue feeling thick.

"Really?" Kiki asked, stepping between Eddie Davenport and me. "You guys couldn't have waited until we got back to headquarters?"

Eddie barely glanced at her. "You know the rules, Kiki."

"But she's sick. There's time for this later, after I've had time to look her over."

"Wh-what's going on?" I asked. Thanks to the morphine, I managed to push myself to my feet though I stumbled a little. Immediately, the two men who flanked Eddie Davenport stepped forward and grabbed my arms. "Why are you doing that? Stop!"

Kiki stepped forward. "Please don't do this," she said. "She could be innocent."

"That's not our call to make," Eddie said, as I tried harder to pull free of the men holding me. The nurses were crowding the doorway of Angélica's hospital room, watching us worriedly. At Eddie's annoyed look, two of his men began to shuffle them out of the hallway so that it was just Kiki, Eddie, and the two men holding me up by the arms left in the hallway.

Sweat broke out all over my skin. First they'd shoved me out of Angélica's room, and then I was being manhandled. Everything began to swim unpleasantly, but I kept my head held high. "Will somebody please tell me what the *hell* is going on!" I said.

"What's happening is that they're being really stupid," Kiki said, scowling as two men disappeared into Angélica's hospital room. "And—oh my god, you're bleeding."

Belatedly, I felt something wet leaking over my lips. Oh. It was coming from my nose. I had a bloody nose. Perfect.

"Let me—" Kiki began, but the man on my left held up a hand. "You're being ridiculous. She's *injured*, and I took an oath—"

"And there are rules." Any trace of the geniality I'd once seen on Eddie Davenport's face was gone as he stepped forward to face off against Kiki. "You know the rules are for our own protection, Kiki. Gail Godwin—"

I stopped listening. The door to Angélica's room opened, and the men reappeared, pushing a sheet-covered gurney. I didn't need super-senses to know what lay under the sheet.

"No!" I shouted. My knees buckled. I went forward, whimpering when my ribs burst into hellfire, but I didn't care. The men tightened their grip; I struggled against them, trying to get to that gurney. This had to be a joke. This couldn't be real. Where was Guy? He was supposed to swoop in and save the day. This wasn't supposed to happen. "No! *Angélica! No!*"

"Kiki, sedate her!"

The gurney was pushed around the corner and out of sight. I lunged with all of my strength and actually broke free, stumbling away. If I could just get to Angélica, maybe this cosmic joke would be over, and she would be okay—

Something pricked my shoulder. Instantly, everything went from wobbly and unpleasant to downright hazy. I started to go backward, only to feel Kiki's arms catch me.

"I'm so sorry," I thought I heard her say, but everything felt surreal. "Gail, I'm so sorry."

The fog threatened to overwhelm me, but at least it made the pain go away. I felt something soft under my back, and opened my eyes to see Eddie Davenport standing over me, frowning. "Gail Godwin," he said, and I blinked sluggishly. "By order of Davenport Industries, on the charges of conspiring with a known villain and on the murder of Angélica Rocha, I am hereby placing you under arrest."

I replied the only way I could: I rolled over and threw up all over his shoes, too. I might have heard him sigh, but that hardly mattered, as I was too busy passing out to care.

TO BE CONTINUED . . .

About the Author

LEXIE DUNNE is a woman of many masks, all of them stored neatly in a box under her bed. By day a mild-mannered technical writer and by night an adventuress and novelist, she keeps life interesting by ignoring it and writing instead. She hails from St. Louis, home of the world's largest croquet game piece, and *Superheroes Anonymous* is her professional debut into the world of caped crusaders, a journey that started when her father took her and her brother to see *The Rocketeer*.

Discover great authors, exclusive offers, and more at hc.com.